Gillian's Island

VAL TOBIN

DEDICATION

Dedicated to Bob, Jenn, Mark, Chanelle, Savannah, and Jack.

ACKNOWLEDGMENTS

Editing by Kelly Hartigan (XterraWeb) editing.xterraweb.com. Thank you, Kelly.

Thanks to Patti Roberts of Paradox (paradoxbooktrailerproductions.blogspot.com.au/) for the amazing cover.

Thanks also to Andrea Holmes; Val Cseh; Michelle Legere; John Erwin; Alis Kennedy; Sergeant Kelly Bachoo, York Regional Police; The Ontario Fire Marshall's office; Mike Foran of Ketchunany Lodge in Temagami, Ontario; Wendy Quirion; Pam Kesterson; Linda Bartash Dowley; Dr. Maral; Amanda David; and Ceri Bladen.

CHAPTER 1

Today, my life changes forever.

Gillian Foster unclipped the last clothes peg and hauled the crisp, white sheet from the line. It went into the laundry basket beside her with the rest of the bedding, all of it done for a man she'd never met.

As resort owner, she'd often done laundry for strangers when an extra pair of hands was needed, but this time, it was different. This time, it was for Daylin Quinn, the resort's new owner, and that made her every motion heavy and reluctant.

The heat didn't help put a spring in her step. The day was uncharacteristically hot, the air oppressive. It was the first of May and felt like the end of June.

She sighed and ran her fingers through her hair, which always frizzed up in humidity. She bunched it into her fist to let a passing breeze cool her neck.

The wind that had dried her sheets so quickly would also blow in a cold front. The puffy, white clouds overhead now showed hints of grey. Sooner or later, a storm would blow in. Hopefully, it wouldn't be until after Daylin had arrived safely on the island—unless it rolled in fast.

Then she could use it to her advantage and delay the visit until tomorrow. Sure, it put off the inevitable, but a storm was a legitimate reason to procrastinate.

She hefted the basket onto her hip and walked from the garden through the sunroom to the large living room. She set the basket on the floor and arched backward, rubbing her lower back.

A stereo system in the corner next to the fieldstone fireplace had a radio, and she switched it on. Eventually, there'd be a weather report.

Damn it, if she was forced to sell her home, why did it have to be to an

1

arrogant developer like Daylin Quinn?

When he'd made the offer through his real estate agent, Gillian had researched him on the Internet. That had been both enlightening and infuriating.

He had a history of buying up properties, demolishing the buildings, and redeveloping the lots. It had made him a wealthy man, but the prospect of her beautiful century home being torn down nauseated her.

She envisioned a cheesy souvenir shop and tacky cabins; the porch swing gone, a snack machine in its place; the quaint restaurant preparing home-cooked meals replaced by greasy fast food. Her blood boiled as she imagined what he might do, and she wished this city boy had stayed there despite how close to her asking price he'd come.

Most of the photos she'd found of him showed a stunningly handsome man with a variety of gorgeous women on his arm—sometimes one on each arm. No mention of a wife or steady girlfriend. Not that it was any of her business, but it was a reflection of his character.

Worse still, he was an American. A New Yorker.

The locals weren't pleased when the news that the Fosters had sold the island to a foreigner spread. Most of them admitted no one living in the area had the millions required to buy the resort. Still, they considered it a betrayal that the purchaser not only wasn't from Ontario but wasn't even a Canadian.

No matter that Daylin's had been the only offer in the two years the island had been on the market. Nor did anyone care that Gillian's ex-husband had forced her to sell so he could get his half of the money. Folks simply expressed their resentment at what she'd done without regard to the extenuating circumstances.

Now he was coming to claim what was legally his.

She carried the laundry basket into the master bedroom to make the queen bed, one of the many pieces of furniture she was leaving here.

She'd already moved most of the possessions she was keeping into a storage unit on the mainland in the town of Fiddlehead. The meagre wardrobe and personal items she'd need for her month here had been transferred into a room in the staff quarters.

Daylin had contracted her to stay on for two months to show him how the resort operated. She planned to live on the island for the first month and then move to the mainland and commute to work for the second month. This would help her transition to life without her island.

The scent of the outdoors wafted from the freshly laundered sheets as she worked. The cozy comforter she spread out on the bed would provide warmth for the remaining chilly nights ahead. She arranged the decorative pillows and stepped back to survey her handiwork.

All was ready.

Daylin would probably claim this room for his own until he destroyed the place.

Stop it. You don't know that's what he wants to do. She shook her head. It wasn't being cynical if history showed that's what he'd always done.

The weather report caught her attention. She cheered and did a skip-dance when the announcer upgraded the storm watch to a warning.

She rushed to the kitchen where she'd left her cell phone and called Daylin's office.

His assistant answered and took the message. She assured Gillian she'd notify Mr. Quinn to stay in his hotel tonight and head out to the island the next morning.

Relief flooded through her as she disconnected the call, and she sent a quick thank you to whatever weather god might be responsible for this turn. Admittedly, it was silly to get so excited over a one-night reprieve. Nevertheless, the rescheduling made her heart soar.

When Daylin stepped foot on shore, the place would be his. Until then, she'd spend tonight blessedly alone, curled up in front of the fireplace with a book and a glass of wine.

First, she'd better batten down the hatches before the storm hit.

***

Daylin Quinn ended his call and started his Mercedes-Benz E-Class sedan, which sat in the hotel parking lot. He gazed up at the sky.

The sun speared through grey-tinged clouds devoid of menace. His assistant had caught him in time to abort the trip to the island, but Daylin wouldn't let a little rain spoil his plans.

Rain seemed a remote possibility anyway, judging by the sky. If he was wrong, it might hit while he was crossing the channel between mainland and island, but so what? His boat was sturdy and would get him across.

He'd waited long enough to visit his new place again. The quick walk-through before he'd bought the island was a faint memory. He had big plans to implement, and the desire to get started was an itch he had to scratch right now.

To hell with rain. Most forecasts were wrong anyway.

Light traffic on the highway ensured he'd quickly get to the marina where he'd leave his car and pick up his boat. From there, it was ten minutes to the island.

He looked forward to meeting Gillian Foster. He'd investigated the former owner of Loon Island Resort and liked what he'd seen.

She'd lovingly cared for the place even after her marriage had broken down and left her to run it alone. Her insistence on putting into the sales contract a clause to honour the reservations she'd taken before the sale had

3

impressed him. He'd agreed to it readily.

If he ran the resort this season, he'd get a feel for the land before he made any changes. The bonus was that her pictures showed a fit, sexy body despite her hiding it under sweatshirts and baggy pants.

As he sped toward the turnoff to Loon Island Marina Road, he cranked the radio and burst into song. Anticipation and joy surged through him, and it was all he could do not to bounce on the seat like a kid on Santa's knee. The start of an important new project always gave him a thrill, and he was on his way to meet with an intriguing new woman.

Could it get any better than this?

CHAPTER 2

Gillian strode from the guest cabins back to the house and paused on the front porch.

The wind had picked up, and large, grey-bellied clouds obscured the sun. The lake's mirror sheen from this morning was now choppy and white capped. Waves hurled against the rocky shore.

When the storm hit, it would be fierce.

She'd make a delicious dinner before the power went out. Then she'd settle in with the book she'd been reading and a nice Cabernet, even if it meant reading in candlelight.

The low hornet buzz of a motor made her halt as she reached out to open the wooden screen door. Who the hell was crazy enough to be out on the water right before a storm? Intuition gave her the answer before she confirmed the sleek speedboat headed toward the island.

Damn him for ignoring my message. The arrogant city boy. Figured Mother Nature had no teeth because they'd covered her with concrete where he lived.

She huffed out a breath and hurried toward the dock. He'd need help securing the boat. If he was lucky, it would survive the storm tied up there. The boathouse had no room.

Silently cursing him, she reached the dock. Water splashed across the cedar decking.

Daylin's craft sluiced through the water, the engine cutting in time to slide the boat into the space to her right.

He tossed her a rope, and she hauled the craft in. She looped the rope around the cleat in a figure eight and then checked to make sure his fenders were in place. They were. One less thing to worry about. She estimated the Vista was worth six figures, and she didn't need it banging against her dock.

Her throat constricted. *No.* Not her dock but his.

5

Another rope landed by her foot. Daylin leapt after it, hauling a duffel bag.

His grin brimmed with delight, and he bounced around the dock in a blaze of energy. He snatched up the rope. Moving to the other cleat, he tied off the boat expertly, much to her chagrin.

Rain pelted them in a sudden torrent, and she motioned him to go ahead of her up the steps to the shore.

Lightning flashed, and five seconds later, the thunder rolled, deep and long.

His bag hanging from his shoulder, he scrambled up the rocky slope, Gillian begrudgingly admiring the way his jeans hugged his butt as he moved.

The wind fought them, and they were soaked through by the time they reached the front porch. She wrenched open the door and led him inside. She secured the screen, slammed shut the main door, and rounded on him.

"What were you thinking? You ignored my message."

Infuriatingly, he grinned and offered her his hand.

"Daylin Quinn. You must be Gillian Foster." His gaze travelled up and down her body.

How must she look with her ratty sweatshirt, faded jeans, and windblown hair? She disregarded the hand, planting both her fists on her hips.

"You shouldn't have gone out on the water. Your assistant promised to give you my message. Didn't you get it?"

He threw her a sheepish grin. "I figured I had time."

She shivered. "Well, you're here now, so we may as well make the best of it. Take your shoes off. I don't want you trekking mud all over my"—she paused—"your house." She kicked her own shoes off and stomped into the bathroom.

When she returned, she tossed a thick terry towel to Daylin and rubbed herself with another one.

"The temperature dropped, which is why this is such a dangerous storm." She smiled, but it felt so fake it probably looked more like a grimace.

Avoiding his gaze, she draped her towel over a chair and walked to the fireplace. "A fire will help me dry off. Did you want to change out of those wet clothes?" She pointed at the duffel bag he'd dropped on the foyer floor. "You only brought one bag?"

He shrugged. "I travel light. The rest of my things will arrive in a day or two."

She struck a match and held it to the kindling until it caught. A scowl on her face, she focused on the fire.

"Ms. Foster, I own this place now." His voice betrayed a hint of anger

6

for the first time since he'd arrived. "If I wanted to come despite the weather, it was my prerogative."

The kindling burned strong, the larger pieces catching. She tossed a small log on top. The reminder her home was now his stabbed her heart.

"I'm sorry if I seem rude, but you took a huge risk. Don't you get how dangerous that was?"

His expression relaxed as he shook his head. "No, I suppose I don't. You're right. It'd be a hell of a lesson to learn the hard way."

She sighed and went to Daylin, who stood with the towel hanging limply in his hands.

"Can we start again? I'm Gillian Foster." She offered him her hand.

He gave her a dangerously sexy grin and reached out.

When their palms connected, his soft, warm touch calmed her, and she wanted to linger in it. His grasp was firm and his handshake strong.

She'd have to be careful around him. His type was charming and charismatic—and nothing but trouble for any woman.

"Would you like something to drink? Water? Coffee or tea?" No way would she open the Cabernet now. She wasn't about to drink alcohol with a strange man.

Whenever she glanced at him, their gazes locked. His eyes were deep brown and ones she could easily drown in.

"Coffee, please." He snatched up her towel. "I'll hang these in the bathroom and take a tour."

She strode to the kitchen, flicking on lights as she went, and tried not to picture him walking around her house.

His house. Damn it.

Tears sprang to her eyes. Good thing he wasn't in the room to see it.

Stop crying like a baby. Put on your big-girl pants and suck it up.

She'd vowed not to grieve over this. It was a setback, and she'd recover. Someday, she'd buy another place on the lake.

Yes, but not this one. This one was lost to her forever.

She set up the coffee maker for two cups though she didn't usually drink coffee this late in the day. She checked the time. Only two o'clock? Her stomach fluttered.

Outside it was dark as night, and the rain poured down in sheets. They'd lose power soon for sure.

Daylin appeared, interrupting her musings. "The place is beautiful. You've taken great care of it."

Gillian smiled. Maybe he wasn't planning to tear it down. He'd said it was beautiful. Surely, he wouldn't want to destroy beauty. "I love a century home, and this one has interesting architecture. The uniqueness attracted Josh and me when we were house hunting. We've added on to it since then but maintained the original look and feel."

"You built all the guest cabins and other buildings?"

"Most of them. The barns were already here."

The coffee maker rumbled to completion, and she grabbed two mugs from the mug tree on the counter.

"We wanted an island large enough to have a resort and built most of the guest cabins ourselves." Years of work, and for what? She forced the sadness away.

He studied her.

She averted her gaze. "How do you take your coffee?"

"One sugar and milk." He took the pitcher of milk from the fridge and set it on the counter.

"It's raw."

He gaped at her, puzzled.

She smiled. "The milk. I have dairy cows." She shook her head. "I guess you already know. You'd have seen them when you went through the place the first time."

He picked up the pitcher again and sniffed it. "Isn't that illegal?"

"No." She laughed, and it brought a surge of joy. "It's for personal use." She finished fixing their coffees and handed him a steaming mug. Motioning for him to follow, she walked back into the living room and sat on the couch in front of the fire.

He set his mug on an end table. As he dropped into an armchair, his cell phone buzzed, and he answered it. "Daylin Quinn."

Gillian stared into her coffee cup while he talked, unsure if she should leave the room.

"I'm sorry, Nichole. I meant to call you … No, I'm here for the night … Settle into the hotel, and I'll see you tomorrow … Yeah, the storm's bad here too … Sure … You have a good night too." He hung up and put his phone away.

So he had a girlfriend waiting for him at the hotel. Annoyed it disappointed her, Gillian stood and moved closer to the fire. She stretched her hands out toward the flames, trying to chase away the deep, gripping chill.

He gave her a rakish grin and joined her, stretching his hands toward the heat. "I'm almost dry. If there's still daylight left when the storm is over, I'd like to check out the barn and cabins."

She moved away as he drew closer. "Sure."

"I don't mean to crowd you." He shuffled back and gave her space. "Do you mind if I ask you a personal question?"

"You can ask."

"I get the impression you didn't want to sell the place. Why didn't you buy out your ex?"

She returned to the couch and sat. "I couldn't afford it."

"You couldn't borrow what you needed?"

"No. I considered it, but I can't run this place alone. Besides, my heart wasn't in it when Josh left." She sighed. "I hate to lose it. I hate losing." She tilted her head. "If I could change my mind now, I would, but it's too late. At the time, it seemed like the right decision, and Josh wants his money."

Daylin joined her on the sofa but kept his distance. He set his feet on the coffee table and leaned back, relaxed. "When are the first guests due to arrive?"

"The Victoria Day long weekend. It's always our kick-off weekend." She curled her legs under her and set her empty coffee cup on the table.

A spark of lightning changed the darkness outside into a momentary blaze of light, and the crash of thunder that followed made her jump.

"It's almost on top of us." The words were no sooner out of her mouth than the lights went out.

The howl of the wind intensified.

She rushed to the kitchen window and peered into the murk.

Waves crashed over the dock, tossing the boat against it. The fenders would help protect it, but the potential for damage remained.

Not her problem anymore. Still, it would be a shame if that beautiful boat was marred.

He put his hand on her shoulder and she startled.

"A little jumpy? I hope it's the storm and not me." He removed the hand from her shoulder.

How was she supposed to respond to that? The truth should work. "Both. I didn't expect to be stuck in here with a stranger." Was that rude? Others had accused her of being too blunt. Josh had accused her of being too blunt.

Daylin's mouth opened and closed. He waited a beat and said, "Okay. Would it help if I told you I'm not a psycho?"

"Not really. Prove it by not attacking me." She checked the fire. "Why don't you throw another log on while I hunt up candles?" She walked toward the closet, snagging the flashlight from a drawer on her way.

He remained in place, studying her. "If you were afraid to be alone with me, why didn't you have someone stay here with you?"

She shined the flashlight on him.

He stood, hands on his waist and a scowl on his face.

Still sexy.

She gave him a frown in return. "I didn't have anyone I could ask. But I did tell a few people you'd be coming out here, and I can handle myself. After Josh left, I took a women's self-defence class. I'd prefer if you didn't force me to prove it. It would be inconvenient, and I don't like to be put out."

"You're blinding me." His voice and expression betrayed amusement.

She swerved the light to the side and held up a bag of candles. "I checked you out on the Internet when you bought the place. Looks can be deceiving, but you don't come across as a psychopath. To save you some time, I won't sleep with you."

"I didn't realize I'd asked you to."

Where had she left the matches? *Oh, yeah.* She spotted them at the back of a shelf and grabbed them. "I'm sorry if that's crass, but I'm familiar with your type. I'm not interested in being another one of a million. I've got enough problems."

And he had a woman waiting for him at the hotel.

Gillian shrugged. "Maybe I'm being presumptuous, and you're in a committed relationship. Your bio didn't mention a wife or girlfriend. It did, however, present you as one of the most eligible bachelors, and there were plenty of pictures of you with supermodels on your arm."

"Does that bother you?"

"No. I don't care what you do with your personal life. But we're stuck in this house alone, and I want to make sure you understand me. I'm not interested in one-night stands—or one-month stands."

She carried the candles to the living room and set a few up on the coffee table, the mantel over the fireplace, and the end tables. After she lit them, she went to the fire and threw a log on it.

Daylin hadn't moved.

She switched off the flashlight and returned to the kitchen. "I'll fix something to eat. We've got nothing else to do."

"Apparently not."

Unable to help it, she grinned.

He shook his head. "Do you overthink everything? I didn't come here assuming you'd sleep with me."

Based on what she'd read about him? Yeah, she'd assumed he'd try. Perhaps that wasn't fair, but no way would she admit it. She jerked her head up and opened her mouth to retort.

He held up a hand. "I did some research on you, too."

Her stomach did a flip. "What did you find?"

"Not much. Your website, with a short bio and some pictures; images of your resort on a couple of Ontario travel sites; photos of you and your husband at the local Chamber of Commerce. It's not like I hired a private investigator." He pressed a finger to her cheek and dropped it again when she flinched. "You play it close to the vest, don't you?"

"Yes." She went to the fridge and opened it.

When the silence drew out, she pulled out of the fridge and faced him. "I'll help you learn what you need to know to run this place. Sorry if I seem abrasive. Josh is the extrovert. You'd have been better off if he'd stayed to show you the ropes. He dealt with guests, with everyone, really." She stopped talking, a lump in her throat. God, she was awful with people. She met Daylin's gaze. "But Josh isn't here so you're stuck with me."

He nodded once. "All right then." He peered inside the fridge as if fascinated. "What were you after?"

She grabbed a tray of cheese and fruit she'd prepared earlier in the day. "This will do. There's smoked salmon, too, and crackers in the pantry." She lifted a glass jug of water from the counter and carried tray and jug to the kitchen table.

"I'll grab some plates."

They worked in silence for a while, Gillian wondering what the hell had just happened.

CHAPTER 3

Daylin studied Gillian while she munched on some fruit and cheese. The short bio he'd mentioned finding on her website was outdated. It still talked about her marriage as if it were intact. When he'd read it, he'd wondered what had destroyed the smiling couple. They'd seemed so much in love. It was hard to reconcile the happy, carefree woman in the photos with the cynical and suspicious one sitting across from him.

She wouldn't be one to let him pry, and she didn't seem the type to enjoy idle chitchat. Safest to discuss the property. Maybe if he revealed his plans to her, she'd perk up. He'd start small—ask about the basic stuff. "Does this place have a generator?"

She finished chewing and swallowed. "Yes. I won't run it for a temporary blackout. We have them frequently here, but they don't usually last long enough to warrant wasting the gas."

"I studied the financials on the resort. You made a good income for three seasons. Ever consider operating it year round?"

She picked up her glass of water and leaned back in her chair. "No. The guest cabins aren't winterized. I like the peace and quiet of the winter months. It gives me a chance to write."

He leaned forward. "You write?" Great. She'd be thrilled when he told her what he wanted to do with the place. For some reason, he wanted to put a smile on her face—crack that armour she had around her.

The long, wistful sigh she emitted said it all. "Yes, but I haven't published anything."

Ready for the big reveal, but wanting to savour it, Daylin decided to tease his way into it. "The phone call I had earlier? My consultant. She's helping me get building permits and secure contractors." His excited grin faded when her face paled, and she leapt from her chair.

"Oh, God. I was afraid of this. You're going to do it, aren't you?"

Confused, he rose but remained rooted to the spot. "Do what? What are you afraid of?"

"You're planning to tear apart my island, my house. So typical. Greedy developer wants to buy up nature, rip it up, and build a huge, commercial monstrosity."

Another assumption. This one scalded.

He scanned the house in the dim light, letting his gaze drift from the large, wooden beams to the fieldstone fireplace, and then on to the hardwood floors. The closets were cedar lined. The original fixtures remained, as did the hand-plastering in the hall and on the bedroom walls.

Tear it down? What an insult.

"It's mine now. If I want to tear it down, it's up to me, isn't it?"

Eyes wide, Gillian gripped the back of her chair. "Why not preserve it? It's a century home."

"Does it have heritage designation?"

Lips curling into a snarl, she said, "You know it doesn't."

He nodded. "Yes, I do. Nothing can stop me from tearing it down."

At the look of despair on her face and the sag of her shoulders, his anger deflated. She'd wounded him, and he'd wanted to wound back.

Ever since he'd arrived, she'd assumed the worst of him. Information she'd read on the Internet had influenced her, but did she have to distrust him completely?

"Gillian."

A rumble like an oncoming freight train interrupted him.

If possible, she grew whiter. She sprang to the kitchen window. "Oh, God."

He reached her side.

A huge funnel swirled across the water, which churned. Trees along the shore bent double. The sky was an insane mixture of green and black. In the distance, taunting, lighter clouds promised sanity.

His jaw dropped. He'd never seen a waterspout.

She stepped backward, bumping against his chest. Automatically, he put his arms around her.

She jolted away, giving him another surge of irritation, but it didn't last.

"Under the stairs. Quick." She rushed to the closet and opened the door. "There's nowhere safer. Hurry. If it makes land, it might hit the house."

The house had no basement. The island was part of the millions of square kilometres of unyielding *Precambrian* rock called the Canadian Shield. The closet was their only refuge.

He followed her.

When he reached the closet, she pushed him inside and slammed the

13

door shut—leaving herself on the outside.

He shoved the door open, ignoring the crash when it hit the wall. "What are you doing?"

She was blowing out the candles.

"Damn it, I'll help."

"Just get in the closet." She waved her arm at him, but he ignored her and helped her complete the mission.

The fire in the fireplace was burning down to coals, and she closed the screen in front of it.

The wind whipped the house, rattling the windows. Lightning flashed, thunder crashing simultaneously.

Heart in his throat, Daylin grabbed Gillian by the arm and hauled her into the closet, slamming the door shut behind them.

She whimpered when the ground shook. Unable to see her in the darkness, he sensed the warmth from her body on his right side. Not caring if it offended her, he put an arm around her shoulders. When he realized she was shaking, he pulled her in and hugged her.

"Are you okay?"

To his surprise, she leaned against him and rested her head on his shoulder. Her hair smelled clean, nothing flowery, and he rested his cheek on its soft cushion.

The house rattled and they both cried out in shock.

He held her tighter, muttering soothing words without paying attention to what he said.

"I'm sorry." Her voice shook.

"For what?" His hand stroked her hair.

Her arms went around him, and she clung to him. "I'm so afraid. You should have stayed at the hotel, but if you had, I'd be alone now. I'm glad you're here. I'm so sorry. It's selfish." She buried her face in his chest.

His body vibrated as he chuckled. "It's okay. I don't intend to tear down this house."

Muffled, her reply floated up, weak, uncertain, and relieved. "You don't?"

"No."

She lifted her head as though their gazes could meet in the dark. "Then why did you say you would?"

A cold, empty space on his shoulder remained where her head had rested. Reflexively, he eased into her and cupped the back of her head so she snuggled into his chest once more. "You assumed the worst of me. I got angry and didn't correct you. I'm sorry."

She pulled away and he fought the urge to touch her.

"I'm the one who should apologize. I've done nothing but accuse you of things I didn't know anything about."

They stood in the quiet dark until Daylin became aware of the silence. "Listen."

She sucked in a breath, and the doorknob rattled. The door cracked open, letting in grey light. She pushed it open wider and stepped from the closet.

***

Pale and drippy daylight shone in through the windows, making the room bright enough to see without lighting candles. The clock showed twenty minutes had passed while they'd huddled in the closet. The storm had been fast and furious.

Gillian went to the kitchen. Envisioning the dock and the boat in pieces, she refused to look outside.

"The house is still standing. That's something." She smiled. It would remain standing.

Daylin smoothed a finger down her cheek. "Right there. You have a dimple."

She didn't flinch.

He helped her clear the table, and when everything was put away, they stood together, gazes locked.

"I guess we'd better see how bad it is." She led the way to the front door. She slipped her soggy sneakers on and stepped onto the porch, Daylin right behind her.

The boat was beached but intact. Planks from the dock littered the ground and floated in the lake. Uprooted trees lay tossed about like pick-up sticks along the shore.

Heart pounding, Gillian ran toward the barn to check on the animals. As she neared it, she relaxed. The destruction hadn't taken this path. Whatever damage had been done concentrated around the shore.

She headed back toward the lake as Daylin reached the boat. He stood gaping at it while she walked toward him.

"I'm sorry. You had insurance, I presume."

"Yes. It's just stuff. It can be fixed." He focused on her as she approached. "I want to tell you what I have planned for the island."

She froze, so he went to her.

"I want to create an artists' retreat. The setting will be as natural as possible. I have no intention of tearing down your house. I want to live in it."

Her heart fluttered. "What are the building permits for?"

"I'll add some cottages. A lodge, where we can give workshops. I want a place where we can have yoga classes, meditation. Artists need spirituality to develop their creativity. I want to build this in memory of my brother. He suffered from depression, but he was a gifted poet. Andy committed suicide. If he'd had an outlet for his creative work instead of wasting his life at menial jobs, he might still be alive. I'd like to offer that to other struggling artists: painters, filmmakers, writers, anyone on the creative path."

Why had the son of a wealthy family, the brother of a millionaire, lived in poverty? None of her business.

"Sounds amazing." She stepped closer to him. Their gazes locked, and a tingle zapped through her solar plexus. If he smiled, she'd be undone.

He didn't.

He stuffed his hands in his pockets and led her back toward the house. "You moved your personal things out of the main house?"

"Yes. I've got the big bedroom in the staff quarters. I have whatever I need for the next month."

He halted and faced her. "I'm not assuming you'll sleep with me, but I feel something for you I want to explore."

She lowered her head, and her hair spilled forward, covering her face. When she looked up again, it was through an auburn curtain. "I'm attracted to you. I can't lie and say I'm not. But I'm not like those supermodels you're used to dating. My life is quiet, and I like it that way. I'm still recovering from a messy divorce. You're impulsive, and I'm not. I won't be your flavour of the month."

"I take calculated risks. Everything about you fascinates and attracts me. When my brother died, I swore I'd never waste time pussyfooting around what I want. When I see it, I go for it. I'm not pressuring you to jump into anything. I'm asking you to take things as they come and see what happens."

Before she could reply, a loon cried out, its haunting call echoed by another.

"Wow." Daylin scanned the water. "Where are they?"

She pointed toward a small island in the distance. "They nest there. Everyone avoids the island so we don't disturb them. We're lucky. With the windows open at night, we can hear them calling to one another. The storm probably roused them."

She inhaled. "I love the way the air smells after a good rain."

He mimicked her and took a deep breath. "I could get used to this." He hooked his arm through hers, and they walked up the steps and into the house.

The arm on hers was strong, comfortable, his body warm beside her. The more he touched her, the more she wanted him to.

When they entered the house, she pulled away from him, afraid to get used to the physical contact. Gillian kicked off her shoes and walked to the kitchen. She peered out the window at the mangled dock and the beached boat. Light from the setting sun streamed in, and she squinted into it.

This morning, she'd believed her life would change forever, and it had but not as she'd expected.

A thud from behind told her Daylin had dropped his shoes on the foyer floor.

"You should see the way the sunlight catches your hair." His voice was as smooth as aged whiskey.

An urge to have him close to her flushed her face with warmth. She looked over her shoulder at him and opened her mouth to ask him to join her at the window.

His phone sounded, shattering their intimacy, and he answered it.

She turned back to the window and listened.

"Hey, Nichole ... Yes, we survived. The shore took the brunt of it ... I'll meet you at the landing at ten in the morning. I'll use the pontoon ... No, Gillian will come with me and show me how ... Okay, I'll see you in the morning." He hung up, and Gillian watched his reflection in the window approach her.

He put a hand on her shoulder. "My consultant is coming tomorrow. She'll be staying for a while, getting a feel for what we might want to do. She can stay in the staff quarters." He stood close behind her, his body near enough to skim against hers.

An image of Daylin, a gorgeous woman on each arm, flashed through her head. Distrust filled her, followed by fear. He was sucking her into his trap. If she stayed here alone with him any longer, she'd sleep with him, and he'd use her. Guys like him considered women to be disposable. She pictured herself clinging to him, competing with this Nichole person for his attention.

She nodded. "Sure. I'll go and prepare a room."

The hand on her shoulder slid away. "Why don't you have dinner with me first, and then I'll help you get the room ready?"

"No, thank you. I need to get to sleep early. I have to be up before dawn to feed the animals and milk the cows. Meet me at the barn at five, and I'll show you what needs to be done." She faced him, pasting a smile on her face.

"Dear Lord, that's early. I'll just watch, right?"

She laughed at his horrified expression. "The animals are yours now. You'll have to learn to care for them."

"Is it too late to get my money back?" Amusement tinged his voice.

She gave him a quick smile. "Yes." She paused. "I have to go."

His face fell when she stepped around him.

She slowed down, though it was difficult not to run to get to her shoes. She slipped them on but not fast enough.

He caught up to her before she reached the door. "What's your hurry?

Surely you can stay for dinner? You have to eat something, don't you?"

She backed away, afraid he'd touch her again, and even more afraid that, if he did, she'd stay, not only for dinner, but for the whole night. "I have food in the staff kitchen. I'm fine. Sorry. I have a lot to do." Gillian stopped short of launching into her to do list. Jabbering would give away her nervousness.

Not giving him an opportunity to reply, she said, "Good night, Daylin" forcing lightness she didn't feel into her voice.

She darted out the door.

When the screen door slammed shut behind her, she whirled back and peered inside. "Five AM. The barn. Be there."

Without waiting for a response, she spun around and ran for the staff quarters.

CHAPTER 4

I t was too damn early in the morning to be sitting on a three-legged stool like a milkmaid with his fists pumping a cow's teats. Daylin didn't know what was more shocking: the position he was in, the fun he was having, or how proud he was he could do it. He dared to raise his gaze enough to sneak a peek at Gillian.

Her flyaway hair was held in check by a ball cap and a scrunchie, and all he wanted to do was rip her head gear off and burrow his hands in the silky softness.

"Watch your aim." She pressed her hands to her gut and laughed, loud and hearty.

A spray of warmth hit him on the ankle, and he returned his attention to the job at hand. "I can't believe I'm doing this."

"You're doing all right. Pretty good with—" She bit off her words.

He stopped squeezing, the shocked horror on her face making him sit up. "What is it?"

She blushed. "Nothing. I'll finish and we'll collect the eggs. Let me have the seat."

Annoyed, he rose and stepped aside as she took his place.

She'd been about to say "Pretty good with your hands." He was sure that's what she'd stopped herself from vocalizing. What was the big deal? They were having fun. She'd been laughing. He was good with his hands. Someday, he hoped to show her exactly how good. At the moment, though, it never seemed less likely to happen.

She was trying to avoid you thinking shit like that. He scowled, but she didn't notice. Was he never supposed to flirt with her?

Ever since she'd refused his dinner invitation and run out on him the night before, he'd struggled against a desire to confront her. At the same time, he was afraid to open the wound she was nurturing. No doubt it had

19

to do with whatever had destroyed her marriage. He'd fallen asleep mentally chewing on it, and as soon as he'd awakened, Gillian was right back in his head.

As she milked the cow, her shoulders hunched over the bucket resting under the udder. If she would relax and get to know him, he'd show her she had nothing to fear. The couple of times she'd let her guard down, it had been fun and easy between them. But then she'd wrapped up inside herself again for no apparent reason.

"Gilly." As soon as he spoke, he flinched. The use of the nickname had slipped out. Despite this chill she'd frosted the air with, he wanted to be close to her.

She removed the bucket from under the cow and faced him. "Yes?" Her eyes were wide, and in the dim light of the barn, bluer than sapphires.

"Everything okay?"

She shrugged. "Yes. Let's get the milk inside. We have to get it chilling."

She led him across the yard to the restaurant's kitchen, located in a building behind the main house. In the sink, she'd set up sterilized glass jars packed in ice. She removed the lids and poured the milk into the jars.

"Old fashioned, I know, but it's simple and fast."

Daylin watched, fascinated.

She finished pouring and capped the jars. "We'll go get the eggs and clean them. By then, the milk and cream will have separated, and it should be ready to refrigerate."

"You do this every day?"

She laughed. "Twice a day."

"I'll pay someone to do it. I don't need to learn this end of things."

She snagged a basket off the kitchen counter, crooked a finger at him, and guided him back outside. "Never mind the excuses. You should know how to do this."

"Why? I'll have someone live here year round who'll do it for me." Suspicion lacing his voice, he said, "What exactly has to be cleaned off the eggs?"

She halted and, hands on hips, faced him. "Are you a man or a princess? What if there were an apocalypse, and you had to live off the land?"

"You could teach me then."

"What if I don't survive, smart guy?"

When he moaned, she nudged him out the door and headed for the chicken coop at the side of the barn. She was smiling again, relaxed.

She opened the gate, and they entered the fenced-in coop area. "I leave the brooders alone to hatch and raise their chicks, and collect from the rest. They don't mind you taking the eggs if they're not interested in hatching them, but you have to watch they don't try to eat them."

While she talked about egg retrieval strategies and cleaning the bloom off them, Gillian collected the eggs from three of the chickens.

"Okay, your turn."

He stepped back, throwing his hands up in surrender. "I'm not touching those things."

"Come on, city boy. Show me what ya got." The corners of her mouth twitched as she indicated one of the hens.

He approached the chicken she pointed at. "It'll peck me."

She shook her head. "You saw me do it. Lift and grab."

"Yeah, but they know you."

"Trust me; they don't care. Just do it. You have to get used to it."

He disagreed—someone else would take over this job as soon as possible—but he didn't want to revive that discussion. Tentatively, he reached out to grab the chicken as he'd seen her do. To end his misery and show her he wasn't afraid, he grasped the bird. When it didn't react, Daylin lifted it, snatched an egg out, and released it.

"Okay." His breath was ragged. "Two more under there. How'd you get them all in one shot?"

She wiped a tear from the corner of her eye and, with visible effort, stifled the laughter. "Good job. Grab the other two eggs and put them in my basket." She held it out.

He managed to do it as smoothly as Gillian had done. When the eggs were in the basket, he grinned at her. "I did it."

"Congratulations. You're not chicken."

He groaned and then chuckled.

The sun had reached the yard, making him squint when they stepped from the coop.

He took the basket from her. "I'll carry that for you. Where do you want it?" He spoke low, gentle, her nearness making his body heat.

Her throat flexed as she swallowed. "Your kitchen. I'll leave some with you and take the rest to the staff quarters. Then I'll put the milk away. The guys from the marina are coming to repair the dock and pick up the Vista soon, so I want to get all the other chores done early."

They went to the main house, and Gillian showed him how to clean the eggs.

Daylin watched her every move, not because what she did was so interesting, but because she was so beautiful to watch. Everything she did had grace, a poetic rhythm.

He shook his head. She was turning him into a lovesick fool. He'd better get some guys onto the island before he went completely soft.

21

CHAPTER 5

Gillian closed the scheduler.

Daylin sat next to her at the desk in the office she'd set up for him in the main house.

"Since most of the regular staff will return, it'll be easy to get the place ready for the guests' arrival. As you can see, we're booked solid from the Victoria Day weekend to the end of the Thanksgiving weekend."

His brows rose. "Thanksgiving?"

"Canadian Thanksgiving. In October."

"Right. I forget you celebrate it earlier than we do."

She checked the time. "It's almost nine-thirty. We should leave to pick up your consultant."

Nichole. Gillian pictured a statuesque blonde, impeccably dressed and wearing impossibly high heels. She'd make Daylin lose that look in his eyes he had whenever his gaze met Gillian's. What should have been a reassuring thought irritated her, as if she resented the competition.

Well, she refused to compete with any of Quinn's hussies. They could have him.

"Let's go." Too abrupt. She'd better tone it down. "You'll like the pontoon boat. It's fairly new. You probably saw it when you inspected the place. We had a smaller one we sold to get this one." Now she was rambling.

She sighed, powered down the computer, and led the way to the dock.

The repairs on it had taken almost no time. She was sure she could have done them, but Daylin had insisted on farming out that task. The Vista would take longer to fix. She could have sworn he'd teared up when the guys from the marina towed it away.

As she guided the pontoon boat to the landing dock on the mainland, she scanned the shore for a sign of anyone who might be Nichole. "Do you see her?"

Daylin kept his gaze on the shore and shook his head.

Gillian eased the boat into the slip, cut the engine, and jumped onto the dock.

He followed, and together they secured the craft.

"Maybe she hasn't arrived yet?" She checked her watch. Ten o'clock exactly.

He shrugged. "Possible. She has a habit of being late."

She eyed the cars parked in the public lot. "What's she driving?"

"A Caddy. Black. Wait. There she is." He strode toward the lot, and Gillian spotted a sleek, black Cadillac pulling in from the dirt road on the other side.

The car tucked into a spot shaded by a cluster of beech and maple trees. The driver's door opened, and a slim foot in a strappy, flat-heeled sandal stepped onto the pavement. The rest of the woman followed, and she was nothing like Gillian had imagined.

Lean and lithe, Nichole was petite instead of tall. Her mane of red hair flowed in waves down her back, and her skin was porcelain and blemish free. Rather than the expected business suit, she wore a body-hugging sundress. Sunglasses, resting on a cute-as-a-button nose, hid her eyes.

Gillian regretted the T-shirt, ratty jean shorts, and running shoes she'd thrown on this morning, but immediately anger replaced self-consciousness. What did it matter if she wasn't decked out like a fashion model? She was comfortable.

Daylin hurried to the car and hugged Nichole, who rose on tiptoes and yanked him down for a kiss. "Darling, I had the worst time finding this God-forsaken place. It was so lonely last night without you." She beamed a hundred-watt smile at Gillian. "You must be Mrs. Foster. A pleasure."

The trunk of the Caddy popped open, and the newcomer waved to Gillian. "The bags are in the trunk."

Daylin's head snapped up. "I'll get them."

"I'd be happy to help you carry your bags, Miss ... I'm sorry ... I don't know your last name."

"Berringer." Nichole frowned.

"Miss Berringer, then." Gillian met Daylin behind the trunk of the car.

A collection of bags and suitcases were crammed into every space. She picked up two carry-on-type bags and moved away. "Shall we go?"

Daylin hefted the rest of the bags onto the pavement and picked up the two large suitcases. "What have you got in here?"

Nichole approached the bags. One more suitcase and a backpack sat on the ground. She made a moue of distaste.

"Make sure you grab everything you want to bring with you to the island and lock up your car. I'll meet you at the boat. Daylin will guide you."

Gillian walked away, smiling. Little miss city gal would find an astonishing lack of servants on the island. Fantasizing, Gillian imagined telling the woman she had to milk the cow herself to get cream for coffee.

Gillian had stowed both bags by the time the other two arrived. Nichole still pouted. Daylin murmured to her until they reached the boat and then clammed up while he set the suitcases on the dock.

After helping Nichole into the boat, he waited for her to sit on the padded bench under the canopy. He then hoisted the bags to the deck one at a time, and Gillian loaded them into the back of the boat.

Nichole goggled at them from her perch.

No one spoke. The boat creaking and water slapping its sides emphasized the silent tension. Somewhere above, a gull screamed out.

Daylin threw the ropes in and hopped aboard. Gillian maneuvered the craft away from the dock and headed back toward the island.

The real trouble started after they'd unloaded the boat and Gillian had returned it to the boathouse.

Once again, Nichole assumed the resort's former owner would take care of the bags. The consultant linked her arm through Daylin's, ready to make the climb up to the main house.

Daylin, to his credit, gave her a puzzled look and went to grab the two large suitcases. Gillian picked up the two small cases, tossed her hair back, and left the other two bags sitting on the dock.

"The staff quarters are beyond the main house, Miss Berringer. You'll be in the room next to mine."

Shock crossed Nichole's face, and she rounded on Daylin. "Staff quarters? Why am I in the staff quarters? Day, aren't I staying with you?"

"No, Nicky. The staff quarters are more appropriate."

She scurried to his side and took his arm again. She lowered her voice, whispering frantically at him.

Gillian stepped back to give them some privacy. She set the bags she held on the ground and waited. Though their words were muffled, she caught the irritation in Daylin's voice, and the undercurrent of whininess in Nichole's.

Why didn't he just take her up to the house? The way the woman touched him and spoke to him gave Gillian the sense the two had already slept together. It was one more reason to keep her distance from Daylin Quinn. The man was obviously a player. He'd been in a relationship with his consultant, and now, ready to move on, wanted to turn his roving eye to Gillian.

A rustling made her look up.

Nichole picked her way back to the dock to grab the remaining bags. Daylin sidled up to Gillian. "I'm sorry. She's out of her element here."

"Will she be staying with you, then?"

24

He looked pained. "No. The staff quarters will be fine for her. She'll have to get used to roughing it."

Gillian ignored that. Compared to what he was used to, the staff quarters might be considered roughing it, but she resented he'd said so.

Through gritted teeth, she said, "Okay."

"She's a friend. She's my consultant because she knows her stuff, and we're friends. She's doing me a favour and giving me a deal."

"I didn't say anything." Gillian widened her eyes, the picture of innocence.

"You're thinking things." His jaw tightened.

"It's none of my business what you do." *Or who.* She smiled, her lips a thin line. "I'll put her bags in her room and prepare lunch. Perhaps she'll feel better after she eats something."

He muttered under his breath.

She tilted her head and raised her brows in mock puzzlement. "Pardon?"

"Nothing. She has a tiny appetite. Don't overdo it."

"Fine. I'll set out food anyway. We'll eat whether she does or not."

Before Nichole caught up, Gillian walked away, leaving Daylin standing alone.

***

Nichole settled reluctantly into the room next to Gillian's in the staff quarters. The three ended up having lunch together, but Daylin had called it correctly: The consultant barely touched the food, eating like she thought it was poisoned. While Gillian and Daylin scarfed down a hearty lunch of Cobb salad, homemade chicken soup, and fresh rolls, Nichole nibbled on bits of lettuce and half a roll.

It was a wonder she had the strength to stand.

After lunch, Gillian left to do chores in the barn, and Daylin and Nichole went to the main house. At last, Gillian was alone.

Lunch had been tense. The remnants of the easy camaraderie that had built between her and Daylin faded away as Nichole, a.k.a. *Nicky*, batted her eyelashes at an accommodating Daylin.

How could men be so easy?

It was a relief to stand amongst the hay and scent of leather and animal in the barn and lose herself in physical labour. While she mucked out the stalls, Gillian struggled not to think about Daylin and Nicky. Whenever Gillian said the other woman's name in her mind, she used a prissy, whiny voice.

I'm so immature.

Whatever it was that poked at her whenever she thought of Nichole, she'd better get over it. Or learn from it. The issue was probably the other woman's relationship to Daylin coupled with Gillian's attraction to him. The sooner she shook off this jealousy—how she hated to admit that's what it was—the better off she'd be.

She set the shovel against the stall's wall. Using her fists, she massaged her lower back. How would she get through the coming months without getting her heart hurt?

Asking that was an admission she wanted to get close to Daylin. Her body did, anyway. Her head was another matter, and her heart? Her heart was what ached constantly ever since he'd pulled up to her dock and disrupted her life.

She groaned.

"You in pain?"

Daylin. You have no idea. She faced him.

"My lower back." She glanced over his shoulder. No sign of Nichole.

He put his hands on Gillian's shoulders and spun her around so her back faced him. His mouth close to her ear, he whispered, "Relax. Let me help you."

His fingers worked on her shoulders and then crept down her back until they massaged and soothed the aching muscles.

She sighed, tension easing. The warm air of the barn made her sleepy, and all she wanted to do was lean into him.

No. She refused to let him seduce her. Back going rigid, she twisted away from him.

"Enough. Thank you." She tried not to sound shrewish but must have failed because he frowned.

"What's wrong? Did I cross a line?"

No, I almost did. "Yes. Please, keep your hands off me." As soon as the words were out, she regretted them.

He remained silent for so long, studying her, she stopped breathing.

"I'm sorry. It won't happen again." He spun around and walked out of the barn.

Tears filling her eyes, she breathed again—hitched, ragged breaths that bubbled up regret. She picked up the shovel again and went back to work.

CHAPTER 6

The Loon's Nest Pub parking lot had plenty of spaces near the entrance, but Gillian slid her Honda Civic into a spot near the edge of the property. To her right, a stream gurgled over rocks, and ducks and geese floated in the water or waddled on the shore on either side. Wildflowers covered the banks. A bridge across the stream led to the pub's walkway and entrance. The lot was packed, the lunchtime crowd getting an early start—it was only eleven in the morning.

Daylin had encouraged her to take the whole day. He had even promised to milk the cows, get the milk stored, and collect the eggs. Leaving him to it made her nervous, but he'd insisted. Of course, he could handle it. They'd taken turns doing the barn chores for the last three weeks, and he'd mastered most of them to her satisfaction. Leaving him alone for a good part of the day would verify it.

She'd spent the morning running errands in town including visiting an apartment to rent.

May was almost over—the Victoria Day long weekend was this weekend—and she still didn't have a place to live. The one she'd inspected this morning had potential, though, and she would likely take it. Leaving the island would hurt, but it would be a relief to detach from Daylin.

Damn it, the man rang all her bells. Every time she was near him, she wanted to touch him, to, well, climb him like a mountaineer scaling a cliff. Each time she kept her distance, she died inside.

Nichole, on the other hand, flirted shamelessly with him, making her interest in him obvious. How could the woman be so uninhibited about chasing a man, especially one who'd demonstrated a lack of interest?

Perhaps she didn't care if he went from one woman to the next or if he used her as a temporary distraction. Maybe that's all she wanted from him.

To Gillian, it seemed a lonely and unsatisfying way to live.

Yeah, and I'm not lonely and unsatisfied?

She grabbed a large, faux-leather bag, stepped out of the car, and walked toward the pub.

Was sex for fun so wrong? What if she viewed Daylin as a passing fling? Just this once, she could have fun, sleep with a man, and move on. Like a man. Let him use her and use him the same way.

The idea horrified her. Was there something wrong with her that she couldn't loosen up like everyone else? Oh, it was so damn confusing and frustrating.

Inside, the pub bustled with activity. Voices mingled with laughter and music. Erika Wolfe, the server, waved to Gillian from across the room. "I'll be right there."

Gillian curled her lips in an attempt at a smile and waved in response. She scanned the room, picking out the faces she recognized. Almost everyone in the room had a familiar face. She'd lived on the island long enough to get to know most of the people living in Fiddlehead.

Keith Harrison, the pub's owner, stood behind the bar serving drinks. He waved to her, and she returned the greeting. Unsure if she should go talk to him, she took a hesitant step toward the bar when Erika reached her.

"Just me," Gillian said.

"Patio?"

Gillian shook her head. "Inside, please. The back, if possible."

"This way, then." Erika snatched a menu from the stand next to the door and spun on her heel. She wove around the tables, heading to the back room. It was quieter and cozier back there, preferable to the crush and noise of the main dining area.

Erika seated Gillian at a small table next to the unlit fireplace. After lighting a candle, Erika asked Gillian if she wanted her usual, the house white wine.

"Sure," she said, absently.

She searched this room for familiar faces as well and spotted a few. Rather than reassure her, it made her nervous. She reached into her bag, pulled out a novel, and opened it. If she kept her head down, maybe no one would bother her while she ate. She didn't dislike these people—she simply didn't know what to say to them.

It had been so much easier when she'd been with Josh. He was the outgoing one, the one people gravitated to and chatted with. Keeping quietly in the background, she'd allow him to monopolize the conversation. Without him as a buffer between her and the rest of humanity, she was exposed. The book was her shield.

She'd perused the menu and read a few pages of the novel when a glass of wine appeared in front of her and Erika asked her if she was ready to order.

Gillian smiled hesitantly. "I'll have the fish and chips—the haddock, please."

"Sure, honey." Erika didn't leave, but leaned over, and in a low voice said, "How are you holding up out there with the new owner and his girlfriend?"

Gillian flushed. "I'm fine."

She didn't want to talk about Daylin to anyone. She'd have to give them something, though. Gossip in a small town was unstoppable; you could only feed into it and hope it didn't come back on you. "He seems nice."

"Will he tear the place down?" Erika tucked an errant strand of her long, straw-pale hair back into her ponytail clip. Light from the candles glinted off rings decorating each finger.

"No. He said he won't."

"He's a Yankee, right?"

Gillian winced. "He's American, yes. He won't tear down the house. He'll add more cabins." Admitting that was likely safe enough. It might reassure anyone giving her grief for selling the island to a foreigner. No doubt, Erika would pass the information along before Gillian even left the restaurant.

"He as gorgeous in person as he is in his photos on the Internet?"

"You searched on him?"

"Of course. Not just me either." She leaned into Gillian's face again. "Well? How is he?"

Not comprehending, Gillian said, "How is he? He's a nice guy?"

"No. Is he hot? Sexy? Do you want to do him?"

Heat rose up Gillian's body and into her face, and she stayed mute.

"Oh, my God. Did you already sleep with him?"

"Stop it. No. Of course not." Why was Erika going on about this? "He just arrived. No." She paused. "No."

Erika grinned. "Oh, but you want to, I can tell. Thou doth protest too much." Her tone was teasing, friendly, but Gillian wished the woman would shut up and leave.

Thinking about Daylin had the blood rushing to her face again. Sweat trickled down her back and her underarms moistened. Damn her stupid body. Did it always have to embarrass her? She picked up her glass of wine, sipped, and managed to set it down again without spilling it.

"Don't worry, honey." Erika patted Gillian's hand. "Your secret is safe with me."

Gillian's gaze darted from side to side like a caged animal's. Why had she decided to have lunch in town? Didn't Erika have to get back to work?

"How you holding up?"

Another question. What did that mean? Holding up what? "Fine."

"Must be hard for you now Josh is living with Candi."

Gillian's mouth dropped open in shock.

Erika raised her brows. "You don't know? Oh, honey. I'm sorry. They moved in together last month."

How had she found out?

"He's not living in Fiddlehead." Gillian knew that much.

He'd moved to Temagami, not far away. Candi's family lived there.

"They come in here sometimes. To visit."

Of course they would. Josh was Mr. Popularity. When he and Gillian had split up, he got the friends, and she got the sympathetic, guilty stares. Everyone had always been closer to her ex than to Gillian, so it was no surprise they'd remained his friends, even if he was a lying, cheating bastard.

She wanted to take another sip of wine but didn't trust her shaking hands.

"Erika!" Keith's shout pulled the server back into her job.

"Coming." She winked at Gillian. "We'll talk later, sweetie."

Not knowing what else to say, she said, "Sure."

When Erika left, Gillian ducked her head back into her book. The words on the page were a blur, but she thought she gave a good impersonation of someone reading.

But her mind was on Josh and his nymphet, Candi, who'd met three years before at the resort. Candi was on summer vacation with her university friends, and they'd rented a cottage on the island. Gillian didn't know when Josh had ended up in Candi's bed, but before the week was up, the affair had begun.

Perhaps it had been while he was at the cabin on one of the numerous maintenance calls he got. Gillian was sure now it had been Candi getting him out there on a pretext to flirt with him, and he'd lapped it up. Almost eight years younger than Josh, she was a striking brunette, slim, and large breasted. Gillian had noted the girl spent most of her days in her bikini on the island's beach within eyeshot of the main house.

The affair continued after Candi had returned to Temagami.

Gillian got suspicious at her husband's sudden desire to run all the errands, leaving her to deal with the resort and its guests on her own.

While she didn't mind the chores, she hated dealing with the guests. Josh had always insisted Gillian get the supplies and run the errands on the mainland, so this flip-flopping had first annoyed and then scared her. He packed a duffel bag and disappeared for almost the entire day. He grew distant with her, and she caught him frequently texting in the evenings.

More often, as time went on, he didn't even come home. He'd call and say he was staying in town "with the guys" and didn't want to cross the lake in the dark after he'd had alcohol. It was the right thing to say to get his straight-laced, cautious wife to agree. Safety first had always been her motto.

Initially, she refused to believe he'd cheat on her. But as the evidence piled up, she was forced to admit it was true. Then she caught the pair in Gillian and Josh's bed together.

They'd screamed at each other; all three had cried. Josh had moved out shortly afterward, first to an apartment in Fiddlehead, and then, last month, to Temagami. And apparently, Candi had moved in with him.

The divorce proceedings had begun six months ago, the sale of the resort closing the day Daylin had arrived to take it over. Closing the sale helped clear the way for Josh to marry Candi.

"Ah, honey, here are your fish and chips." Erika's lilting voice cut into Gillian's brooding. "Can I get you anything else? Water?"

"Sure. Water with lemon, please."

Erika didn't linger this time, to Gillian's relief. But just when she thought she'd be able to eat in peace, Keith appeared and asked her if he could sit down.

CHAPTER 7

Gillian didn't want Keith to join her but was unable to say no. "Sure."

Keith Harrison had owned The Loon's Nest the last ten years, inheriting it when his father had died. Single, Keith had let Gillian know he was interested in her about a year after Josh had left.

Tall and sandy-haired, Keith had a quiet strength about him she liked, but she didn't feel any chemistry between them. He'd never made her heart race the way Daylin did with a simple glance.

Gillian picked at her piece of fish. It was hot, crispy, with a hint of grease to give it flavour. She loved pub food, but her appetite had disappeared.

Keith sat across from her and leaned back in his chair, an elbow on the seatback behind him. "How are you?" His tone was casual.

"I'm fine. Thank you."

"Come on. I know how difficult it must be for you. If you need to talk, I'm here."

"Thank you. I'll keep it in mind." *Please, go away.*

What was she supposed to tell him? That she was depressed? She wasn't depressed. She wasn't even sad. After the dust had settled on her marriage, the only thing she missed about it was having someone around to do the heavy lifting. When she considered it, she wasn't surprised it had come to that. She and Josh had been growing apart for years.

"There's talk of that Yank. I've seen his bio on the Internet." Keith sat up and leaned forward. "He causing you any trouble?"

Her mind went blank. "Trouble?"

Why did everyone have to interrogate her? She didn't know what to tell them. Josh should be here to do the talking. Anyone should be here to do the talking.

"He's a hotshot developer. A city man. Are you okay over there with him? I know you. Is he making you uncomfortable?"

Not as much as you are.

"No. It's fine. I'm showing him how to operate the resort. He has his consultant out there, so I'm not alone with him. He's in the main house, and I'm in the staff quarters. I assumed at first Nichole was his girlfriend, but he put her in the staff quarters, so I guess she isn't." That was way more than she'd wanted to tell anyone about Daylin and his personal business, but nerves were making her ramble.

Go away. Go away. Please, go away.

He continued to sit there. "How have you been? Tell me the truth."

Did he consider her to be his friend? They'd known each other for twelve years, but not socially. She and Josh used to come here to eat often, especially in the winter when the resort was closed. They'd hang out, Josh laughing it up with everyone who came into the bar while Gillian sat quietly and bided her time until they left. Sometimes, Keith would sit and chat with her, ask her about her interests.

Yes, he probably assumed they were friends.

"It's hard." Something released inside, and she dropped her gaze to the plate in front of her.

"I know. You don't come around much since Josh left. We miss you."

Miss her? No one missed her. She'd kept them all at arm's length. The only one she'd let in was Josh, and it had ended in disaster. "I'm sorry. I like my privacy."

He nodded. "Okay. But you shouldn't close off." His face brightened as though struck with an amazing idea. "Have dinner with me. I bet you haven't been out for a long time. How about it? I'll take you to The River Inn."

Her stomach constricted. The River Inn was the closest this town had to a fancy restaurant. Close to the lake, it had a gorgeous view year round, and the food and service were first class. "I'm sorry. I don't think so. But thank you for asking."

"Maybe it's too much for you right now. Okay. What about a walk on the trails tomorrow afternoon?"

"I'm busy tomorrow afternoon. Another time, okay? I'm not saying no." *Because I don't know how.* "Just give me some time, okay?"

"All right. I'll let you get back to your meal. If you want company, you can always come here, okay?"

"Yes. Thank you." A weight lifted from her at his words, and when he stood up to leave, her appetite returned. She tucked into her fish and chips and the side dish of coleslaw.

By the time she left the pub, her anxiety had dissipated. She'd even approached a few people in the bar to ask them how they were doing. It had taken an effort of will on her part not to dart past them without a word, but she'd done the polite thing.

When she reached her car, she was ready to return to the island and face Daylin and Nichole again.

"Gillian," a male voice called.

She turned.

Bruce Pankowski jogged across the parking lot toward her. Pankowski owned a construction company.

She suspected she knew what he wanted.

"How are you?" he said as soon as he reached her.

"I'm fine, thank you. You?" She hated the social niceties. If she were dying, she would tell him she was fine, and he'd likely do the same. What was the point of it?

"Good. How are things with the new owner? He settling in all right?" Pankowski removed the ball cap from his head, scratched his bald spot, and put the cap back on.

"Yes, everything's fine. What's up?" She pressed the button to unlock her car. She had no desire to talk to this man. He had a reputation for being arrogant and aggressive. His temper had landed him an assault charge once, though it had been dropped the next day.

"He'll need work done, right?"

"Yes." Best not to sidestep the question. She'd already told Erika Daylin would be adding buildings. Pankowski would hear about it soon enough.

"Put in a good word for me?" He smiled like a shark, all teeth and dead eyes.

"I'll tell him you're available. No promises. He'll make up his own mind."

"Sometimes these guys come in and bring their own crew, you know?" He scowled. "Doesn't make for good community relations."

Irritation flickered across her face. "No doubt he'll do what's best for his operation."

Pankowski put a hand on her arm, his grip strong and tight. "Encourage him to go local. It's in your best interests."

She tugged her arm but didn't shake him. "What's that supposed to mean?" Was this a threat?

"Might have problems you don't need if you don't go local."

"Let go of my arm. I said I'd tell him you're available. The rest is up to him." She'd tell Daylin all right—she'd tell him to stay well away from Pankowski. Other local contractors who weren't assholes existed.

Pankowski leaned into her face, and for a second, Gillian thought he meant to kiss her.

She swallowed, her stomach twitching with nerves.

His face softened, and when his lips curved into a smile, it was more leer than threat this time. "You want some company? We can have dinner tonight." The grip on her arm relaxed, and he tilted her chin up so they were eye to eye.

He was asking her out? Was he crazy? He'd threatened her.

"No. Thank you." Her voice shook, and she wanted to kick herself. No. She wanted to kick *him*.

"How long has Josh been gone?"

"Two years." Why had she answered him? It was none of his business. But she was frozen to the spot unable to think clearly.

"Must get lonely out there on the island." Pankowski rubbed his chin as though contemplating.

She took a step toward the car, and he grabbed her arm again, gently this time.

"Don't go. We'll have some fun tonight."

"No. Thank you." At last, anger replaced the confusion and timidity, and she acted. Gillian twisted, wrenching her arm free. She leapt to the car and opened the door.

"Hey. Wait."

All she wanted was to be back on the island, as far from Bruce Pankowski as possible, but her anger rooted her now. She held up a hand. "Enough. Back off. I'll talk to Daylin, and if he wants to interview you, he'll call you."

She climbed into her car. "See you around." She slammed the door in his face.

Tires squealing, she pulled out of the parking lot and drove to the landing.

Once the car was parked in her assigned spot and the engine was off, she dropped her head into her shaking hands and allowed the shock to hit her. Aside from her natural tendency to get nervous around other people, Pankowski had frightened and intimidated her. He must have been a bully in school.

Gillian had never spoken about anything personal to Barbara, his ex-wife, but if he'd treated her the way he'd treated Gillian, it was no surprise Barbara had left him.

Nerves back under control, Gillian grabbed her things, locked up the car, and headed to her boat. Halfway across the lake, it dawned on her she'd shaken off an aggressive man on her own. For the first time since Josh had left, she felt capable and whole.

CHAPTER 8

Purse hanging from her shoulder and bags of supplies dangling from both hands, Gillian stepped from the boathouse. Relieved to be home, she made her way up the bank toward the main house. She'd cut through the backyard and head straight to the staff quarters. This way, odds were better she'd avoid Daylin and Nichole.

The heat from the afternoon had faded to a pleasant warmth. A slight breeze rustled Gillian's hair and cooled her neck. She inhaled, relishing the clean, lilac-scented air. There was no place she'd rather be than on her island, away from the social pressures being around people always brought.

Except, it was no longer her island, and she'd never be alone on it again.

She refused to let that stir up her emotions. She'd managed to get back here after the ordeal on the mainland, and she planned to lose herself in some physical labour. That always cleared her mind and soothed the tension.

A low hedge of spiky green foliage demarcated the main house's back garden, and she walked behind it. Unable to help it, she peered over at the back porch.

She and Josh had had good times there, taking a break from chores and responsibilities with a cold lemonade or cup of tea and a chat.

At one end of the porch hung a hammock. She'd spent many warm evenings there, reading a book and enjoying a glass of wine while Josh puttered in the garden. After the sun had set and the mosquitoes came out, they would retire to the sunroom. Sometimes they'd make love on the sofa under the velvet, star-sprinkled sky.

Movement on the porch caused her to halt and stare.

Nichole sat at the round, glass table under the kitchen window. A laptop and a scattering of papers sat in front of her.

Daylin stepped from the house, carrying a tray with drinks and plates of food. Nichole raised her head, smiled at him, and cleared a spot for the tray.

His voice floated across the yard, but his words were too low to understand. She responded with a whoop.

Then Daylin lifted his head and met Gillian's gaze.

Her breath caught; her heart pounded. Heat rushed into her face, and she wanted to hurry away, but he smiled and waved to her.

"Come join us. We could use your help over here."

Nichole stared, expression irritated.

Gillian cleared her throat. "I can't. I have to put away these supplies I bought." It was a flimsy excuse but the only one she had.

"If there's nothing perishable, bring them with you. Come on. You've been away almost all day. Come and see what we've done." Daylin's face reflected delight and excitement.

Part of her hoped it was the sight of her returning that did it. *Don't be such an idiot. He's excited about your island, not you.*

"I should go get some work done."

"The work will wait. I milked the cows and got the eggs for you, exactly like you showed me."

"Did you chill the milk?"

He grinned. "Yes, it's in the fridge. Come here and have a drink and something to eat."

She tried one more excuse. "I ate in town." Even she heard the hesitation in her voice.

"That's okay." His voice was soft, and he held her with his gaze. "Have a cup of tea."

She wanted to. It hurt how much she wanted to. Head swivelling right then left, she calculated the closest way in.

Before she could move, Daylin leapt off the porch and jogged to meet her.

***

"Hand me the bags." Daylin held out his hands, and Gillian surrendered everything. He set them on the ground at his feet.

"Let me lift you across." He reached his arms toward her and his hands waved her closer. "It's okay." Half-afraid she was still skittish from what had happened between them in the barn, he wanted to reassure her.

She stepped close to the hedge.

He leaned across it and lifted her over.

A squeak escaped her as he took a large step backward to keep his balance. To his delight, her arms, warm and soft, wrapped around his neck. His breath shallowed and quickened, and he had an urge to kiss her while she was so close. He fought it and set her on her feet, but he didn't release her.

"Okay?" His gaze held hers, and she swallowed audibly.

Her arms had slid away from his neck but her hands lingered on his shoulders. Her body, so close, radiated heat, and he caught the scent of clean that always followed her. He ached to run his hands over her body.

Her eyes had glazed, and he wanted to cheer. Desire. It had to be. Her cheeks flamed with red.

He softened his voice and broke the lengthened silence. "Gillian?"

"Yes?" It was a gasp, vague and distracted.

He gazed into her eyes, captivated. "I asked if you were okay."

She nodded. "Yes. Thank you." Her hands slid to her sides, and she stepped backward. She shivered.

"Tea will warm you up." The chill had hit him, too. His body wanted her warmth on it.

He bent to retrieve the bags he'd set on the ground and forced normal into his voice. "Nicky made some great suggestions for the redesign of the restaurant. I want to have everything together: the studio and the dining room in the same building. Wait until you see the plans."

Gillian picked up her purse and the remaining two bags, and he led her back to the porch.

When they were seated, Daylin went back into the house to grab another mug.

The women's low voices floated out through the open patio door as Nichole showed Gillian the roughed out plans for the various buildings.

His morning with his consultant had been difficult, and he was glad Gillian was back and had joined them. Nichole hadn't wanted to let up on him, even when he'd made it clear he didn't want to continue with their physical relationship. She hadn't been hurt—they'd never been exclusive, and she'd had other partners between their trysts—but she didn't want to stop having sex with him.

To Daylin, she'd been companionship and physical release, and he'd assumed she'd felt the same way. Long periods of time passed between their hook-ups, and he was happy with the arrangement. They'd both seen other people and neither had cared.

When he'd first asked her to consult on this job, he'd figured they'd pick up where they last left off whenever she came out to the island. But meeting Gillian had changed his mind about who he wanted to spend his nights with. The attraction had been instant and electric, and she'd taken up residence in his mind as well as his staff quarters.

Nichole's unwillingness to make the relationship platonic complicated whatever was developing between him and Gillian. So did the gossip rags, which had him sleeping with women he'd never even met. Because of what Gillian had read and heard, she saw him as a commitment-phobic cad.

God help him, he'd had enough of casual sex—had lost his appetite for it before he'd even come here.

So what do I want now? Formal sex?

The real pisser was Nichole wanted him and Gillian didn't, yet he was holding out for the slim possibility she'd change her mind. He'd never gotten so twisted up over a woman before. But damn, who'd have thought watching a woman milk a cow or snatch eggs from under a chicken could be so hot?

He shook his head. If his buddies could see him now, they'd never believe it, especially if they'd seen him milking said cow and collecting said eggs earlier this afternoon. The chickens had almost won that round. He smiled and absentmindedly rubbed the souvenir pecks they'd left on his hands.

He returned to the porch, handed Gillian the mug, and sat next to her.

She smiled her thanks and poured the tea, but her hand shook as she held the pot.

Friction hung in the air between the two women. A scowl twisted Nichole's face, and Gillian's shoulders tensed toward her ears, hunching her posture.

Afraid to ask, he spoke up anyway. "Is there an issue here?"

"The contractor I'm recommending." Nichole's face clouded further, and the hands resting on top of the table curled into fists. "They're the best."

Gillian shook her head. "They might be the best, but they're not local. If you don't use a local contractor, you'll have trouble."

"We'll hire some local workers," Daylin said.

"Not good enough," she replied. "Both Fiddlehead and Temagami have excellent contractors."

"I want the best. Donaldson's always manages my builds."

She shot him a worried look. "How many small-town developments have you done?"

He hesitated. "This'll be the first."

She leaned back in her chair and sighed.

His eyes narrowed. He sensed he was about to be patronized. Under the table, his hands curled into fists.

"It's different in a small town, especially when you have to live there. People don't just want you to support local businesses, they expect you to. If you don't, you alienate everyone in town, not just the contractors you snub."

His hands unfurled. What she'd said hadn't been so bad, and it was delivered without condescension, though the snub comment wasn't endearing. "I need a high level of expertise."

"You'll have it—and you'll have tradespeople who can get you deals on locally sourced materials." Her hand moved, and he thought she would put it on his, but she lowered it to her lap instead.

Nichole jumped in. "The people we do business with can get great deals. And if the locals don't want to work for foreign contractors, we don't need them."

Gillian sighed, exasperation bleeding through, as though she was tired of rehashing the same argument. "I told you it'll cause problems for him. Daylin has to live here."

Nichole frowned. "No, he doesn't."

Gillian's head swivelled around to face Daylin. "I don't understand."

He glared at Nichole and opened his mouth, but Nichole responded first. "He lives in New York. Just because he bought this place doesn't mean he'll live here permanently."

"Now, wait a minute." He held up a hand. "Nothing has been settled. I planned to spend at least two years here."

"You won't live here?" Gillian spoke in a whisper, and he almost didn't catch what she'd said.

Irritated he had to deal with the question right now, he hedged. "I haven't decided. My place in New York is my home base. Originally, I planned to spend most of the next two years here while I get it to where I want it to be."

"Then after that?"

"I'd planned to go where the next project took me, with New York continuing to be my main residence."

Her face blanched. "I understand. You should still use locals to do the work. Support the economy here. It's the right thing to do." She rose. "I have work to do. Thank you for tea."

Panic rising, he leapt to his feet and gripped her arm. "Gilly, wait."

She stopped, and her expression relaxed. "It's okay. The plans Nichole showed me looked great. I'll give you the names of some local builders. Talk to them. The final decision is up to you, and if you're not planning to make this your permanent home, then it doesn't matter, does it?"

When he'd first arrived, he'd mentioned living in the house. She probably believed now he'd lied to her to try to get her into bed. This wasn't the time to explain—he wasn't sure he could explain it to himself entirely—but he didn't want her to continue to believe he'd lied.

"The original plan was to make this a temporary home. Plans can change."

Nichole sucked in a breath and scowled but didn't comment.

"I'll see you in the morning." Gillian slung her purse over her shoulder. When she reached for the bags, Daylin snatched two of them from her grasp.

"I'll help you carry these." If he could get her alone, he'd ease her mind.

Nichole spoke up then. "If we're done here, I can help carry your bags back to the staff quarters." She stared pointedly at Daylin. "After all, that's where I'm staying."

No one spoke. The women stared at Daylin.

"Yes. Fine. We're done here. Go ahead." He helped the women pick up the bags, and when they were gone, he sat down on the chair at his laptop but couldn't get back to work.

In the distance, Nichole and Gillian walk toward the staff quarters. When Nichole dropped the bags she carried and planted herself in front of Gillian, his stomach clenched.

CHAPTER 9

Gillian walked silently beside Nichole, unsure what to say to the other woman. The silence grew to uncomfortable proportions until Daylin's consultant broke it.

"He has feelings for you."

Throat constricting, Gillian had to clear it before she said, "Excuse me?"

Nichole's bags dropped to the ground. Arms rigid and hands fisted, she blocked Gillian's path.

"Daylin has feelings for you. If you don't see it, you're blind or ignoring it."

"I don't know what you expect me to say."

Nichole relaxed her arms and tilted her head to the side. Lips pursed, she contemplated Gillian. "Do you really have work to do?"

"Why?" She narrowed her eyes.

"We need to talk." She put a hand on Gillian's arm. "It's time we had a girls' night. Got to know each other."

"I'm not the girls' night type." Nerves twitched in her gut. How could she get out of this? The last thing she wanted was to spend time alone with Nichole. They had nothing in common, and she made Gillian self-conscious—like most people did.

"Honey, it's time you joined the sisterhood. We have a man problem, you and I. This has gone on long enough. There's only one thing to do: drink until we clear the air."

Gillian glanced toward the house. Daylin stood on the porch, staring as if contemplating running over. A surge of sadistic pleasure flooded her. Nichole could answer a lot of personal questions about Daylin Quinn.

Gillian shrugged. "Okay, I'm in."

"Excellent. I'll make us some blender drinks. You can't have a girls' night without at least a pitcher of margaritas." Nichole picked up the bags she'd dropped and led the way.

Gillian followed, anticipation making her mouth go dry.

Daylin remained on the veranda, one hand shading his eyes.

For a moment, she pitied him and considered telling the other woman to forget about it. But then Gillian shrugged it off. One drink with Nichole wouldn't hurt. Then Gillian would finish the work she needed to do and go to bed, no harm done.

An hour later, the women sat in the staff quarters' communal living room, a pitcher of margaritas on the coffee table in front of them. Gillian had fixed snacks while Nichole made the drinks. They'd chatted as they worked, and some of the frost hanging between them since Nichole's arrival melted away.

Gillian learned Nichole worked for a large architectural firm. Her expertise in project management and structural engineering, and her long-time friendship with Daylin, had him turning to her for help on many of his projects. She openly admitted to sleeping with him every time they worked together.

She now sat curled up in an armchair, legs tucked under her. She sipped her drink and then set it on the end table next to her. "I get my presence and my past with Daylin chaps your ass."

Gillian cringed at the crass expression. Unable to think of anything to say, she picked up her drink and sipped.

"We haven't even come close to getting it on this time. He's not into it." Nichole sighed. "It pissed me off. I was looking forward to some sack time with him."

"You don't have to explain." Why was she talking about this? It forced the image of the two together into Gillian's head, and she was afraid she'd never get it back out.

"I do. You should know he's acting like a monk, and it's your fault."

Gillian set down her drink and stood.

"Sit down. I'm not trying to pick a fight. I'm trying to tell you he's into you, and you must mean more to him than a casual lay because he's cut me off."

"I'm sorry. I have no intention of coming between you and Daylin." Who tossed aside a friend to chase another woman? And after what Josh had put her through, she'd rather die than make another woman endure such pain.

"You're not. We're friends and we always will be. But we won't have sex anymore. Sit down. It's okay."

"But …" Gillian trailed off, unable to think of anything to say. She sat and picked up her drink.

"Relax. I've got other guys to fill the void." She shrugged. "They'll do whatever I want. Sure, I got riled up when I realized Daylin and I would shift to platonic, but I cooled off when I saw the way you two moon at each other."

Gillian's face went hot. "I don't."

Nichole snorted. "The hell you don't. When your eyes meet, it's like we're in a corny romance movie. I've never seen him fucked up over a woman before." She picked up her drink and sipped, her long, red nails a stark contrast to the cobalt-blue glass. "I can't fight it. You should know how he feels about you. I don't want him to get hurt."

"You don't?"

When Nichole frowned, Gillian said, "I didn't mean it to sound the way it did. I don't understand casual sex. I've never indulged in it. I can't." She lowered her head, ashamed, and then realized the absurdity of it. Her chin rose, and her gaze met Nichole's. "If I were you, I'd be hurt and angry."

Nichole gulped from her glass and nodded. "I get it. But we weren't in love. We both enjoyed the physical relationship. We travel a lot. It worked for us. I assumed we'd pick up where we left off when I got here, and I was disappointed when he didn't want to." She smiled. "Nah, disappointed is an understatement. I was hurt and pissed off, so I had a hissy fit."

Gillian smiled back. "How'd he take it?"

"He wouldn't cave. I tried to seduce him. I should be insulted he found me resistible, but I can tell he's thinking about you all the time."

Gillian focused on her drink. "I can't be casual about sex."

"I doubt he wants to be casual with you. Has he tried to get you into bed?"

"No. I made it clear I wouldn't sleep with him."

"Yet he still refused me. You don't want him?"

Gillian shook her head but couldn't meet the other woman's gaze. What right did this stranger have to question her like this?

She stood. "I've had enough of this. I told you I'm not a girls' night type. Daylin's reputation is warning enough. I won't get involved with him. He's all yours." Her breath hitched, and, horrified, she fought back tears as a sense of loss hit her.

Nichole chuckled. "It's obvious you're attracted to him. Forget his reputation. Do you believe everything you read on the Internet?"

Gillian sat again and folded her hands in her lap. She understood how a whack-a-mole mole might feel. "Of course not. I'm so confused. What am I supposed to do?"

Nichole smiled. "I have to head back to New York tomorrow. It'll be you and Daylin here. I would love to be a fly on the wall for that, but, sadly, I have business to attend to."

Gillian stared at the hands in her lap. How the hell would she face Daylin in the morning?

CHAPTER 10

The speedboat's motor cut out as Gillian put the morning's milk into the fridge. Daylin had returned from taking Nichole to the mainland. The women had said their goodbyes the night before, Gillian thanking Nichole for giving her an outlet about the new resort owner.

While Gillian was indeed grateful for the chat they'd had, she still hadn't figured out what she was supposed to do with the obvious crush.

If Nichole had noticed it, Daylin must have, which worried her. She refused to get involved with a man who gravitated to casual sex. He was better off with someone who shared those values, someone like Nichole.

According to Nichole, their relationship had worked because it wasn't intimate. Gillian wanted intimacy and love. After her disaster of a marriage had ended, she was convinced it would never happen for her—certainly not with someone like Daylin Quinn.

Then with whom? Keith Harrison? She shook her head as she set the last bottle of milk into the fridge. He was nice, but she needed the chemistry. Every time she went near Daylin, anytime she even looked at him, he scorched her, electrified her. When he wasn't around, she continued to be consumed by him.

She absently wiped down the spotless counters and then picked up the broom to sweep the clean floor. She and Daylin were on the island alone for the first time in three weeks. She'd have to face him sometime. Not now. Now, she should change.

She looked down at her sweatshirt and cut-off shorts. Her "Gillian's Island uniform," Josh had called it. He'd said it derisively. When had his affection for her mutated to contempt? She thought it'd been before he met Candi; Gillian just hadn't noticed it until only mockery and derision had broken the silences between them.

Damn Daylin. She refused to change. If Daylin Quinn couldn't accept that you didn't muck stalls and milk cows in high heels and a sundress, then so what? Why did making him notice her appearance matter this morning? She hadn't cared before her conversation with Nichole.

The kitchen door opened and Daylin entered.

So much for changing into something more attractive. He'd have to see her, warts and all, now.

"Did Nichole get away okay?"

He nodded. "Amazingly enough she didn't even complain about carrying her own bags." He smiled. His eyes were more black than brown in the early morning light. "She tells me you two had quite a chat last night."

Gillian's heart thumped. What had Nichole told him?

He approached Gillian and stopped close enough for her to catch his scent: soap and spicy masculinity.

"She suggested I talk to you and clear the air about my personal life."

"You don't owe me any justifications." She backed away from him and went to the closet to put the broom away.

"I told you once before I go after what I want. What I want has changed over the years. People change, wouldn't you agree?"

She stood, back against the closet door, and considered the question. "People don't change, but they can modify their behaviour."

"You don't think changing your goals means you've changed?" He strode over to her, taking long, confident steps.

"I guess." A breeze blew in through the open windows and made her shiver.

He took her hands in his. "Come and have breakfast with me. We'll talk. I want to get to know you. I don't want to add to the hurt you're so obviously trying to heal."

"Daylin." As it rolled off her tongue, his name raced heat down her body. She envisioned them sitting at the kitchen table in the main house, the way they'd done the day he arrived. It'd been pleasant, even if she'd resented his presence.

Anyone else could have bought the island. Yet Daylin had, and he had wonderful plans for it.

"Okay."

They left the staff quarters, and he took her arm as they walked to the main house. She was again reminded of their first day together. They'd returned, arm in arm, to the house after the storm, and his touch had soothed her frazzled nerves. It had the same effect now.

In the house, Daylin went to the fridge and stuck his head inside. When he didn't come out again, she stepped behind him.

"Having trouble finding your way back?" Laughter tinged her voice.

"I guess I'm not sure what to make. You should know I can't cook."

She did laugh then. "Move aside, city boy. Let me take care of it."

He stood, relief evident on his face. "I'll clean. In my zeal to get you to have breakfast with me, I forgot I can't cook. I can make toast." His eyes went wide in appeal.

"Okay, you make toast. I'll make some omelettes and ..." She dug in the meat keeper. "Here it is: bacon. Let's see what veggies you have."

They worked together in silence, Gillian drawing comfort from the routine.

Soon, the air filled with the aroma of bacon frying, coffee brewing, and toast browning. His stomach rumbled and she smiled, pleased he'd get enjoyment from what she was making.

She started cracking eggs for the omelette.

When she and Josh had been together, they'd divided the kitchen duties the same way: She cooked; Josh cleaned. One of the red flags at the end of her marriage was Josh's sudden interest in learning how to cook.

He'd started asking her questions about what she was doing and had taken over the tasks. The bastard. He'd been willing to learn how to cook for another woman and had used Gillian to teach him. When she found her jaw clenching, she pushed the thoughts out of her head.

Behind her, Daylin switched on the radio, and rock music spilled out. The tune was upbeat rather than raucous, but she would've preferred her folk station. He reduced the volume to background music and went to set the table.

She peeked at him sporadically as he moved around the kitchen.

He had on jeans and a T-shirt and wore them well. He'd wear anything well.

He caught her peeking and grinned. "It smells wonderful."

The scent of frying bacon now dominated.

She checked the omelette under the broiler and removed the skillet from the oven. "Everything is ready. I hope you have an appetite."

He wiggled his brows. "I do."

When the double meaning of their words hit her, she scowled. Was this how it was done? Flirtation, double *entendre*, and sly touches until the woman gave in? Was that how Josh had seduced Candi, or was that how Candi had seduced Josh?

"What?" Daylin stared at her, puzzled.

"It's nothing." How could she tell him harmless flirting made her suspicious?

She'd believed she was well over Josh. They'd been apart for more than two years now. Daylin's presence had aroused the desperate rage Josh had left her with that she'd believed she'd long ago released.

"Did I offend you?" He drew close to her, and she involuntarily took a step back, nudging into the fridge as she did.

His eyes narrowed, and he sighed in frustration. "Do I frighten you?

Didn't we establish when I arrived that I'm not a psycho?"

Some of her tension evaporated in a gasp of air, and she managed a smile. "For the most part, we did, yes." She turned back to the stove and lifted the cast iron frying pan of eggs with an oven mitt. After setting it on a trivet on the table, she went to get the bacon and toast from the warming tray.

"Wait." He laid a hand on her shoulder.

She managed not to flinch, even when he gently spun her around to face him.

"What puts that fear in your eyes, Gilly?" His hands rested, one on each of her arms. The touch was light and warm.

"It's not you." His name caught in her throat. Afraid if she said it, he'd hear the desire, she kept it inside.

"What can I do to help you relax?"

Thoughts flicking to the moment in the barn when he'd massaged her shoulders and she'd snapped at him, she shook her head. "It's not anything you can help me with. I need to work through this on my own."

"You've stayed isolated, haven't you? He hurt you so badly you've locked yourself away. I'll make you forget him." He leaned toward her. "I want to kiss you. If you don't want me to, tell me."

The darkness of his eyes filled her vision until she couldn't see anything else. His desire engulfed her until she couldn't feel anything else. His scent, his voice. He became her craving, her lighthouse in a sea of fog and storm.

"Yes." She choked it out, and a second later, he captured her mouth with his.

CHAPTER 11

He was hungry and demanding, but then, so was she. The more he poured into her, the more she wanted to take, and the more she took, the more she had to give. Her head spun and her body quivered. A moan escaped her. How long had it been since she'd been with a man?

Years, her body answered. *It's been years.*

Daylin lifted his mouth from hers, raised a hand to stroke her cheek, and smoothed a stray lock of hair from her forehead. "Tell me you don't want me, and I'll never touch you again."

Arms wrapped around his back, hands clutching his shirt, Gillian clung to him. "That's not fair. You can't kiss me like that and then ask that of me."

He dropped his head again, and the tsunami of desire returned, wave upon wave of it, dragging her under. She battled an urge to pull him to the floor, to ask him to take her right there. The ache for him was unbearable, and another moan escaped her.

She broke the kiss. "I do want you to touch me. I want it. But I need …" She trailed off, uncertain what she wanted to say.

He hugged her to his chest. One arm held her close while his other hand stroked her hair.

"Okay. We'll let it go for now." He shifted her back until their eyes were level.

"You have the most intense gaze of any woman I've ever met." Tilting her chin up, he kissed her on the nose and then planted another one on her lips. It was tender, yet playful.

He grinned. "Our food is getting cold."

"I guess we should eat then." But she remained still, and he had to step away from her to the frying pan.

As soon as his back was turned, the spell broke, and Gillian followed him.

Together they put the food on the table, and as they ate, he talked to her about his plans for the resort. He seemed happy, excited, and she'd played a part in making him that way. She refused to destroy it by reminding him her time with him was almost at an end.

After breakfast, she helped him clean up. It was something she liked to do anyway. They enjoyed a second cup of coffee on the back porch, the rising sun making the water sparkle. The breeze had picked up, swaying the birches and cedars and spicing the air with their scent. A hummingbird darted among the flowers Gillian had planted in the garden.

Her hummingbird. Her flowers. She still considered them hers, even if Daylin owned the land under them now.

She set her empty mug on the table and smiled at him. "We'll have to get the rooms ready for the staff. I'll show you the administrative stuff. Housekeeping will get the restaurant ready and the cabins cleaned and aired out."

They didn't talk about the kiss or what would inevitably follow. When they rose to go inside, they both knew they weren't heading to the office, though Gillian talked about the files they'd access when the computer booted up, and Daylin nodded as if interested.

He steered them toward the bedroom—he took her by the hand as they passed by it and guided her to stand next to the bed.

Neither spoke.

He led and she let him.

His hands stroked her arms and her face, slowly and gently, but the strain of holding back showed in his expression.

"Gilly." His voice, hoarse and low, vibrated through her. "Tell me you want this."

Her hands fluttered across his chest, and she ran her palms along his shoulders and down his arms. His muscles were solid, his body tight and taut. Lust speared from her chest to her loins. Her arms went around him, and she raised her chin to invite his kiss.

"Yes, I want this. Now. You can touch whatever you want right now."

He groaned at the invitation and accepted it, lowering his mouth to cover hers in a fierce, hungry capture. His hands gripped the bottom of her sweatshirt, and in a flash, it was off her and on the floor.

Her fingers struggled to tug his shirt over his head, and for a comical moment, he was trapped in it as she yanked at it.

"God, just rip it off." The words floated, muffled, from under the shirt.

She wrestled it up until his face appeared. They both laughed with delight when their gazes met again.

He pulled her to the bed and eased her down on it.

"Your breasts are beautiful." He palmed them through the practical material of her bra.

"I'm small." She said it without apology. It was a fact.

He unhooked the plain cotton garment and removed it.

"You're perfect." His head dipped and he sampled the nipples, pulling a groan from her when they hardened under his lips.

His tongue teased. His teeth nipped and tormented.

Pulsing with sensation, she rolled out from under him and clutched at his jeans.

Clothes scattered around them as they undressed each other in a frenzy of need. Naked, they rolled together on the bed, wrestling, fighting for union. They explored each other's bodies, both rising higher on a wave of pleasure.

Before her mind was totally lost, Gillian cried out, "Condom," and Daylin lunged for the table next to the bed. In seconds, he was ready for her, and when he finally entered her, it was with a ferocity that mirrored her own.

She couldn't recall such an aching need to be filled, such a desire to be conquered. Her hands stroked his face and his hair. She wanted to touch every part of him and opened to receive him.

The pressure of his body on hers wasn't enough.

She wrapped her legs around him and thrust her pelvis up to meet him. Her cries echoed in her ears.

"Gilly. Oh, my God. I can't hold on any more."

"Then let go. Just let go."

They floated away together until, unable to go any higher, they released.

He collapsed on top of her, his lips seeking hers again. His palms cupped her face, and she held his eyes with her gaze.

"Daylin."

"Shh. Let me look at you."

She tried to be quiet and still to let him enjoy the moment. Odd she considered that important. She couldn't remember doing the same for Josh. Perhaps that had been part of the problem.

Daylin kissed her forehead and her cheeks.

She wrinkled her nose when he kissed it.

The weight of his body pressed on her and became uncomfortable, but she didn't want to ask him to move. Once they disconnected, she'd have to confront the implications of what she'd done with him.

"I'll move so I'm not crushing you." He rolled away from her and lay on his back.

She shivered, chilled from the loss of his body heat. When she made a move to get up, he sat up and restrained her with a hand on her arm.

"Where are you going?" A hint of worry laced his voice.

It made her strangely jubilant.

"To shower. Get dressed. I guess it'll be the other way around. I'll have to get dressed before I go to the staff quarters to shower." *Staff quarters.* It echoed in her ears and hung between them. She was staff.

"Shower here. You don't have to leave. If you want, we can shower together."

She hesitated. What, if anything, would that mean? Did it have to mean anything? Nichole, carefree, laid back, wouldn't overthink something like this—she'd do what she wanted.

It would be faster to shower here. A compromise might work.

"Okay, I'll shower here. But I'd like to get in and out quickly. If you don't mind, I'll go first."

His face remained neutral. Was he disappointed or indifferent?

"All right." He lay back in the bed and pulled the sheet across his abdomen.

Gillian hesitated.

Was there something more she should say now? "Thank you" came to mind, but she was afraid it sounded too formal.

In the end, she simply picked up her clothes from the floor and strolled into the bathroom.

CHAPTER 12

When the shower started, Daylin stretched and got out of bed. He hunted for his cell phone and found it on the floor with his clothes. The display showed a missed call from his mother. Guilt welled up. He'd forgotten to call her this week. Might as well do it now.

Sandra Quinn's warm voice responded after the second ring. "Hello?"

"Hi, Mom. I'm sorry I haven't called you for days. I've been preoccupied."

"That's okay. I always assume you're busy."

He smiled. "I should have called anyway, and I apologize. Nichole got the building permits we need and returned to New York to get the blueprints formally drawn up. I want to line up a local contractor, which will take time, but I think I can get the work started soon."

"Wonderful. Your brother would be so proud of you."

"When will you and Dad come and visit?"

There was a long pause. She was probably thinking of what excuse to give for why his father wouldn't be joining her. *She'll go with "busy."*

"Your father is busy ..."

Nailed it. "He can't take a few days to come and see what I'm building here in honour of his dead son?"

"Honey, try to understand. He's still grieving."

Daylin bit back the retort, not wanting to take his anger at his father out on his mother. Patrick Quinn's stubborn pride had cost him a relationship with his youngest son. Now it threatened to destroy the one with his eldest.

"Okay. We'll leave it alone for now. When will you come? You can meet Gillian Foster." Enthusiasm raised his voice and had him pacing around the room, still naked.

Behind him, the water in the shower cut off. The plastic curtain rasped as it tugged aside. Gillian would be stepping out of the tub, her skin damp and her hair dripping. An urge to burst into the bathroom and lick the droplets off her body almost made him disconnect the call.

"How's Tuesday?" His mother's voice dragged him back to reality. "Daylin?"

"Sorry. I got distracted." Had he ever. He should cover up before Gillian appeared and saw how much he missed her. He grabbed a robe from the closet and wrestled it on while he talked to his mother. "Sounds fine. Staff will have settled in by then. My assistant will call you and make the arrangements. Wait until you see what I've got planned."

The bathroom door opened. Gillian walked out, dressed, her hair slicked back from her face, emphasizing her large eyes and sensual lips.

He gulped. "I've got to go. Gillian just walked in." *From my shower after we made love.* His throat constricted.

After he ended the call and set the phone down, he went to her and cupped her face in his hands. "You look good enough to eat."

She laughed. "I'm back in my sweatshirt and cut-offs."

"If you wore a garbage bag, I would still want to ravish you."

"The shower's all yours, and we've got work to do."

"Killjoy." He covered her mouth with his anyway, tasting and savouring. After he drew a moan from her, he pulled away. "That'll have to hold us."

He released her and went into the shower, happy she'd finally opened up to him. She wouldn't regret it—he'd make sure of that. No more heartbreak. No more pain and loneliness. She deserved better than she'd had, and he'd make sure she got it.

While he showered, Daylin sang as if no one was listening.

***

Gillian listened to the full-throated warbles emanating from the open bathroom door and smiled, affection for Daylin growing. He made her laugh, eased her stress, and filled her with his infectious joy. Her body tingled at the memory of his touch. If she wasn't careful, she'd fall in love, and she refused to let that happen.

Since Josh had left her, she hadn't slept with another man. She hadn't even dated. Daylin had taken possession of her heart as well as her island. She'd have to proceed with caution. Nichole might be able to go in and out of a man's life without emotional repercussions, but Gillian couldn't.

She went out to the kitchen and put the kettle on. When she was growing up, her mom always made tea when Gillian had an emotional crisis to deal with. A longing for her mother overcame her, and Gillian prepared the tea in a travel mug. While it steeped, she scribbled a note for Daylin and left it on the kitchen table, along with a fresh pot of tea.

The shower shutting off put her in a panic. She didn't want him following her right now. She grabbed her mug of tea and charged out the door.

***

Daylin left the bathroom, a towel wrapped around his waist. Everything was quiet. He got dressed, putting on a clean T-shirt and jeans, and went to find Gillian. In the kitchen, he discovered the pot of tea and her note: *I'll be back in an hour. Enjoy the tea.*

Would she have gone to the mainland without telling him? They were planning to head there later anyway, so it didn't make sense.

He fixed a cup of tea and took it outside.

The first place he checked was the boathouse. All boats were where they should be, including the newly repaired Vista. So she hadn't left the island. Maybe back at the staff quarters? Why had she run out on him?

Frustrated, but realizing he was being petty by making assumptions and taking it personally, he headed back to the house. If she'd wanted him to follow her, she'd have told him where she'd gone. He'd get some paperwork out of the way, and when she returned, he'd get some answers.

***

Gillian was at her private place on the bluffs overlooking the lake on the other side of the island. Long ago, she'd set up a couple of wide-armed, cedar-slatted Muskoka chairs and a small table. Solar fairy lights decorated the trees behind her. A gazing globe stood in the midst of a small garden of wild flowers.

It was a perfect place from which to watch the lake or the sunset—with Josh, when they'd been together, and now, alone.

Five years before, she and her brother had scattered their parents' ashes on the rocks below after a car accident had taken their lives. Whenever she missed her mother, Gillian came up here to talk to her.

The tea was hot and comforting, exactly like her mother used to make. Gillian curled up on the chair and leaned back, letting tension and sorrow drain out. "I had a wonderful morning with a new man, Mom. You'd like him. I hope you see him with me. Well, maybe not this morning." She smiled, remembering. "He makes me feel good, and I haven't connected like this with anyone in such a long time."

God, she missed her mother. They used to talk on the phone at least once a day.

The sun, high above, beat down. A breeze blowing up from the lake brought scant relief from the heat.

Gillian rolled the sleeves of her sweatshirt up. She was overdressed for the current temperature, and exposing her arms did little to cool her off. After scanning the lake to make sure no one was around, she removed the sweatshirt. She leaned back and let the sun and air hit her exposed skin.

"I think I might be falling in love with him." The admission was easier if she pretended her mother listened. She sipped her tea and imagined her mother relaxing in the chair beside her. Mom would have joined in the sunbathing, but she'd have worried at the lack of sunscreen.

"I won't stay out here much longer, I promise. It's difficult to concentrate with Daylin nearby. I had to clear my head, and it's been weeks since I've come up here. I'm sorry for not visiting sooner. We've been so busy."

The fact was, the time had flown, and she'd forgotten to come up here. Daylin had become a friend to her, as had Nichole, and they'd monopolized her free time like no one else ever had.

"It's lonely on the island sometimes. It never bothered me to be so far away from people before. I like the solitude. But Daylin's got me so mixed up I need someone to talk to."

What about Erika? No. Erika wasn't a good friend.

Gillian didn't have good friends. She was used to keeping her own company or the company of her family: her parents, her brother, her cousins, and Josh. Anytime she'd needed them, they'd been there.

In high school, she'd had one or two girls she'd hung out with, but when they left for university, she lost touch with them. She'd hung out with her brother and his friends until they moved away. Then she'd married Josh, and he'd brought friends to the marriage. It had never bothered her that the people who came into and out of her life did so because she was with someone they knew.

"I'm a loner. I've always been a loner. I like it. I don't dislike people ..." Then what was it?

No man is an island. Her father used to repeat that cliché. *"No man is an island, Gilly. You need people."*

Her dad certainly had. He was never happy unless he had a crowd around him.

Gregarious Radley Foster had made friends wherever he went. Too many, in Gillian's mind. A huge crowd had turned out for her parents' funeral, overwhelming her. Thankfully, her brother and Josh had run interference, shielding her from the press of the crowd and the small talk.

What did buying an island to live on say about her?

Out on the lake, a fishing boat trolled past. She followed its progress, lazily sipping her tea.

She must stop agonizing over Daylin—too high school. The day she'd met him, he'd suggested taking things as they came. It was a good idea.

Whenever the panic rose, she'd have to remember that.

"You know, Mom, I think you'd tell me I don't have to tie myself to him forever because I slept with him. I don't even have to love him forever. But you'd want me to love him and not use him. That was your style, and you taught me to treat my lovers with respect."

With Josh, it had backfired on her.

Daylin isn't Josh. Something else to keep in mind.

Gillian stretched and yawned. She bunched her windswept mane in her hands and twisted it up on her head, letting the breeze hit her neck.

Out on the lake, the fishing boat drew close to her shore.

She squinted, focusing on it.

A man in the boat aimed binoculars in her direction.

First, she blushed, her face heating in a rapid wave of embarrassment. Then she snapped her shirt up and dragged it on. This was her private space, and some creep was playing peeping Tom with her.

While part of her told her she'd been asking for it, the other part insisted she had a right to privacy.

"I'm sorry, Mom. It's time I got back anyway. Daylin will be wondering what happened."

She said her goodbyes and returned to the house.

CHAPTER 13

Daylin heard her come in but didn't get up to go meet her despite the overwhelming urge.

Like a puppy greeting its master.

He shoved the thought aside. She wouldn't see it that way, so neither should he. Still, letting her come to him allowed her the space to do it in her own time.

"Hi. Did you get a lot of work done while I was gone?" Gillian stood next to him and peered over his shoulder.

He caught her glance and she flushed.

"I'm sorry. For all I know, you were watching porn."

He laughed. "After this morning, what would I want with porn?" He wrapped an arm around her legs and pulled her into his lap.

She squealed and grabbed his shoulders. Her cheek came to rest against his neck, her hair tickling his chin.

He squeezed her to him. "Where did you sneak off to?" He hoped it sounded light, casual, even though that question had distracted him the entire time she was away.

"I went for a walk."

Uneasy, he lifted her up so they faced each other. "Are you sorry we had sex?"

To his great relief, she leaned in and kissed his lips. "No, not at all."

"Did I do something to make you want to get away from me?"

She shook her head. "No. I honestly just needed time to think. Josh used to accuse me of overthinking things, and I guess I'd agree. But it doesn't stop me from needing to do it. I took the time out."

"You could've told me, and I wouldn't have stopped you." His voice was gentle. It was true. He would've let her go. He wouldn't have tried to stop her and drag out of her the reason for the need to walk away from him right after they'd made love. And yet ...

"I'm lying. I'd have tried to find out why you ran away from me."

"Thanks for that. I wasn't running away from you, though. I was running to something: my private thinking place. It had nothing to do with you. Sometimes, I need my space. This was one of those times."

"Okay. I'll accept that." He had to, for now. Perhaps over time, after he'd gained her trust, she'd no longer have the need to escape.

"Thank you." She wiggled in his lap, attempting to stand.

"Keep that up, and I'll drag you back to bed."

Her laughter rang out again, and he grabbed her and tickled her to keep it going. Breathless, she struggled and fought, but the giggles continued. When she'd had enough, he manoeuvred her in for a kiss before he helped her stand.

"I'll run home to change before we go to town. We should leave so we can get back in time to do the afternoon chores."

Ah, the milking and collecting of the eggs. It had lost all its charm. He anticipated the day when the staff could take over those jobs. It was still sexy to watch her do it though.

"I'll meet you at the dock." Daylin looked forward to going into town. It would give him an opportunity to finally meet the locals and see what they thought of the new owner of Loon Island Resort.

***

Initially, Daylin attributed the stares to curiosity. People gave him and Gillian surreptitious glances as the two went about their business in Fiddlehead. Often, someone waved a greeting to Gillian, but didn't approach. A few people shouted a quick hello to her and continued on their way. The townsfolk were polite, but not friendly.

After a morning of shopping for supplies, Gillian and Daylin returned to her Civic, which was parked in a lot near the centre of town. They stashed their purchases in the back, when he noticed the time and his growling stomach.

"What's a good place to eat around here? My treat."

She paused. "The Loon's Nest. Good pub fare. There's fine dining at the hotel, but it's more for dates."

He took her hand. "We could have a date."

She flinched and tugged at the hand he'd clasped.

"What's wrong?" He looked around. "You don't want people to see me hold your hand?"

A flush spread up her face, and she shook her head, but she extricated her hand from his. "It's not about you. Right now, I want to keep whatever is going on between us private."

"I don't understand." What did these strangers matter to him? What did they matter to her? Since he'd landed on the island, she hadn't had a single visitor from town. He'd never heard her chatting on the phone. She didn't text in front of him. "Do you have a problem with the people here?"

"No. They don't need to know my private life."

"What do you care? We're consenting adults. These days, holding hands in public is accepted. We don't need to rent a room to do it." He injected humour into the tone but didn't get the expected laugh.

She hesitated. "Josh was friends with a lot of them."

"So? You're divorced. Aren't you?"

"The final papers still have to be signed, but my marriage is certainly over."

"Then what does it matter if you move on?"

"I've moved on. I don't want to do it publicly yet. Please?"

He forced down the rising irritation. "Okay. Let's go to the pub. I'm hungry. Are you hungry?" He fought an urge to touch her. To be safe, he stuck his hands in his pockets.

She smiled. "Yes." A long pause followed, during which she gazed down at the pavement. When she raised her head, her eyes betrayed guilt.

"Thank you. I'm sorry, but I don't want them prying into my personal life. They were already asking questions the last time I was in town. I want to be left alone."

His arm twitched with the need to comfort her. "Let's walk, then. Which way?"

She led him down the sidewalk. "It's close—down by the stream that flows out of Lake Temagami. There's a patio."

As they walked, he observed the people. Again, he noticed stares, some sneaky, others overt. A few people waved to Gillian. One or two called a greeting. No one approached her.

"Do you have friends here in town?"

"No. Acquaintances, I guess." She didn't sound sad, but she didn't sound thrilled about it.

"Don't you miss hanging out with people? Spending time with them? It must get lonely on your island in the winter." As soon as he said it, he realized he'd referred to the island as hers.

"I've always had family. After my parents died, Tony, my brother, got married and moved to Toronto with his wife. She's a lawyer. He's a teacher. They followed the jobs to the city. He likes it. They visit me when they can, and once a year, I'll visit them."

"But you don't like the city?"

She shuddered. "No. It's so noisy and crowded. I love being surrounded by trees, water, plants, and animals. All the company I need—well, that and books."

The Loon's Nest sat apart from the rest of the buildings in town. It reminded Daylin of the pubs he'd visited in Ireland when he'd gone there on vacation with his family as a kid.

The stream ran under the street and behind the property. A wrought-iron railing hemmed in the patio. Colourful umbrellas poked up between tall, potted shrubs. Flowers and ivy wove around and through the bars of the fence.

"Can we get to the patio from outside, or do we have to go through the restaurant?" Perhaps he'd spare her the walk through the crowded place.

"No, we have to go inside." She said it meekly, as if she was nervous. Her gaze darted around the parking lot as though searching for something—or someone.

"You okay? Is this an ordeal for you? Do you dislike people so much?"

She shook her head. "There's someone I want to avoid. His truck's parked in the lot."

Daylin put a hand on the small of her back and guided her to the door. "Don't worry. You're with me." He opened the door and held it for her.

She stepped inside, giving him a smile as she passed by.

A server met them at the door, and when she recognized Gillian, she grinned.

Finally, someone who appeared overjoyed to see her.

"Gill, hi."

"Hi. Can we get a table for two on the patio?"

Right to the point. No small talk.

Erika grinned and stretched out a hand. "You must be Daylin Quinn. I'm Erika. Nice to meet you."

He returned the smile and clasped the woman's hand in a firm grip. "Nice to meet you, too, Erika. How's the patio today? Not too crowded to add two more people?"

"Not at all. This way." She led them to a table in the shade. "Does this work? If you prefer the sun, I can relocate you."

"This'll be fine, thanks," Daylin replied.

"Thank you," Gillian said.

She sounded steadier. Whoever she was trying to avoid probably wasn't around.

Daylin and Gillian sat, and Erika handed them each a menu.

"Drinks to start?" Erika shifted her weight to one foot and rested a hand on her hip. Her breasts strained against the tight material of her T-shirt.

He forced his gaze up to meet her eyes. "I'll have a beer. Whatever you have on draft is fine."

Gillian ordered a white wine.

After Erika left, he scanned the menu. "What do you recommend?"

"The food here is good. Whatever you order will be fine." Her eyes shifted, her gaze restless.

She's jumpy again.

Her menu lay open on the table in front of her, one of her hands resting on it.

He fought the urge to take her hand and kiss it. Whenever she was near him, he wanted physical contact with her—even the lightest touch. What was wrong with him? He was turning into a love-struck loon.

"You nervous? What's wrong?"

"Nothing. The guy I'm trying to avoid is out here, and he makes me uncomfortable. I don't want to be rude to him, but he won't listen to me when I ask him to back off." Surprise crossed her face. "I didn't mean to spill that."

Happy she'd opened up even a little, Daylin succumbed to the lure of her soft, slim hand and covered it with his. When she didn't pull away, he squeezed gently, then let her go, not wanting to push his luck. "Where is he?"

She focused on a spot behind him, and he threw a quick look over his shoulder.

Four tables, all occupied, stood in the area he deduced her gaze had covered. One of the tables held a likely candidate, but he didn't want to be obvious, so he faced Gillian again. "No one will bother you while I'm here."

Her mouth widened into a grin. "Because you're so intimidating?"

"I have a steely gaze that will terrify him."

She laughed, leaning back in her chair.

Pleased he'd been able to make her relax, he returned to studying the menu. By the time Erika brought their drinks, he'd drawn Gillian out of her shell. They talked about the plans for the resort, something he knew would keep her chatting.

They ordered, Gillian getting a soup and salad and Daylin selecting heartier pub fare.

Shortly after Erika left, a man appeared at their table and greeted Gillian. His voice was smooth and friendly.

Daylin went on alert.

The smile she gave the newcomer seemed genuine, though nervous, and Daylin relaxed.

"Keith, this is Daylin Quinn. He owns the island now. Daylin, Keith Harrison owns this pub."

The two men shook hands, and Keith asked Gillian how she was.

Daylin sensed a more than casual interest from the other man, who chatted with her until the food arrived. When Erika deposited their meals, Keith left.

"He's interested in you." Daylin jumped on that.

"He's asked me out a couple of times since Josh and I split up. I've always turned him down."

"Does he bother you? If so, I must be losing my touch, because I didn't get that vibe."

"No. Keith is a nice guy. He said he'll continue asking me out, but he's not aggressive or arrogant about it. I needed him to give me some time, and he respects that."

Daylin shifted uncomfortably. "Are you considering dating him?"

She could if she wanted to, of course, but hopefully, she wouldn't. Surely, the intimacy they'd shared this morning meant as much to her as it did to him.

"No, I'm not. Especially not after this morning."

"Does it make me less of a man if I tell you I'm happy to hear it?"

"Of course not. What happened between us was important to me. Significant. I don't jump into bed with anyone who asks." She focused on her salad then, a flush spreading prettily across her cheeks.

"From what I can tell, you don't even speak to just anybody. I'm flattered you do all of the above with me."

Her eyes narrowed, and she set her fork down. "I'm not a snob."

"I didn't mean to imply that. I know it's difficult for you to deal with people. You're doing fine today, by the way."

Her shoulders, which had tensed, lowered again, and she breathed out a sigh. "I'm sorry. People make me nervous. I don't know how to connect with them. Josh—"

Daylin cut her off. "Josh was the people person. If you tell yourself that, it'll be true. You're smart, beautiful, and have a lot to contribute. Recognize it. And don't hide behind others. You don't have to."

"You don't understand. There's something wrong with me. I don't know how to fix it."

He set his fork down and took her hand again. "You're not broken. To get comfortable with people you have to be around them. When you cut yourself off from others, you only hurt yourself."

"Well, isn't this cozy." The rough voice broke into the conversation.

Gillian flinched and drew her hand away from Daylin's grasp. "Bruce." She said the name under her breath, and her eyes got the look of a trapped animal.

"You must be Daylin Quinn. I'm Bruce Pankowski." He held out a hand. "Has Gillian told you about me?"

Not sure what Pankowski expected her to have said, Daylin responded with veiled sarcasm. "She mentioned you, yes."

Pankowski missed it. "Excellent. Then we can do business."

Daylin's gaze shifted to Gillian and noted the look of horror on her face.

"Leave me your card, and I'll be in touch. We're in the middle of lunch."

"Oh, yes. Sorry." Pankowski frowned. He reached into his back pocket and pulled out a slightly wrinkled card. "A business lunch, I assume. Gillian, stay in town. We'll go for that dinner I suggested last time you were here."

"No, thank you, Bruce."

"When will you be back? We'll go out then."

"Sorry. I'm not interested." She said this through gritted teeth, as though struggling to remain polite.

"Sure you are." He glanced from Gillian to Daylin and back to Gillian. "I saw your little show this morning. Thank you for making my day."

"You?" Her face paled.

Enough. Time to end it. "Mr. Pankowski, Ms. Foster said she's not interested. I suggest you back off."

Pankowski's face darkened, but he got it under control. His hands bunched into fists, he gave them each a nod. "Enjoy your lunch. I'll expect to hear from you soon, Mr. Quinn." He stroked a finger along Gillian's cheek, making her flinch and infuriating Daylin, and walked away.

"You okay?"

She nodded and sipped from her wine. "Last time I came to town, he asked me to recommend him to you. He's an independent contractor and wants to work on the resort. I planned to mention it but only to advise you not to use him."

"After what he did here, the warning becomes unnecessary. What did he mean about the show this morning?"

Her face flaming red, she tilted her head down. Haltingly, she told him about her private place at the bluffs. She described how, when the heat became unbearable, she checked the lake for boats and removed her sweatshirt.

"At some point, a boat came close to the island. A man was in it, and he had binoculars trained on me. That was Bruce's way of telling me he's the one who saw me. I doubt he expects me to tell you about it. He probably meant it to be an inside joke. He has this delusion I'm fighting an attraction to him. It obviously doesn't occur to him I'd prefer to ruin his chances of getting the contract."

"Son of a bitch." Daylin scowled, fury taking over. He picked with his fork at his plate of half-eaten steak and kidney pie.

"It's okay. Don't take him seriously. He's not worth the trouble. I wasn't naked—I had my bra on. Not much of a show, honestly. I'm almost flat enough to be a guy."

"Don't."

"What?"

"Belittle yourself. He was spying on you. What was he doing coming close to the island anyway?"

"It was early. Maybe he was fishing. I took a risk. He got an eyeful. I'm more upset that I didn't hear the motor or notice the boat getting close." She sighed. "Don't let it ruin our lunch."

"Great suggestion. We'll finish eating and go for a boat ride. I haven't taken the Vista out since it got repaired."

"The chores."

"We'll do them. Before or after we go out—whatever works best. But I want to cruise the lake. Take you out." Gratified when her face lit up, he tucked back into his meal.

When they were done, they strolled back to the car, enjoying the afternoon heat. Daylin couldn't wait to get out on the lake. They'd take bathing suits and go swimming. Gillian probably knew the best spots.

As they left town, she drove past a truck with lettering for Pankowski Contracting on the side. Her gaze remained on the road, her expression neutral.

Daylin took her hand, and when she looked in his direction, he said, "Don't worry. I'll hire the locals. But Bruce Pankowski is not coming anywhere near the island."

CHAPTER 14

Gillian insisted on taking care of the chores first, but by four o'clock, they were out in the boat. Daylin guided it around the island and through a narrows into the wider section of the lake to the east. When they hit the deep water beyond the islands, he opened it up.

Wind whipped Gillian's hair, and she ducked behind the windshield where she sat on the leather seat beside him. The speed and freedom energized her, cleansing away the stress of their encounter with Pankowski.

She hadn't intended to tell Daylin about her shirtless sunbathing experience, but she'd been so shocked and horrified Pankowski had seen her she'd spilled it. Getting it off her chest, so to speak, had relieved some of the internal tension.

Daylin cut the engine and let the boat drift.

The sun had started its descent toward the western horizon, but it was still bright and hot. Soft, thin clouds scraped across the sky, occasionally dimming the light. A breeze blew strong and cool, whipping her hair around her face. Water surrounded them, but in the distance, land peeked out, lush and green with new growth.

"There's a kids' camp on an island nearby I'd like to take you there. I visit them at the beginning of every year and give them coupons for ice cream. The counsellors give one to each kid, and the kids come to my island for a free scoop. The children are from low-income homes, and various charities fund the camp."

"How nice." He swivelled around in his seat and kissed her, a soft, gentle kiss that went straight to her solar plexus.

"Mmmm." Unable to speak, she ran her fingers through his hair.

He broke the kiss and took her hands in his. "Thank you for everything. I want this resort to be the best. You're helping me stay true to those goals."

"You're welcome." Unsure what else to say, she fell silent.

Somewhere, a gull screeched. Water slapped against the boat, little thuds that rocked and swayed them.

"I hope you have your sea legs." His lips curved up, sexy and tempting.

She leaned in and brushed hers against them.

He swept her into his arms then, and it was rough and hot. They stumbled their way into the small cabin under the bow.

The air was close and dusty, but the bed was soft and welcoming.

Unable to keep her hands off him, she stroked and teased him even as he stroked and teased her. For a second, she tensed. Another boat might come by. But the things he did with his mouth on her body pushed reason far away. She quivered, all sensitivity and need.

Her hands in his hair anchored her to him when his mouth let her go. Intense desire throbbed in her loins, and an ache to be filled became unbearable.

"Please, now." She moaned.

He snatched a condom from the compartment next to the bed and rolled it on. "Gilly, you're for me. Tell me you're for me."

"Yes. I'm for you." The words confused her, but she spoke them, sensing the truth behind them. She was committing to him, and she wanted to do it.

He entered her and any residual thoughts swept away, leaving only sensation. She wanted him deeper, deeper. She insisted on it.

"Daylin." When she cried out his name, she asked him to give her more, more, and even more. When she touched him, it was to give back. She steadied his face with her hands, and pressed his lips to hers. All of her wanted him in her, moving together and joining. Sweat-slicked and breathless, they rose and peaked, until they collapsed together, exhausted and sated.

"You do things to me." She held him in a tight embrace.

"And I want to do them often."

She giggled.

His head rested on her shoulder, his hair soft and damp against her cheek. Her hands sifted through the waves. "You have great hair."

His voice floated up, lethargy thickening it. "Thank you. I can't move or I'd kiss you."

The thrum of a motor closing in on them compelled Gillian to attempt to sit up, but Daylin squeezed her back down.

"A boat's coming this way. They might think we're in trouble and come aboard."

"I *am* in trouble. You've knocked me flat." But he raised his head, kissed her, and then slipped off the bed.

They dressed hurriedly, if not awkwardly, considering the cramped space, and went above decks.

The motor she'd heard belonged to a small fishing boat.

Her heart skipped a beat in fright. What if it was Pankowski? But it was two men dragging fishing lines.

She waved a greeting to them, and they carried on their way.

Daylin came up behind her and slid his arms around her waist. "The sun's getting low. This would be a great place to watch the stars. Let's stay out here. We've got enough food, drinks—a functioning commode."

She chuckled. "Sounds wonderful." She hesitated. "It'll get chilly as the sun goes down."

"I've got extra blankets stashed below. We can set up on the prow. There's enough room on it to lie down."

She agreed, and after they'd had something to eat from the provisions they'd brought, they set up the blankets and pillows and got comfortable as the remnants of sunlight disappeared below the horizon. Her head rested on his chest.

A safety light glowed at the back of the boat. The black velvet sky, dotted with countless pinpricks of light, spread open above them. When a shooting star flew across the heavens, she made a quick wish on it, a habit she'd had since childhood.

She caught herself wishing to stay on the island with Daylin. At first, it amused her, but the more she considered it, the more it worried her. She was getting too attached to him.

There was one way this could conclude: he'd finish the work on the resort, and when it was running successfully, he'd leave. Even if he loved her, he'd want to leave here and return to New York, to his real home.

Sure, he might ask her to go with him. But she couldn't trade the clean open spaces of lakeside living for the smog, bustle, and stress of the city. They'd split up then, and she'd be left more wounded than when Josh had left her.

The relationship with Josh had died a slow death even before he'd abandoned her. With Daylin, the love was blossoming, intensifying each time they were together. If he were to rip that love away, she'd be left broken, unable to recover.

"Day?" The use of the shortened name heightened their camaraderie. She liked the way it sounded.

"Gilly?"

She returned the smile he flashed.

I'm afraid this will end. Instead, she said, "The staff arrives tomorrow. After that, we'll have little time to ourselves. I'm glad you suggested this. Thank you."

"I'm glad I did, too. Nichole will be back Thursday, and my mother will be arriving next Tuesday."

"Oh." How should she respond to that? What would his mother think of her? They'd have nothing in common, and Gillian would be tongue-tied. *Oh, God, how will I get through this?*

He rolled onto his side, easing Gillian to the blanket, and studied her face. "You're worried already."

She attempted a smile, failed, and simply nodded.

"Don't be. I know it's difficult for you, but you'll love my mother, and she'll love you."

"What did you tell her?"

"That I wanted her to meet you because you two would hit it off."

"Did you tell her we …" She didn't know how to say it.

"I didn't tell her we slept together."

She laughed and slapped him lightly on the arm. "What did you tell her about us?"

His grin turned sly, and his eyes lit up with mirth. "I told her you threw yourself at me and I couldn't resist you."

"You did not." She slapped him again, harder this time, but still lightly.

"Geeze, you hit like a girl." He buried his face in her neck and nibbled.

"You think so? How do you like this?" She pushed him, attempting to roll him over, but he'd anticipated.

He straddled her, his thighs gripping her hips. He grabbed her wrists and pinned them above her head. Belly to belly now, he nipped at her neck. "Did I mention I'm a vampire?"

Helpless, Gillian laughed until her stomach ached. "Please, stop." She gasped, and though she tried to be serious, the giggles spilled out.

His tongue tickled her ear. "Do they have wet willies in Canada?"

"Oh, my God, are you twelve?" She squirmed and bucked her hips. "Is this a male thing, an American male thing, or a New York male thing?"

"Keep fighting me. It's turning me on."

"A male thing then." She forced a frown but couldn't hold it. "Let me go. You'll be sorry, Yankee, if you don't."

"Ah, a battle between the U. S. and Canada. What do I get if I win?"

"Remember the War of 1812. You guys didn't do so well."

"And you Canucks are always throwing it in our faces. Tell you what: if I win, you have to stay overnight in the house with me. If you win, I have to stay in the staff quarters with you."

"I can see how both of those scenarios would benefit you." She yanked her hands and got one free, but he captured it again. Immediately, she bucked and rolled, and he tipped over. And kept going. The last thing she saw before he splashed into the water was the look of shock on his face.

CHAPTER 15

Gillian scrambled to the side of the boat and hung on as it lurched under her weight.

"Daylin!" She shrieked it, her voice echoing across the lake.

"I'm here."

She climbed off the bow and grabbed the life preserver. Leaning over the starboard side, she spotted him paddling toward her. She tossed the ring to him. Using the line to guide him, she helped him swim to the stern where it would be easier to climb aboard.

"Your plan to get your island back by drowning me won't work. You're not in the will yet." He stood dripping on the deck while she dug out a towel and handed it to him.

"You'll have to let me know as soon as you've updated it." She tugged at his T-shirt. "Take off your clothes. You'll be more comfortable. This air is damp."

"Ah, so this was a ploy to get my clothes off. You were after my body, not my money." He yanked her to him and planted a kiss on her lips while she struggled to escape his soggy mass. "Sweetie, you can have me naked anytime you want."

She was laughing again. Damn, it was good to be so carefree. "Let me go. I can't stand it."

"Nuh-uh. You're mine now."

"Wait a minute. I won that round."

He released her. "You're right. Then I'm yours now. You won't make us sleep in the staff quarters, will you? Not when we have a big house to sleep in."

That sobered her up. "You want me to sleep in the house with you?"

"Sure. If you want to."

She sank into a helm seat. "Daylin." *Tell him you will. Be like Nichole.*

"Okay." She wrinkled her forehead and frowned.

He sat next to her and took her hands. "What's happening? You tell me yes, but your face says no."

To her horror, she burst into tears. And laughed through them when he started to strip.

"What are you doing?" The words escaped from her in a grunt-wheeze.

"I'm soaked. It's inconvenient, and I want to hold you without getting you wet."

"Oh, Daylin. I love—" Shocked, she buried her head in her hands.

In an instant, he eased into the captain's chair next to her and wrapped his arms around her. "Easy. I asked you to spend the night, not marry me. I'm not trying to trap you, and I'm not using you for a one-night stand. Whatever you're afraid of, tell me."

Still sobbing, she rested her head on his naked shoulder. When she lifted her chin to gaze into his eyes, he kissed her. The tenderness of it drew more sobs out of her.

He lifted her gently and pulled her into his lap, which was wrapped in the terry towel.

"Oh, you're wearing a towel."

"I can take it off."

She chuckled, and a surge of joy followed happiness followed a rush of melancholy and more tears. "I'm so sorry. I don't know what's wrong with me. The happier you make me, the more emotional I get."

"Was it Josh who did such a number on your head you fall apart at the prospect of spending the night with me?"

"I won't lay the blame on Josh for all my insecurities, but he can take the blame for the trust issues."

Daylin stroked her hair and her back. "Are you saying you don't trust me?"

"Maybe. Or I don't trust me."

"Listen to me: we'll return to the house. You'll spend the night with me. We don't have to have sex. As a matter of fact, sex is off the table. We'll just be together. In the morning, we'll discuss what it means until you're satisfied I'm not manipulating you and won't hurt you."

"I'm not a virgin you need to coax into bed, and I'm not frightened of sex. I enjoy it, more so with you than with anyone else. That's what scares me." She agreed to spend the night with him, interested to see if she could stick to his no sex proposal. Already hungering for his body, she suspected she'd be the one begging for it.

***

As soon as they reached shore and put the boat away, Gillian's cell phone chimed incoming messages. While Daylin unloaded the boat, she checked her voicemail.

He froze when her expression went from mild interest to horrified shock.

"What's wrong?" He dropped the duffel bag he carried onto the dock and rushed to her side.

"We'll have company tomorrow." Her throat clicked as she swallowed. "Josh and Candi are coming to the island."

"Why?"

"I have some records in my file cabinet he needs. Tax stuff. We're finalizing the divorce so they can get married. They'll be here in the morning and don't plan to hang around."

"Will you be okay? Do you want me to be there when you talk to him?"

"I'll be fine. It's a shock. I haven't seen him in months nor spoken to him in weeks. Erika mentioned him when I had lunch in town. He's living with Candi." She shook her head at his unspoken question. "I don't care if he's with her. He hurt me when he cheated on me, mostly ego bruising. I got over it and wouldn't take him back if he begged me, which he won't do." She tucked her phone away and stepped in close to Daylin. "I'm glad you're here and we'll spend the night together."

He brushed a finger lightly across her lips. "Let's go inside. I'll pour us a glass of wine and we can relax before bed."

"Okay." Her voice was soft, a slight tremor in it. "About tonight?"

He tilted his head, puzzled. "Yes?"

"I'm putting sex back on the table." She rose up on her toes, clasped her fingers behind his neck, and pulled his mouth to hers.

***

Gillian lay in the dark, Daylin curled around her, his deep, even breath blowing lightly on her neck.

His skin was warm and his body hard and smooth. He'd exhausted her, even though his lovemaking had been slow and tender. They'd enjoyed each other, and the pleasure she'd given him had returned to her three-fold. His loving touches had awakened in her emotions that had lain dormant for years.

Tired as she was, sleep eluded her. God, she was falling in love, and she was unable to stop it. She didn't want to stop it. She wanted to enjoy it, revel in it.

Her right leg prickled, and when she shifted, his arm slid away. She rolled to face him and draped her arm across his chest. His bare shoulder was level with her mouth, and she gave it a quick kiss.

The time showed just shy of one o'clock.

She closed her eyes.

Somewhere in the distance, a motor hummed out on the lake. A fishing excursion at this time of night? Someone heading back to the mainland after a cottage party?

Five minutes later, still unable to sleep, she slipped out of bed. She grabbed Daylin's robe on the way to the kitchen.

No need for lights—she could walk the place blindfolded. Moon glow gave her all she needed to find the kettle, fill it, and plug it in. She opened the cupboard.

As she reached for the box of tea, the world exploded around her, and she screamed. Unable to comprehend what had happened, she stood in her bare feet amidst glass, shaking.

The lights flicked on, and a bleary-eyed, naked Daylin ran into the kitchen.

"Gilly, what happened?"

"I don't know." Her voice trembled. Wide-eyed, she stared at him.

"You're cut." He rushed toward her, but before he reached her, she stuck her hand up.

"You're barefoot too. I won't move. Get some shoes on." The fright had passed, and her head had cleared.

A rock on the floor and a gaping hole in the kitchen window explained everything.

Daylin hurried back to the bedroom.

He returned wearing a T-shirt, sweat pants, and sneakers and carrying the first aid kit. He rushed to her side and lifted her in his arms.

From below the house, a motor sputtered and roared to life. It grew fainter as the boat sped away.

Daylin stepped around the glass and carried her to a clear spot on the kitchen floor. "Let me examine you. You have blood on your feet." He crouched down.

"A piece of glass hit my ankle. It stings, but I'll be okay. Glad I borrowed your robe. I could have been out here naked."

"Why were you up? Did you hear something?"

She flinched as he cleaned the cut and covered it with an adhesive bandage.

"No." She sighed. "I couldn't sleep. Worried about tomorrow, I guess. My brain wouldn't shut down. I came out to make a cup of tea."

He stood and hugged her. "It's just a small cut. I'm sorry you got hit, but it could've been worse. You were lucky you weren't standing in front of the window when it happened. Whoever threw the rock wouldn't have seen you in the dark."

Gillian squeezed against him, relieved she'd decided to spend the night. Certain Daylin was the target, she was glad he wasn't alone when it happened. "We have to call the police."

"Any idea who'd want to do something like this?"

She lifted her head from his shoulder and met his eyes. "Bruce Pankowski comes to mind, but he'd be stupid to attack you when you haven't told him you wouldn't be using his services."

"Maybe he read between the lines. You're assuming this is about me." Daylin released her. "Sit on the couch. I'll make the call."

"It could be about me. Some people hate that I sold my island to a foreigner." She went to the couch and curled up on it, her legs folded under her. She shivered. The hole in the window was letting the chilly night air in. "Mind if I light a fire?"

"Help yourself."

Her gaze followed him as he crouched next to the rock to examine it without touching it.

"You think the cops will dust for prints?"

He shrugged. "I'd be surprised if they bothered to investigate."

"Is that how it is in New York? You report vandalism and they ignore it?"

"Even the cops in a small town like Fiddlehead must have better things to do than find out who busted my window."

While he called the police, she focused on getting the fire started, piling up kindling and small pieces of wood. "Whoever it was knew the windows in this house don't all have screens."

"Why is that?"

"It's an old house with old windows. They're custom. The one on the landing leading to the second floor is stained glass. I'm glad they didn't break that one. It's valuable. Josh and I were replacing them a couple a year." Gillian touched match to paper and lit the kindling. Soon, she had a cheery fire going.

She made tea while Daylin covered up the broken window. By the time the police arrived, it was after three o'clock in the morning.

CHAPTER 16

The officer, a tall, slender woman named Purdy, resembled a ballerina more than a cop. She arrived after Gillian and Daylin gave up on the idea of sleep and got dressed. The cop took down their story, dusted for prints, accepted the rock as evidence, snapped a few pictures of the window and the outside of the house, gave them a report number, and left.

"They won't try to find out who did this," Daylin said later as he and Gillian walked to the pontoon boat.

"They won't pretend it didn't happen. It's a small town. People talk. You'd be surprised at how quickly they might catch the person."

"So, police investigation via the rumour mill."

"It's an effective mill."

"I'll install security cameras. They'll be a deterrent. You could've been hurt."

She sat on a bench under the canopy and let him drive. "But I wasn't, and I'm sure whoever did it had no idea I was there." Wind whipping her hair, Gillian leaned back and let the energy of the fresh air and water ease her tension.

The dynamic of the island was about to change. It would no longer be her and Daylin. Most of the staff was young adults working their way through university or college. The chef was a resident of Fiddlehead and would commute every day. A few of them were brand new to the resort, and others had already done a year or more.

On the weekend, the first guests would arrive, and then her island bubble would burst with people and activity. Every year at this time, she looked forward to it, though the thrill wore off quickly and she'd be ready to hide after a couple of weeks. It gave her a safe taste of socializing, especially since Josh would handle most of the people-related duties. This year, she'd throw Daylin into the deep end and let him deal with it.

**

He studied her as they sluiced through the water. Every time he pictured the rock coming through the window, he wanted to hit someone. They were lucky it had only resulted in a minor cut.

He fantasized about catching the guy and cleaning his clock. He imagined it was Pankowski. If he was putting a face to it, may as well make it someone he disliked.

They arrived at The Landing and Daylin helped Gillian dump the garbage and recycling into the bins provided. She waved to a group of young people, who smiled and approached the pontoon boat.

Gillian made the introductions and left Daylin to get everyone on board while she retrieved the mail from the community mailbox.

Four young women and three young men herded onto the boat, along with their bags and supplies. The chef would arrive mid-morning. A couple approached the docks, and Daylin recognized Josh from the online photos.

Daylin spotted Gillian on her way back from the mailbox, a stack of letters in her hand. When she recognized Josh and Candi, she froze.

"I'll be right back." Daylin didn't wait for anyone to reply but jumped onto the dock and hurried toward Gillian.

Josh and Candi reached Gillian first. "Morning, Gill. We're early, I know. My boat's still moored here. We can meet you at the resort."

Face pale, she nodded. "All right."

Daylin held out his hand, and Josh clasped it in a firm grip.

"Daylin Quinn. I assume you're Josh Foster?" He turned to the woman. "This must be Candi." He shook her hand.

She smiled. "Nice to meet you. So, you bought Gillian's island?" She looked at Gillian. "How have you been?"

"Fine, thank you." She didn't ask how Candi had been.

The four-inch heels Candi wore made her tower over all the other women there. Her walk up the slope on the island would be a spectacle. A bleached-blonde pillar of hair gave her yet another few inches. The tight, scoop-neck T-shirt showcased perky breasts, and a denim mini skirt ended a hair's width below the curve of her butt.

If Josh is driving a convertible sports car, we know what this is all about. Daylin scanned the parking lot but didn't see anything resembling a mid-life crisis-mobile.

"Shall we go? The staff must be anxious to get settled." Daylin placed a hand on the small of Gillian's back and guided her to the pontoon boat, while Candi and Josh made their way to a small speedboat docked farther along the shore.

When Gillian's ex was out of earshot, Daylin said, "Will you be okay?"

"Yes, don't worry." She stopped walking and faced him. "Thank you for being here."

He smoothed a rebellious curl from her face. "You're welcome."

He studied Josh. What had Josh been doing early this morning? Daylin dismissed the idea. There'd be no reason for Josh to have thrown the rock.

Anyone who crossed Daylin's path now would be a suspect.

***

Back on the island, the staff went to settle into their quarters while Gillian took Josh and Candi to the main house. Gillian went to Daylin's office to retrieve the file folder of papers she'd prepared. He followed her.

"Want me to stay close?" he said as she headed out of the office, folder clutched tight to her chest.

"I'm fine." She kissed him on the cheek and went to the kitchen.

She considered putting the kettle on but didn't. She wasn't in the mood to be hospitable to her ex and his slutty home-wrecker.

Josh and Candi both exclaimed over the broken window as soon as Gillian entered the room.

"What happened?" Josh said.

"Someone threw a rock through it during the night. The police are investigating."

Candi's eyes went wide, and she minced her way to the couch and sat. "Must've scared Daylin."

Gillian didn't comment. Best not to mention she was here at the time.

"Any idea who did it?" said Josh.

"Someone who doesn't like the idea that Daylin bought the place," she replied.

Josh set the briefcase he'd brought on the table and opened it. His gaze met hers as she placed the folder next to the case.

She motioned for him to look inside. "Make sure everything you need is in here. I made copies for my files, so you can take it all. If I missed anything, let me know."

"I'm sorry, Gill. I didn't mean to hurt you." Josh put his hand over hers.

She snatched it away. "Yet everything you did was guaranteed to do just that. I don't want to discuss this with you. Take what you need so you can be on your way."

He riffled through the papers and nodded when he was done. "Seems like everything's there." He closed the folder and directed his gaze at Gillian. "I've heard talk in town about this guy. Are you sleeping with him?"

She scowled. "Not your business."

"Which means you are. What are you thinking?"

Candi stood. "Why does it matter? We've got what we need. Let's go home."

Josh fired a glare in her direction and then focused again on Gillian. "What are you doing? You can't get involved with this character."

"Not your decision." Rage making her tremble, she smacked her palm onto the table. "We're done here. You can go."

He stepped toward her. "That rock might be the first attack. People aren't happy you sold this place to a Yankee, but most of them can understand the circumstance that made you do it."

"Circumstances you put me in," she said through gritted teeth. "And *we* sold the place to Daylin. We owned it together; we sold it together. Lest you forget, you wanted it done quickly so you could get your money out."

He held up his hand. "All right. They understand we had to sell. But they don't want him here, and if they find out you're involved with him, you'll be under attack."

"I'll take my chances." She snatched the folder from Josh and tossed it into the briefcase. "See you around."

He closed the case and clasped her hand in both of his. "You were my whole world once. I'm looking out for you."

"Josh?" Candi sounded nervous. She moved behind him and put a hand on his shoulder. "We should leave."

Gillian yanked her hand away. "I don't need you to look after me." How dare he? He'd betrayed her, hurt her, and now he was playing white knight?

"I'm warning you. They're talking about you behind your back. I've tried to tell them you're only fulfilling your obligations. But there'll be backlash against you if you get involved with this guy."

"What are you saying? Do you know something about this?" She pointed at the window.

"No." He grimaced. "But it's obvious how people feel about him. He'll have problems. Do what you have to do and then get out."

"I'm involved with him." Anger made her spill it, but she wasn't sorry despite giving them grist for the gossip mill.

"Jesus. Are you stupid?"

"Everything all right, Gilly?" Daylin stepped into the kitchen, coffee mug in hand, and strode to the coffee maker. Casually, he went through the motions of making a pot of coffee, but she'd seen the storm brewing in his eyes.

She joined him and rested a hand on his shoulder. She gave it a gentle massage. "I'm fine, thank you." She tilted her chin at Josh and Candi. "They're leaving."

Daylin put his arm around her, and his mouth curled in a frosty smile aimed at Josh and Candi. "Nice meeting you both. Sorry to cut it short, but we've got chores to do. Those cows won't milk themselves, right, darling?" He kissed her cheek.

"That's right, dear." She kissed his lips.

Josh glowered at them.

Candi shifted from one foot to the other. "Josh. Come on." She whispered it, as though she didn't want anyone else to hear the begging in her tone. "Please."

Josh grabbed his briefcase from the table, spun around, and stalked to the door, Candi mincing along behind him. "Josh, wait."

He stopped at the door and took her arm when she caught up.

"Goodbye, Gill," he said. "Don't say I didn't warn you." The door slammed behind them.

Gillian peered out the window.

Candi and Josh picked their way down to the dock. Josh helped Candi into the boat, started the engine, and they sped away.

Gillian sighed. "Cat's out of the bag now. Even if he doesn't publicize it, she'll tell everyone I'm sleeping with you."

"Does that bother you?"

"No, and I'm sorry I wanted to hide it before. You make me happy. I don't care who knows we're together."

His arms wrapped around her, and he held her close. "Is he right? Will a relationship with me make it hard for you?"

She stepped back. "Does it matter?"

"Of course. I don't want to cause you problems."

"If you don't want to be with me, I understand. But I won't stand for you getting chivalrous on me. I can take care of myself." She paused "As long as there aren't too many people around."

He laughed. "Don't worry. If we have to, we'll take them on one at a time."

She threw her arms around him and kissed him. "The cows are waiting. We'd better go."

He groaned. "What about the staff? Why can't they do it?"

"Don't worry, you'll be spared the ordeal when the guests arrive. You'll be mister personality, schmoozing and glad-handing. I force you to do it now because you make such a sexy farmer boy."

He grinned. "As you wish."

Laughing, she led him out to the barn.

CHAPTER 17

As the staff settled in and helped Gillian prepare the cottages for guests, she fell into the routine easily and happily. Daylin got acquainted with the newcomers and worked with the chef to get the restaurant up and running.

In the midst of this bustle of activity, Nichole returned, bringing with her an entourage of assistants and engineers. This time, Gillian welcomed her back as a friend.

The afternoon before the guests were to arrive, the two women sat on the back porch of the main house.

Daylin was at the docks, tinkering with his boat. He'd left them with a pitcher of margaritas and a stern warning to Nichole not to get Gillian tipsy.

"He doesn't trust me with you, you know." Nichole stirred her drink with a cherry red-tipped finger, which she then licked clean. She looked cool and comfortable in a halter dress and strappy espadrilles.

"What do you mean?" Gillian kicked off her Birkenstocks and stretched her long legs out in front of her. She should have put on something nicer for the afternoon, but it didn't occur to her to wear anything but shorts and a T-shirt or sweatshirt when she was working. Next to the sexy New Yorker, she looked grubby. She examined the dirt under her fingernails and cringed.

"He's worried I'll girly you up."

"I don't understand."

"Daylin wants me to leave you alone." Nichole skimmed her finger around the rim of the glass, scraping up bits of salt. The fingertip poked back into her mouth, and her cherry red lips enveloped it.

"He told you that? Why would he leave us out here then?"

"He wants us to get along, but he doesn't want me to force my style on you."

Gillian sipped her drink. It was cold and sour and went down smoothly. "Why does he think you'd do that?" Uneasy, she sat up. "What did you say to him?"

"Nothing. Okay, something. I bought you a few things in New York."

"You did? Why?"

Nichole smiled. "I love shopping and figured you might enjoy some new clothes."

Gillian's face warmed. "Like what?"

Her friend giggled. "Don't worry. Nothing radical. A few pieces to add to your wardrobe."

Shock warred with curiosity. Curiosity won. "Show me."

Nichole jumped up and ran into the house. She returned with a bag from a well-known New York clothing store.

Gillian rose and accepted the gift. "If all you gave me was the bag, I'd be happy. It's a great souvenir." She laughed, the buzz from the drink making her giddy.

Inside the bag were a sundress and a summer blouse and skirt set. The colours were bold and the style feminine.

"I don't dress up often. Chores make me filthy and sweaty, so I wear what's functional."

Nichole laid a hand on her friend's arm. "You can still dress up sometimes. You're not always doing chores."

Josh's voice intruded into Gillian's head. *Maybe sometimes I need a woman who dresses like one. Do you always have to look so dumpy?*

Would Daylin get tired of the farm wife look after a while? Dresses made her uncomfortable. She hated worrying about keeping them clean, and they forced decorum and ladylike behaviour. Who the hell wanted to be ladylike?

Be polite. "They're pretty. Thank you."

"Try them on."

The fright must have shown on her face, because Nichole laughed. "Come on."

She dragged Gillian into the bedroom. "Okay, strip."

Self-conscious but intrigued, she peeled off her T-shirt and shorts.

"The bra too. The sundress needs you braless."

"I'll try the blouse and skirt first, then." She snatched up the top before the other woman could convince her otherwise and slipped it on. The gauzy material lay soft against her skin. She peered into the mirror over the dresser. The bright pink of the shirt brought out the blue in her eyes and draped around her curves.

She picked up the turquoise skirt and stepped into it. When she zipped it up, she stuck a leg out in front, testing the hemline. It stopped above her knee. She peeked into the mirror again and preened, smoothing her hands over her hips.

"You have legs like a giraffe. Heels would punch up your outfit. And a necklace."

She winced. "I don't wear heels. They make walking difficult."

Nichole shook her head. "Next time I go to New York, you're coming with me, and we're getting you a pair of decent heels."

"No." Gillian stumbled backward in horror. Go to another country? To buy *shoes*? Was Nichole crazy? Gillian didn't even like leaving the island to go into town.

Yet soon she'd be moving there.

"Stop worrying. You'll be with me. What can go wrong?" Nichole's mouth quirked up.

"Ladies?" Daylin's voice preceded the sound of the front door banging open. "Hello?" The thud of his shoes hitting the floor reached them.

"Come on. Show him your new outfit." Nichole grabbed Gillian's arm and hauled her out of the bedroom.

She stumbled out, and when his gaze met hers, she flushed, embarrassed. She gripped the hem of the skirt on each side and tugged down, as though attempting to lengthen the hem.

He whistled, and her gaze darted around, searching for the nearest exit. If only she could disappear or sink into the ground.

Nichole gave her a gentle shove in Daylin's direction.

So ridiculous. They were adults, and her appearance shouldn't matter to anyone. Nichole might be a vain exhibitionist, but Gillian considered herself better than that.

"You do look nice. Let's go into town and have dinner at The River Inn," Daylin said.

"Oh, no. Guests arrive tomorrow." She shuffled toward the bedroom and the safety of her old clothes.

"It'll be fine. We're ready for them. I'll treat. The three of us can go."

Nichole clapped her hands. "Great idea. You can show off your new clothes, and I'd love to get out for a nice meal." She paused and wrinkled her nose. "Sorry. You know what I mean."

"Sure," Gillian replied, but her hands had gone clammy and her heart rate accelerated. She examined her dirty fingernails. "I have to milk the cows and gather the eggs. I'd better change back into my work clothes."

She held up her hand at the concern on Daylin's face.

"I'm fine. We'll go out for dinner. I need to do the afternoon chores first. Most of the staff is finalizing the cabins, restaurant, and grounds for tomorrow. I'll take care of my animals."

She hurried to the bedroom and studied her reflection in the mirror. The outfit made her look like a different person. She scrunched her hair up in her hands and piled it on her head, revealing an elegant neck. Lips pursed, she made the duck face she'd seen teenagers make in their selfies. Ridiculous. She giggled.

The floor creaked behind her and she startled, dropping her hair and sobering her face.

Daylin's arms went around her. His fingers brushed the hair away from her throat, and he nuzzled her neck. "You're so beautiful. Why do you hide from it?"

"I don't hide." Her voice sounded thick and heavy. His touch made her belly tickle and her body quiver.

He kissed a trail down her neck, and she shivered.

She faced him and slipped her arms around his neck.

His body pressed to hers, lips hungrily capturing hers, he soothed the ache inside her.

"You hide your beauty." The words came out hoarse and insistent. "You can't hide it from me. It doesn't matter what you wear." Gently, he forced her around to face the mirror. "See that gorgeous body? The thick fall of hair?" One of his hands tangled in her hair and the other held her around the waist, pulling her in tight against him.

"Nichole told me you didn't want her to girly me up."

"I don't want her to make you think you have to change who you are. She's wonderful the way she is and so are you. But you don't have to be afraid to put on a dress."

She struggled to swallow, her throat tightening. "I'm not afraid. I prefer comfort."

"I see it in your eyes, in the way you self-consciously tug at these clothes." His lips pressed the top of her head.

Her hands clutched at his arms. Heart thudding, sweat beading at the back of her neck, she gulped in air and forced her head to clear. She spun around and buried her face in his chest.

"What happened?"

"I have to get changed." She wrenched away from him. With shaking fingers, she unzipped the skirt, yanked it off, and threw it on the bed. She grabbed her shorts and hauled them on.

Daylin sat on the bed and pulled her into his lap. "Are you okay?" His voice was so kind.

In her mind, Joshua's voice intruded. *Sometimes it's like I married a guy. Are you sure you're not gay?*

She tucked her face into Daylin's neck, and her fists grabbed his shirt. "Bad memories. I don't feel comfortable in skirts and dresses, but I'll be fine."

"It's okay." He stroked her hair and held her close.

"I'm sorry."

"It's all right."

She lifted her head, their eyes meeting. Her fingers played with his shirt, clutching it, smoothing it out again. "Where's Nichole?"

Her friend must be wondering where they were and what took them so long.

"She went to her room to change for dinner."

"I'll wear the new blouse and skirt. It looks good."

"Are you sure you're okay with it?"

She nodded. "I can't wear heels."

"No problem." His face showed concern and compassion.

He tilted his chin down until their lips met and then tenderly kissed her. "We'll go out for dinner and have a good time. I'll help you with the chores and we'll go."

"Okay." She stood. "Thank you." She folded the skirt and packed it up in the bag with the new sundress. She switched out the blouse for the T-shirt. "I'll run these back to my room and meet you in the barn. It won't take long."

She gave him a quick kiss and hurried from the room.

CHAPTER 18

They got a table for three on the terrace overlooking the lake. Gillian sat across from Daylin, and Nichole sat between them. To Daylin, his old friend appeared solicitous toward Gillian. He didn't know what she'd told Nichole about the skirt—perhaps the truth, whatever that was. Gillian wore a hint of makeup, and no doubt, Nichole had influenced that decision as well.

The waiter served them the drinks they'd ordered as soon as the hostess had seated them. Gillian sipped on a white wine and Nichole on a red, while Daylin nursed a vodka martini.

The lush gardens and a warm spring breeze cutting through the humidity soothed the atmosphere.

Silverware shone in the setting sun, the blinding-white tablecloths adding to the glare. All three wore sunglasses. Daylin suspected Gillian was happy to be outside where she had an excuse to hide behind her shades.

Eager to keep the conversation off his girlfriend's wardrobe, he brought up the subject of contractors. "I've narrowed my options down to two companies: Tidal Limited and Borealis Construction. Gill, you've mentioned you favour Borealis. I sense that's because you know the owners better."

She set her wine glass down and smiled at him. "Yes. Both companies do exceptional work. I've known the Andersons since I was a kid. The Forans own Tidal, but I didn't meet Mike and his family until I was in high school. They're all good people."

The waiter appeared and gave them the specials. After he left, silence fell as each perused the menu.

Daylin had an urge to keep Gillian talking, so he caught her eye and asked, "What do you recommend?"

Her smile widened to a grin. "Everything."

"Be more specific."

"You like meat?"

"Yeah." No denying he was a meat and potatoes guy.

"Try the beef tenderloin."

He'd been leaning toward the ribs but had decided he'd order whatever she recommended.

"I'll have the green salad." Nichole closed her menu.

The waiter returned, and when he came to Gillian, she ordered the salmon. Daylin waited for the man to leave before he continued the conversation.

"I'm leaning toward Tidal. Nichole did some digging. They have a larger operation. All other things being equal, I think they can handle the project better. I want it begun by mid-June so it can be finished by the time the snow flies."

Since Gillian hadn't reacted negatively to his choice of Tidal, Daylin pressed on. "We're getting Kelly-Marie Kennedy to do the interiors."

Gillian gaped at him. "A decorator?"

"Sure. She'll do the whole resort including the house." He kept talking, unable to stop. "She's local. Nichole researched her and Kennedy has an impressive portfolio."

The waiter arrived with their food, and they ate in silence for a while. Nichole broke it this time. "It's not a slight on your home."

Daylin tensed, but Gillian appeared unperturbed.

"What Daylin does with his home is his business." She sipped her wine. "I'm not offended. It's normal for people to want to make a new place their own." But her gaze darted around the room, and when it settled on her plate, she picked at her food.

"I'll show you whatever she has planned," he said. "And if I get rid of any furniture, you'll get first dibs."

She kept her head down, but she smiled. "Thanks. That's considerate."

The rest of the meal went smoothly, the conversation mostly on business. Gillian relaxed and participated in the discussions, much to his delight. He slid an arm around her as they left the restaurant. When her arm slipped around his waist, he smiled the smile of the deliriously happy.

Nichole walked ahead into the parking lot.

Night had fallen, and the gentle glow of solar lights guided them down the path. Daylin's Mercedes sat near the inn's back entrance. As Nichole drew near it, she froze and cried out.

Daylin released his hold on Gillian and caught up to his friend.

"What is it?"

Speechless, she pointed.

Words, in red spray paint, covered the car. *Fuck you yankee* was the tamest of the suggestions.

Beside him, Gillian gasped.

"Who would do this?" Nichole said.

"Someone who doesn't know 'Yankee' should have an initial cap and there should be a comma after 'you.' " Daylin tried humour. It was either that or hit something. He pulled out his cell phone, and for the second time in a week, called the police.

***

For Gillian, the next two days passed in a whirl of activity and work. The police had taken their statements and were investigating the latest vandalism, though she didn't expect them to catch the perpetrators. There had been no progress on finding who'd smashed the window, and while everyone assumed it was the work of the same person, they had no proof.

Daylin had cameras installed on all the resort's buildings and a security system on the house.

Guests arrived, registered, and made themselves at home. Though Victoria Day was officially on Monday, celebrations would be held on Sunday to ensure the most guest participation.

Daylin bought fireworks, and Gillian invited the head of the nearby island kids' camp to bring the campers around. He told her the resort would no longer do this when it was an artists' retreat, but he planned to compensate by donating money to the camp every year.

That this was the last Victoria Day fireworks celebration on the island to include the kids made her sad, but she understood the reasoning behind it. In the meantime, the weekend flew by, giving her no time to worry about anything or even to sit on the bluffs and commune with her parents.

The night of the fireworks, Gillian and Nichole sat at the edge of the crowd in the clearing behind the main house. Daylin and Rico, one of the staff members, had prepped the site and were now setting alight the first one.

"Come with me to New York." Nichole kept her gaze on Daylin and Rico.

Chills carved a path up Gillian's spine. "No, I can't."

Nichole whirled to face her friend. "You can. He can get along without you for a few days."

A gasp from the crowd had them turning back to the fire burst.

Gillian shook her head. "He needs my help. The first guests arrived two days ago. It hasn't been long enough for me to leave him." She grasped at another straw. "Besides, I'm under contract to help him."

"He'd let you take a side trip with me. The staff can help him." Irritation clipped Nichole's voice.

"I won't abandon him." A firework blast made Gillian jump. Up in the sky, sparkles of colour flashed and sprinkled back toward earth.

"You have to leave this place sometime. I'm only asking for three days. We'll shop. I'll show you some sights. I promise, you'll have fun." Nichole put a hand on Gillian's arm. "Have you ever been to a spa? Becca's is fabulous. I'll take you. We'll have a champagne brunch and get mani-pedis."

What would it be like to go to New York? Gillian had only been out of the country once, to visit cousins in New Jersey, but it had been short and sweet. She'd visited her brother in Toronto, of course, but that, too, had been a quick trip.

A longing to let some excitement and adventure into her life almost had her agreeing, but it honestly wouldn't be fair to Daylin.

"I can't this month. I have to stay here." She took a deep breath and, before she changed her mind, said, "But I'll go with you next month. Three days. We'll go to the spa and get our nails done. I'm looking forward to it."

Nichole leapt up, dragging Gillian with her. "Oh, it'll be great." She spun around, laughing, and whirled Gillian along.

"You're crazy." Her heart thudded with a combination of joy and fear. She laughed, breathless.

"You won't be sorry." Nichole threw her arms up as another burst of colour showered down from the sky.

Smiling, Gillian turned toward Daylin.

He lit another aerial shell and stepped back.

A shriek and bang sent an emerald streak into the sky. It burst high above, an explosion of shine and smoke.

When there was another pop from Daylin's direction, she looked at him, puzzled he'd light another when they were still enjoying the last one.

But he wasn't crouched before the next banger. He stood, swaying slightly, his hand cupping his shoulder. Rico hovered nearby, grabbing at Daylin's hand.

"Help." Rico's voice echoed across the grass. "He's been shot."

CHAPTER 19

Fright skewered Gillian's heart, and she bolted across the lawn to Daylin's side. He stood, one hand pressed to his shoulder, looking perplexed. Blood oozed between his fingers.

"Oh, God." She put an arm around him and squeezed her eyes shut, trying to cut through the haze. Smoke stung her eyes and the acrid scent filled her nostrils. Behind her, people shouted.

Someone pressed a cloth into his hand, and he used it to cover the wound. One of the guests rushed over, shouting he was a doctor.

The guest, Dr. Ray Horowitz, gently removed Gillian's arm from around Daylin's waist and, with a nod of his head, made her step back.

Something tickled her cheek, and when she brushed her fingers across her face, they came away damp.

"How bad is it, Doc?" Daylin's face was white, but his breathing was steady. "It hurts like a bastard."

"It's a pellet. I should be able to remove it in your infirmary. Why don't we relocate there now? Can you walk?"

"I think so."

Nichole elbowed her way through the crowd and reached Daylin's side.

Blood seeped through the cloth he held.

She paled and bit her lip.

Gillian called to Rico and asked him to take over. He'd been with the resort for four years, and she trusted him as a second in command. "We're cancelling the celebrations. Encourage people to go back to their cabins. I'll call the police."

What would this incident do to the resort? She couldn't have guests at risk, though she was sure the target was Daylin and no one else.

As Rico took control and directed the guests back to their cabins, she hurried after Daylin, Nichole, and Dr. Ray. Along the way, she took out her cell phone and called the police.

The infirmary, a small room with first aid supplies and an examination table in the staff quarters building, wasn't staffed. Gillian and the employees she hired all had first-aid training and could handle the minor burns, cuts, and scrapes the resort typically dealt with.

She reached the staff quarters as Angela, Dr. Ray's wife, arrived with his medical bag. "Don't worry, honey. Ray will take care of your man."

An older woman, stout and solid, Angela's motherly demeanour soothed Gillian.

"Thank you, Mrs. Horowitz."

Angela patted Gillian's hand. "Please, call me Angela."

The two rushed into the infirmary where Daylin lay on the table, shirt off, cloth pressed to the wound. Dr. Ray stood by the table, hands already scrubbed and covered with surgical gloves.

Gillian went to Daylin's side and clasped the hand on his uninjured arm.

His eyes were glassy with pain, but he smiled when it dawned on him she was there.

She lifted her gaze to the doctor. "Thank you, Doc." She spoke calmly. She turned back to Daylin. "Don't worry. The police are on their way."

"Ladies," Dr. Ray said, "please wait outside. He'll be fine." He nodded to his wife. "If you'll stay and assist, we can get this done quickly."

"Of course." Angela set the medical bag on the counter next to the sink and washed her hands.

Reluctant to leave, Gillian and Nichole exchanged glances.

Daylin squeezed Gillian's hand, getting her attention.

She leaned over and kissed his forehead.

"Go on," he said. "I'll be out soon. Let the doc do his job."

"All right. We'll be right outside." She met the doc's gaze again. "You need anything, call."

He nodded in acknowledgement, and she let Nichole lead her into the living area. Gillian dropped into an armchair, head in hands, and Nichole sat on the couch.

"What did the cops say?"

Gillian dragged her head up to meet her friend's gaze. "They're on their way." She sucked in a breath. "It's okay. You don't have to keep me talking. I don't need it."

"Is it okay if I keep me talking? I need it."

She nodded. "I'm sorry. Would you like a tea? Maybe it'll keep our minds off what's happening with Daylin right now."

"Sure. I'll help you." Nichole went to the kitchen.

Gillian rose and followed her. They made tea while Nichole chatted about her work and her family, though Gillian found it difficult to focus on the conversation.

As they returned to the living area with their mugs, Rico opened the main door and stuck his head inside. "The police are here."

"Thanks. Bring them in here."

Rico stepped aside and ushered the officers in. Before Rico retreated, Gillian stopped him and asked him to stay. He'd stood beside Daylin when the shooting occurred. Perhaps he'd seen something that might help the police.

She recognized Officer Purdy but not the man accompanying her. Purdy introduced him as Officer Nolan. She took out her notebook and grilled Gillian on what happened. When she finished, Purdy questioned Nichole and Rico as well and then said, "I'll have to interview Daylin and the other guests."

"I understand," Gillian replied.

"I'd also like to go out to the site, take a look around."

"Sure. Rico can take you."

The door to the infirmary opened, and Angela stepped out.

Gillian's heart shot into her throat. "How is he?" She held her breath.

"Fine, dear. Ray's giving him some care advice. He'll need to take it easy on the arm, but he's fine."

Gillian brushed past Angela and raced to Daylin's side.

Shoulder bandaged, he sat on the table, legs dangling over the side.

The odour of antiseptic overwhelmed her, and she wrinkled her nose. She brushed a hand through his sweat-damp hair.

"You okay?" It came out a whisper. "I was so worried."

He leaned over and kissed her cheek. "Yeah. The doc did a great job. I'll have to take it easy for a while. No milking cows and gathering eggs. Sorry." He grinned.

"You'll do anything to get out of that." She returned the grin but then sobered up again when Officer Purdy appeared in the doorway. "The police are here to talk to you. You okay?"

He nodded. "Of course."

When Purdy moved to enter the room, he held up his good hand. "I'll come out, Officer. Too crowded in here."

Gillian helped him from the table and hovered over him as he made his way to the living area. When he'd settled onto the couch, she kept busy making another pot of tea while he talked to the police. He sounded calm, though an undercurrent of anger tinged his tone, and his posture was tense.

"I was getting ready to set off another aerial shell when something hit my shoulder. The pain didn't register at first. When it did, I thought the shell had misfired."

"Did you see who did it?" Purdy asked.

"No. I was focused on the fireworks and Rico, making sure he was a safe distance away from me. Once I saw the blood and the pain took over, I noticed nothing else."

The doctor and Angela both contributed what they could, which wasn't anything significant. The officers took their statements and dismissed them.

Gillian gritted her teeth as she set the tea service on the coffee table.

The violence was escalating. Whoever had thrown the rock probably hadn't realized she was nearby and could have been struck. But he'd meant to wound Daylin.

"The cameras wouldn't have picked up anything." She muttered it to herself, but everyone in the room stared at her. "Daylin installed security cameras around the house, but they wouldn't have picked up anything out in the field."

"It won't hurt to take a look at what they might have recorded anyway, Ms. Foster." Purdy rose. "We're finished with the interviews for now. I'd like to get the recordings from the cameras. If whoever did this went near the house while everyone else was out in the field, we might be able to identify him."

Hope rising, Gillian stood. "I'll bring whatever we have over to the station tomorrow."

After the two officers and Rico left, she eased onto the couch next to Daylin's good side.

His eyelids drooped and red rimmed his eyes. Almost empty, his cup sat neglected on the coffee table.

Nichole yawned and stood. "I'm going to bed. Call me if you need anything during the night."

They said goodnight and Nichole went to her room.

Gillian kissed his cheek. "You must be sore all over. Did the doc give you some painkillers?"

"Yeah. I have some samples in my pocket, and he gave me a prescription I'll get filled tomorrow."

"Why don't I take you to bed? If you don't want to go back to the house, we can stay here."

He put his arm around her and squeezed. "Sounds nice. We can get an update from the cops and then go back to the house."

She stood, ready to take his arm.

He scowled at her. "I'm not an invalid."

She stepped backward and lowered her eyes.

"Ah, I'm sorry." He went to her and put his arm around her shoulders. "That was rude, and there's no excuse for it. I'm tired and cranky."

She allowed him to comfort her, nuzzling his neck, pressing his warmth against her body. "It's okay. Let's go to bed. We'll both feel better after a good night's sleep."

She collected a few things from her room to take back to the house, and they went outside. The air was soft and muggy. Mosquitoes dogged their steps, swarming around them as they walked. As they neared the field where they'd had the celebration, Purdy and her partner appeared. Both cops swatted at the bugs and quickened their pace when they spotted Gillian and Daylin.

"Rico took us through it. Based on where you were standing, the perp fired from the direction of the lake," Officer Nolan said. "Bugs are awful. We'll walk you back to the house."

"What happens now?" Gillian asked.

"We'll do what we can to track down the pellet gun. It would be easier if it was bought in Fiddlehead, but we can branch out to Temagami and other towns if we have to."

"If you find the gun, can you trace it to the pellet that hit Daylin?"

Purdy shook her head. "No, not to a specific gun. But we can track down local gun owners and question them."

They reached the house.

Purdy shook Daylin's hand and then Gillian's. "Get some sleep. Make sure you turn on your security."

"Thank you. We'll come by the station tomorrow," said Daylin.

The officers walked toward the dock and their boat, and Gillian and Daylin went inside.

She helped him remove his shoes, and he dropped onto the couch.

"It's hot in here. Do you want me to get you a cold drink?" She walked to the kitchen without waiting for him to respond.

"Okay, thanks." He sighed. "You Canadians are even polite when you shoot someone. An air gun. Not how we do things in New York." He chuckled.

She spun around. "Not funny. It could have taken your eye out. You know pellet guns are dangerous." She burst into tears.

"Easy." He stood, and when he approached her, she buried her face in her hands.

She hadn't meant to lose control. The sobs continued to jerk out of her even as she tried to subdue them. "I'm sorry. I'm sorry."

Aware she was close to hysteria, she grabbed a glass and poured some water into it from the water purifier on the counter. Her hands shook as she raised the glass to her lips and sipped.

He gently gripped her arm and spun her around. "Shh. It's all right. I didn't mean to upset you." He pulled her into a one-armed embrace, and she put her head on his good shoulder.

"God. You could have been—"

"Stop. I'm sorry you're upset. I shouldn't have made light of it. It's my habit when the trouble's passed."

She raised her face to meet his gaze. "The trouble hasn't passed. They'll come back, and it'll be worse. Maybe they'll have a real gun next time."

He kissed her. "Come on. Let's go to bed. We'll feel better after a good night's sleep." He sighed. "My mother will arrive on Tuesday."

The reminder sent a pulse of anxiety through her. What would his mother think of her son being shot by some crazy local? What would she think of Gillian?

She got him a glass of water and then let him walk her to the bedroom.

Problems with the locals aside, it was comforting to be with him. As she got ready for bed, she studied him.

He winced whenever he moved his injured arm no matter how he tried to control his expression.

"Don't be such a hero. I know it hurts. If it were me, I'd be whining at you, so go ahead. Cut loose." She grinned as she spoke.

It worked. He snorted a laugh and let her baby him.

She enjoyed the intimacy of putting toothpaste on his brush for him and of helping him out of his clothes and into bed. Little moments like this solidified a relationship, though with Josh, they hadn't solidified it enough to keep him from straying.

She climbed into bed and spooned around him, avoiding his injured arm. "Wake me if you need anything during the night."

"Thanks. I appreciate everything you're doing for me."

Under her hand, his chest rose and fell with each deep, even breath. She nuzzled against his back, savouring the warmth. A light breeze blew in through the open window. She'd had a screen put on this one years ago so they could capture the night breeze.

Peepers sang, a steady violin chorus in the woods and small bogs on the island. From the darkness, somewhere across the lake, a loon cried out and another answered.

Some considered the call of the loon to be sad, but she'd always found it reassuring. She closed her eyes.

As she drifted off, she realized they'd forgotten to set the security alarm.

Her eyelids were so heavy and her body so weary. She'd get up soon and activate it. All she needed was a minute longer.

And she drifted off to sleep.

CHAPTER 20

The scream of the smoke alarm wrenched Daylin from sleep. Smoke invaded his nose and made his eyes water. It rolled in through the open bedroom door, thick, black, and oily.

"Gillian." He leapt out of bed.

She jumped up, almost tripping on the covers in her haste. "Smoke? Fire?" She blinked at him in groggy confusion.

He rushed to her side and shook her, wincing when pain stabbed his shoulder. "Get outside." He didn't wait for a reply but ran into the hallway toward the kitchen.

"I'm not leaving you." Fully awake now, she followed him.

He cursed. "Get out. Call nine-one-one." Smoke fingered across the ceiling, moving lower through the hallway in billowing puffs. Daylin crouched down to get below it.

Behind him, Gillian screamed for help to the emergency operator.

He reached the kitchen, grabbed the fire extinguisher, and hunted for flames. The thick smoke belched from outside the wide-open front door. He ran to it and dropped to the ground.

On the porch, a pile of rags smoldered in a metal bucket. Flames licked at the material, growing and spreading, consuming. He aimed the fire extinguisher at the mound and sprayed, smothering the small blaze. More smoke belched up as the white froth hit it.

Gillian crawled out to the porch, a wet dishcloth pressed to her face and another one in her hand. She handed it to him when he sank to the floor next to her. Grateful, he pressed it over his nose and mouth.

"Your shoulder." Her voice registered fear and concern.

He looked down. Blood seeped through the bandage. Nausea and vertigo teamed up on him, and he leaned back against the wall of the house.

"I'll be okay." He swallowed, a metallic taste in his mouth increasing the urge to vomit. Icy sweat broke out on his body. "Fire's out. The smoke's worse than the fire. Whoever set it wanted it to smoke us out, not burn us down, thank God." It came out in a gasping wheeze.

"You're pale. We have to get away from the smoke." She tugged on his good arm.

Shit, she was naked. "This smoke will attract attention. You'd better put something on."

She smiled. "You too. The fire department and police will arrive soon." She stood but kept to a crouch.

With Gillian's help, he struggled to his feet. Dizzy, he leaned against the wall. He sucked in smoke, and a coughing spasm staggered him into the house.

She kept a firm grip on his arm and led him into the bedroom. She opened the sliding door to let fresh air in.

They dressed in silence until Gillian broke it. "It's my fault."

"Are you saying you set the fire?" He sat on the bed to pull on a pair of sweatpants without falling on his face.

"No." She gave him a tiny grin. "But when we got into bed, I remembered we hadn't set the security alarm. I meant to get up and activate it, but I fell asleep. It's my fault someone was able to come up to the house and set a fire."

Dizziness hit him again. The craving for more air had him gasping, but if he stood, he might pass out. "Help me get outside."

She rushed to his side and grasped his good arm.

Together they hobbled to the sliding doors and stepped out onto the back porch.

Pink and gold stripes of light in the sky heralded sunrise.

She led him to one of the deck chairs and eased him into it.

God, he was such an invalid. He used the dishtowel she'd thrust into his hands earlier to soak up some of the blood from his wound. He would need more stitches if it didn't stop oozing. While he'd fought the fire, he hadn't noticed the pain, but now it came roaring back.

"Don't move." She went back into the house and returned with a glass of water and his pain pills. "You might not want to take the pills on an empty stomach."

He sighed. "I'd love a coffee."

She wrinkled her nose and frowned disapproval. "To be honest, I'd kill for one right now, so I won't argue about it. But make sure you eat something first. I'll get one of the staff to bring you some breakfast."

"Yes, Mom." He laughed and then winced when his shoulder jiggled. "Ah, it hurts to laugh."

"Then don't." But she smiled as she said it.

"Hello?" A voice from inside the house had Gillian rushing to the door.

"Don't move," she shouted back to Daylin as she stepped into the bedroom.

He leaned back in his chair and closed his eyes. Resentment simmered under gratitude. She handled things while he struggled with his injury and the smoke he'd inhaled.

Her voice floated out to him, drawing nearer as she returned through the bedroom with whoever had arrived.

When the patio door slid open, he opened his eyes.

A firefighter, weighed down with gear, followed Gillian from the house. "The paramedics are on the way, Mr. Quinn. I'd like the two of you to stay outside while we make sure the fire is out."

Daylin nodded, and when the firefighter stepped back into the house, Daylin focused on Gillian. "You shouldn't have followed me." The words tumbled out. All he saw was her getting hurt.

She stiffened. "Then you shouldn't have followed the smoke."

"I wasn't going to take any chances."

She stomped across the patio and dropped into the chair beside him. "What are you talking about? You were already taking a chance. We had no idea how bad it was."

He raised his voice, giving fury and frustration free rein. "What do you suggest I should have done? Let fire gut the house?" He tried to sit up but groaned and settled back when his shoulder screamed in protest.

Fear flashed across her face. Slowly, she got on her knees in front of his chair and clasped his good hand in hers. "I love this house. I've lived in it for almost a decade. But it's just a house. It's not worth risking your life to save it. I care about you more."

A tear slid down her cheek, and she stifled a sob. "You could've been seriously hurt by the pellet. That was bad enough. But you walked into a possibly deadly fire. You didn't know if it would spread or blow up." She rested her head on his knees. "I can't handle the thought of losing you. I just found you."

He slipped his hand from under hers and stroked her hair. "I feel the same way. When you came after me, I got angry because you put yourself at risk."

She raised her head and silently met his gaze.

Despite the pain, Daylin leaned forward and brushed her forehead with his lips. "I can't fault you for it since it's what I did. But if anything would've happened to you, I'd have never forgiven myself for leading you into it."

"Okay. Sit back. You'll hurt yourself." With one hand, she pressed him back in the chair.

Footsteps made them both look toward the edge of the house where the garden met the pathway to the front.

A paramedic approached, carrying a medical bag. She jogged up the steps and set the bag down on the table. "Mr. Quinn, I hear you need some attention. Mind if I have a look? I'll need to check you as well, Ms. Foster." She angled her head toward Gillian.

"Sure." She stepped back. "Please check his shoulder first. He's bleeding through the bandage."

The shoulder would be fine.

After the young medic cleaned and redressed the wound, she treated the pair for smoke inhalation with a portable oxygen tank. When they were done, she warned Daylin to baby the shoulder, made them promise to see a doctor by the end of the day, and left.

The firefighter stepped from the house as a policewoman and a man in a suit came around the side of the house.

"Fire's out. You've got smoke damage, which'll be costly enough," the fireman said. "I've opened the windows on the first floor, but you'll want to go around and open them all. Contact your insurance company right away."

The officer and the man with her climbed the steps to the porch, both displaying badges. The woman looked young—probably new to the force. Her blonde hair was tied back in a ponytail, accentuating her large eyes, straight nose, and full lips. The uniform couldn't hide the muscles she sported. She rushed ahead of the man and held her hand out to Gillian, who shook it.

The man, older, greyer, more out of shape than the cop, held his lips in a thin line. He wasn't wearing sunglasses and squinted at Daylin and Gillian as he crossed the patio.

The woman spoke first. "I'm Officer Randall." She inclined her head to the man in the suit. "Detective John Samuels. He's an arson investigator working out of the Criminal Investigations Bureau. He's lead investigator on this fire."

They shook hands with Samuels and Randall. Daylin waved his hand, motioning for them to sit. Both took seats, and Gillian remained standing.

"Would anyone like a coffee or tea? Water?" Her hands fluttered. Daylin caught one in his as it flitted past his face.

"Nothing for me, thanks," Randall said.

Samuels shook his head. "Thank you, no."

The firefighter also shook his head, told them he was leaving, and left through the house.

Daylin squeezed Gillian's hand. *Nerves taking over. Better give her something to do.*

"Coffee for me, please, Gill. You were going to ask someone to bring breakfast down?" He'd deal with the cops. She had enough to cope with.

Her lips twitched into a smile. "Of course. Sorry."

"It's okay," he replied. "Whatever's quick will be fine. I'm feeling a bit weak. Food will help."

She slipped her hand from his and nipped across the patio.

When she disappeared from sight, Randall said, "We'd like to ask you a few questions."

"Sure." Daylin eased back in his chair, resting his hands on the arms.

Randall got a pen and pad ready while Samuels leaned back to listen.

"Tell us how you discovered the fire."

Daylin explained how he'd awakened to the smoke alarm and saw the smoke. He'd jumped out of bed to investigate.

"Where was Ms. Foster when you were in bed?"

He hesitated. They were a couple, and he didn't care who knew they were sleeping together. Gillian might, despite having come out in front of her ex and his girlfriend. "Here—in bed with me. But it's nobody's business."

"They won't hear it from me." Randall got up and walked to the screen door. She peered into the bedroom. "Which side of the bed were you on?"

"The side nearest the patio doors. Gill was closer to the bedroom door."

"She was in bed when you awoke?"

"Yes."

"What was she doing?"

Daylin frowned, his eyes narrowing. "Waking up to the racket from the smoke alarm."

"Are you sure she wasn't already awake?"

"What are you implying?"

"I'm not implying anything, Mr. Quinn. I want to establish where everyone was and what they were doing when you discovered the fire."

"I know the alarm woke her up, because when I screamed at her to get outside, she was groggy and I had to prod her to get her moving."

"All right. What happened when you left the bedroom?"

"We argued as I headed to the front door. Gill refused to leave out the back, but she used her phone to call nine-one-one." He paused. "The front door had been propped open. The fucker left the door open so the smoke would pour inside."

Daylin jumped up and rushed into the house, ignoring the pain in his shoulder.

Randall and Samuels followed him.

Daylin went to the front door, which was now closed. "The fucker broke into my house."

"We'll find him. Keep going. What happened when you got to the kitchen?" Randall guided him out of the hallway, and they stopped by the fridge. The window he'd had replaced was wide open, and it now had a screen in it.

Everything stank of smoke and oil. Black had settled on the bright

99

couch and the quaint cloth lamps Gillian had probably bought and lovingly placed. Daylin gritted his teeth. If he ever found out who'd done this, he'd make the bastard pay.

His gaze landed on the coffee table. "What the hell is this?" He stormed over to the pine coffee table, which was now covered in graffiti. "Like my car."

The messages cursed the damn Yankee and made lewd suggestions.

He gulped in some of the smoke-scented air and coughed, hacking.

"Mr. Quinn? Let's talk outside," said Randall.

"I'm fine."

Randall touched Daylin's arm. "You'll be better off outside."

He shrugged her off and cleared his throat. "Let me finish. Then you can go do your job."

Randall squinted at him, and after a moment, said, "Okay. What happened in the kitchen?"

"Smoke poured in from the porch. I guess I grabbed the fire extinguisher from the kitchen on the way out, but I don't remember doing it. It was in my hands, though, so I must have. Or maybe Gillian gave it to me?" He couldn't focus. A brain-splitting headache built up behind his eyes, making them throb.

"I saw the bucket on the floor. The smoke originated from there. There were flames but mostly smoke. I blasted it with the fire extinguisher." Daylin cursed and his eyes went cold. "The bastard was inside my house."

"Oh, my God."

Gillian. She stood behind them, eyes wide, face pale, and gaped at the marred coffee table.

CHAPTER 21

"You okay?" Daylin rushed to Gillian's side.

"He was inside the house? Oh, my God. We were asleep and he was in here." She dropped her head to his chest, and when his arm went around her, she nuzzled there, savouring the contact. He was so beautiful, so alive. The idea someone wanted to harm him sickened her.

"He's just trying to scare us."

Samuels's throat clearing brought her back to the present. "Excuse me, Ms. Foster. I need to question you as well."

"Okay," she replied, her voice subdued. "Let's go out onto the patio. There's food."

The group returned to the back porch.

A serving tray of food stood to one side, a silver dome covering each dish.

Gillian opened them to reveal tastefully prepared eggs, toast, fruit salad, and bacon. There were condiments, milk, and sugar on the side, as well as a thermos of tea and one of coffee.

"Join us for some breakfast, Detective Samuels, Officer Randall. The chef here makes a wonderful omelette, and there's plenty of everything."

Samuels licked his lips. "Well, maybe a taste. I was out of the house too fast for a decent breakfast. Thank you."

Randall declined, saying she wanted to get photos in the house. She took a camera from her bag and went back inside.

Motioning the two men to sit, Gillian began to set the table and serve the food.

Daylin eased into his chair, favouring his injured arm. He winced when he lifted it to pick up his fork. The injury was on his right side, and he was right-handed.

101

Anger bubbled up inside Gillian. He was in too much pain. They'd have to go get the prescription filled as soon as possible.

Thank God, the staff here could pick up the slack for her for a few hours. Two of them were already doing the farm chores. She'd have to remember to ask Daylin to give everyone a bonus at the end of this week. They were all helping the resort get through this.

After everyone had full plates and she'd poured coffee, Gillian sat and faced Samuels. "What would you like to know, Detective?"

"Mr. Quinn told me you spent the night with him last night, is that correct?"

"Yes." She smiled reassurance at Daylin's worried expression. "It's okay." She turned to Samuels. "I don't care if it gets out now."

"Your call. I need to know for the sake of the investigation." He took her through the steps from the time she awoke to the moment they left the house.

"I didn't notice the graffiti." Her worried gaze once again landed on Daylin.

He leaned over to skim a finger along her cheek. "The police will arrest someone for this." He eased back into his chair and spoke to Samuels. "I hope you nail the bastard."

"We'll do everything we can. I won't let it go." He spoke again to Gillian. "Those are all the questions I have for now. Thanks for breakfast." He went inside the house.

She caught a whiff of smoke when the screen door slid open and closed while Samuels stepped into the house. Her breath hitched, and she choked back tears. Repairs would be costly, the furniture would have to be replaced, and worst of all, that asshole had been in the house with them. Would she ever feel safe again in this place that had always been her refuge?

"We're okay. We'll stay okay." Daylin covered her hand with his. "I'll make sure of it."

She nodded, unable to speak.

"Hey." The voice was Rico's.

She dabbed at her eyes with a napkin and raised her head.

He stood at the base of the porch, staring up at them.

"Come up. Sit. Have some coffee."

"I heard about the fire. I'm sorry." He climbed the steps and sat next to her. "You okay?" He glanced from Gillian to Daylin.

"Yes." She sighed. "It could have been much worse."

"The police are investigating," Daylin said. "Anything else you need? How are things in the restaurant? Guests okay?"

Rico shrugged. "No complaints." He shot Gillian an apologetic look. "People are talking about the fire. They're curious." He faced her straight on. "They're talking about how you spent the night in the house instead of the staff quarters."

"Don't tell us about the idle gossip," Daylin snapped. "Ignore it. You don't need to keep it alive by passing it along."

Rico frowned. "I thought Gill would want to know." His tone was defensive.

She set a cup of coffee in front of Rico. "It's okay. They can speculate all they want. Daylin and I are together. We don't need to keep it a secret."

Rico stood, his gaze still focused on Gillian. "I'm glad you weren't hurt." He turned to Daylin. "Everything is running smoothly. We've got it covered."

"Thank you," he replied. "Gill and I will be gone for a few hours this morning. I appreciate all your help."

Rico gave a slight bow and wave as he left to return to the restaurant.

"He's been a big help," Gillian said.

"He has." Daylin scowled.

"What's wrong?"

"I hope whoever has it in for me doesn't go after you or the staff or the guests. Each incident escalates in violence and severity." He let out a frustrated puff of air. "I don't even know what the point is. Does he expect me to leave? To sell the place back to you? Is it revenge for some imagined slight? What does he want?"

"I don't know." She rose, went to him, spread his knees apart, and knelt in front of his chair again, wrapping her arms around his waist. Lifting her chin up, she smiled at him. "I'd sit in your lap, but I'm afraid of hurting your arm."

He rested a hand on her head and stroked her hair. "God, Gill, you make me love you."

Affection and love for him flooded through her. "I'll get ready to go, and we can leave." As she stood, she leaned over and kissed him. "I'll be back in a few minutes."

She hurried toward the staff quarters. Nichole hadn't come over yet. She wasn't a morning person. But when she learned what had happened, she'd be pestering Daylin. It would be best to head her off.

***

Daylin's gaze followed Gillian.

He couldn't recall a time when he'd wanted a woman more. She'd gotten to him, made him crave to be with her. The models and movie stars he'd dated didn't ignite him like this tomboy woman did.

Her hard, fit body had curves. She was soft in all the right places, and her small breasts fit perfectly in his hands.

He sat up and drained his coffee. What was he doing sitting here mooning over a woman?

His brother would have laughed at him. Andy had been gay, so he wouldn't have understood Daylin's attraction to a woman, but he'd have understood love.

Christ, Andy, why did you have to do it? Why didn't you come to me?

He'd never get answers to those questions. God, but he missed his brother.

Daylin stood and went into the bedroom. He'd have to shower and get ready to go to town.

If they ran into the saboteur, would they see it on him? Or her? The vandal might be a woman, though he doubted it.

His mother would be arriving tomorrow. What if the person harassing him hurt her to get to Daylin? Worry piled on worry. No one here was safe.

Anger replaced worry. That bastard wouldn't rule his life. Surely, there would be something on the security recordings to help find the culprit, but if not, Daylin would make it difficult to take another shot at him—literally and figuratively.

He grabbed his cell phone and called New York.

CHAPTER 22

Daylin scanned the parking lot for his mother's car and spotted it amongst the crowd of vehicles. Her window down, she sat in the driver's seat, her face angled toward the lake spread out on her right.

Sandra Quinn wore her red-tinged brown hair short and sassy. Sunglasses hid her wide, charcoal eyes. Her elbow rested on the door, her hand supporting her head. She was a dreamer, frequently off in her own little world.

Andy had inherited that trait. They were both artists, but neither had pursued it as a career. While it hadn't seemed to bother their mother, it had crushed Andy.

"She's there." Daylin waved his hand in the direction of the car, and spoke to Rico, who he'd brought along to help with the bags.

When they drew near the rental she'd picked up after landing in Toronto, Daylin called out to her.

She lifted her head and smiled at him. "Hi, honey."

"How was the drive from Toronto?"

"Good. Long. Where's this young woman I've heard so much about?" Sandra stepped out of the car and opened her arms, inviting a hug.

He complied, giving her a quick one-armed squeeze and a kiss on the cheek. "She's back at the resort. Rico will help us with the bags."

Sandra held her son at arm's length and frowned. "How's the shoulder? Does it hurt?"

"Some." His mouth curled up in an attempt at a reassuring smile.

He'd told her everything about the fire the day before, but that wouldn't stop her from grilling him about the injury.

"The pain meds take most of the edge off, and Gillian makes sure I don't do any physical labour. You don't need to worry. It's healing fast."

She turned to Rico. "Nice to meet you, Rico. I'm Sandra."

The two shook hands and exchanged pleasantries.

Sandra opened the car trunk and Rico unloaded her bags. Together they managed to carry everything to the pontoon boat in one trip.

Along the way, Sandra quizzed Rico about his schooling. He spent his winters studying math and engineering at the University of Waterloo and worked at the resort through summer breaks.

"It's a long way from Waterloo to Fiddlehead. How did you land a job at the resort?"

"My family lives in Temagami. I've known Gillian's family all my life. Josh and Gillian hired me a few years ago, and I've worked there every summer. I like it."

Daylin listened with half an ear until Sandra brought up the subject of the fire. "Mom, let's not discuss it right now. Contractors are working on it, and by the end of the week, you won't be able to tell it happened."

He'd had to toss out a lot of stuff, but what was the point of being rich if you didn't throw money at a problem? The dominant odour in the place now was fresh paint and new carpeting.

One of the security cameras had also been replaced. The arsonist had destroyed it. This implied he'd known something of the setup. That pointed to either staff or someone who'd scoped the place out beforehand.

His mother's voice pulled him out of his musings.

"All right, dear. I wanted to hear Rico's thoughts on it."

Rico cleared his throat before he spoke. "I was asleep when it happened. The police talked to us after. If anyone saw something, I didn't hear about it. We're all upset, but we're glad no one was hurt."

They reached the boat, and Rico hurried ahead to load the bags on board.

***

Gillian had finished the chores, and while Daylin was still on the mainland retrieving his mother, she stole some time to visit the bluffs. She'd left Nichole and Trevor, Nichole's personal assistant, working on the computer in Daylin's office. Phone pressed to her ear, Nichole had been arguing with someone over the cost of materials.

The day was sunny and brilliant, but rain was in the forecast. Right now, it was difficult to believe storm clouds were on the way. Gillian set her travel mug of tea down on the wide arm of the Muskoka chair in which she sat and gazed out onto the lake.

Dressed in a short-sleeved T-shirt and denim shorts, she'd have no need to take off her shirt. Even so, she scanned the lake for nearby boats. Nothing disturbed the water's glassy surface.

High above, a hawk circled.

She caught a whiff of pine and cedar from the nearby forest and the fresh, clean scent of the lake.

"I'm afraid for Daylin, Mom." Admitting it out loud was a relief. "Someone might be trying to kill him. I can't lose him." She wiped at the tears rolling down her cheeks with the back of her hand. "Even though I've only known him for a month, I love him. He's gotten to me."

When she'd met Josh, it had been a long, slow courtship. He'd pursued her, and she'd allowed him to draw her out of her shell.

They'd met in high school, since his family had moved to Fiddlehead from Toronto when his father had retired. Josh was the youngest of five and had two brothers and two sisters. His city cool had impressed her, as it had many of the other girls in her class, but she'd also been shy and intimidated.

He approached her for tutoring, and she was both flattered and terrified. As they worked together, they became more intimate until finally he convinced her to sleep with him.

The night he took her virginity, he broke through more than her hymen. He cut through her social anxieties and made her feel confident and at ease. Teased and aroused, she wanted him to touch her, kiss her lips, and run his hands over her body.

Her parents were away and Gillian forgot about the books on the coffee table in front of them as his tongue probed her receptive mouth, a thrill of anticipation knotting her belly.

He eased her to her back on the couch, one of his hands sliding up her blouse to skim over her breasts. Murmurs of reassurance, affection, and love whispered into her ear. He loved her. Just her. He would always love her. Just her.

The reminiscences brought with them unbearable pain. She'd worked hard since they'd separated to avoid these memories. Sobs wracked her body.

He hadn't lied. At the time, he meant it.

They'd dated, married, bought the resort, and built a life together. Their intentions had been honourable.

She'd meant it too when she'd told him she loved him. In reality, she'd lied to both of them. He was the first guy to pay attention to her and to love her. Afraid he'd be the last, she loved him back—a shitty basis for a marriage.

With Daylin, it was different. She hadn't wanted another man, but he'd come along and knocked the air out of her from the instant he'd stepped off his boat and onto her dock.

His dock. The correction flashed into her head out of habit, but she barely noticed it.

She loved his physical beauty and his inner beauty. She understood in her core now the meaning of the word attraction. He attracted her like no one else had.

"I love him. What should I do, Mom? I didn't want to fall in love again, but I have." She wiped her tears, sipped her tea, and sought answers in the cold water below.

***

Daylin had Rico take Sandra's bags into the guest room on the second floor of the main house, and Sandra went up to freshen up from her long journey.

Nichole's voice drew Daylin to the office.

When he stepped through the door, she glanced up and held out a finger, signalling for him to wait. "Yes. I understand, but we're buying in bulk … I'd appreciate it, thank you … Yes … Goodbye." She disconnected the call and smiled. "We're getting an excellent deal on materials for the new cabins. I've got them where I want them. Don't worry." She stood. "They'll speak well of us. I'm not taking advantage of them. It's a fair trade, and they'll get to brag you're their client."

"Thank you." He scanned the room as though expecting Gillian to jump out from her hiding place, but Nichole was alone. "Where's Gill?"

"She took off. Went for a walk."

His throat closed. "Where?"

"I don't know." Nichole strolled past him. "Want coffee? I'll put on a pot."

He grabbed her arm. "She went alone?"

What if the lunatic who was gunning for him had followed her? Or what if that pervert was watching her from the lake again?

"Yes. She's a grown woman. We're on an island. She can't go far, and no one comes here without …" Her words trailed off. "You think whoever set the fire is after Gill?"

He paced between the window and the office door.

"They might hurt her to get to me." That spurred him into action. "I'll find her even if it pisses her off."

He ran from the room, and Nichole didn't try to stop him.

CHAPTER 23

G illian stopped crying and dried her tears.
My eyes must look awful. They were probably red-rimmed and her face blotchy. She sniffled and wished for a tissue. Leaning forward, she rested her head in her hands and yawned. Sometimes, there was nothing like a good cry.

A sound to her left made her lift her head. Daylin approached.

When he was close enough so she wouldn't have to shout, she said, "What are you doing here? Why aren't you with your mother?"

His face was dark, stormy, but when he drew near, his expression changed to concern. "You've been crying."

She averted her head to face the water.

What could she say? After years of stoicism, she was finally mourning the death of her marriage? Or that she was terrified of loving him and having him grow cold like Josh had? Why did honesty always have to be the more difficult option?

Daylin sat on the other chair and took her hand.

"Tell me." His voice was so gentle and kind.

The ache in her heart that yearned for him grew.

"I love you." She said it with a mix of wonder and trepidation.

He gave her a half-smile. "That made you cry? Should I be alarmed?"

Her lips twitched as she tried to remain serious. "I was scaring myself with comparing how it ended up with Josh and what might happen with us."

"I'm not Josh."

"I know." She sighed. "He broke my heart—or rather, we broke one another's hearts. It's not something I want to risk again, but I can't help loving you."

He stood and with his good arm drew her up to cuddle her into his body. "I'll never hurt you like that. I've never felt about any woman the way I feel about you. Even when you make me angry, I love you." He paused. "Speaking of that, why are you out here by yourself?"

She had to laugh. "Nice segue. Is that why you're here? You followed me?"

"Of course. You shouldn't have come out here alone." He looked around. "Nice view." His tone was even, casual.

She tried to keep hers the same. "I come here to get away. If I'm up here, it means I need privacy."

"I don't want to intrude, but under the circumstances, you shouldn't be alone." He pulled her in tight. "Someone's trying to hurt me. The best way to do that would be to hurt you. I can handle almost anything but that. When Nichole told me you were walking around alone, I couldn't wait around for you to return. I had to make sure you were okay."

Gillian rested her head on his shoulder. His body was warm, his encircling arm a haven.

"How can I resent that?" She raised her head to meet his gaze. "I'm glad you've found this place, anyway. I didn't show it to you before because it was too personal."

She indicated the little shrine she'd built. "I come here to remember my parents. I miss them, and this place lets me feel close to them." She rose on her tiptoes and kissed his lips. When she drew away, she said, "They'd have liked you. This is the closest I'll get to having you meet them."

"Ah, Gilly. It's a wonderful place." His voice was thick. "But promise me you won't come here alone until they catch whoever is causing us trouble."

She eased her head back onto his chest and sighed, happy to have him with her. "I promise."

"Come back with me now? My mom's anxious to meet you." He stroked her cheek with one finger, and she playfully nipped at it.

"Okay." She took his hand. "Thank you."

Puzzled, he stared at her. "For what?"

"For coming after me. It's nice to know you care." She put an arm around his waist, and they walked into the forest.

***

The man watched them leave and then left the shelter of the trees to retrieve the travel mug Gillian had left behind. His hand curled around the warmth of the insulated cup. Milky tea collected at the spout and along the edge of the lid. He stuck his tongue out and swirled it around the rim, getting hard at the thought her mouth had pressed there recently.

He'd held her in his sights before Daylin entered the scene, but he hadn't come here to harm her. Another day, perhaps, but not this time. Right now, he simply wanted to observe her. He'd still be doing that if jerkwad Quinn hadn't come along.

When he'd first been called in to sabotage Daylin's new investment, one of the reasons he'd agreed to do it was because Gillian had been offered as a reward. Sure, there were flashier babes around, but he'd watched her undress the time or two he'd been on the island and knew she hid her assets well. Anticipation at uncovering them and ravishing her kept him focused.

The rock through the window had been a spur-of-the-moment act. He'd been watching the place, fantasizing about how to drive the asshole out.

She'd been with Quinn that night. Imagining what they were doing together burned. Images of sweet Gillian willingly writhing under Quinn infuriated the man, and so he'd hunted for a rock.

He'd found out later he'd almost hit her.

She'd been standing in the dark, making tea. He was shocked and frightened at first. But then he'd imagined the pain it would have caused Quinn, and he'd regretted he'd missed the shot.

Missed the shot. Yes, he'd missed the shot all right. The pellet had been meant for whoever was assisting Daylin with the fireworks—in this case, Rico.

Oops, sorry. Got Quinn instead.

Fucking Quinn. Moved when the pellet gun went off or he'd have lost an eye. Wouldn't look like such hot stuff with one eye. Women wouldn't be falling all over him then, the gullible twits. Gillian was just as gullible.

What a shame. She was supposed to be different, not just another bimbo ready to fall into bed with the rich guy from New York. Quinn wouldn't be such a hotshot if he didn't have his money and his looks. That was all these women wanted.

But he'd make sure Quinn didn't walk away with Gillian. No, in the end, she'd learn Quinn wasn't the man for her—with help from yours truly, of course.

Thrusting his hands into his pockets, he turned his back on the water and followed Gillian and Daylin's trail into the forest.

CHAPTER 24

Gillian sat on the back porch, revelling in the stories Sandra Quinn told about her two sons. The brothers had been close, especially after Andy came out as gay and their father disowned him. Though Sandra avoided talking about Andy's death, grief infused her eyes and voice as she finished the last story.

Daylin put a hand on Sandra's shoulder. "I miss him too."

Sandra teared up then, and he handed her a tissue from the box on the table. She accepted it and dabbed at her eyes. "I'm sorry. Every time I talk about him, remember the good times, I get all weepy. He was a good boy. It still breaks my heart. Your father—" She choked.

He rubbed his hand down her arm. "I know. I'm sorry his pain is hurting you."

"He made me put away all our pictures of him, everything I had of him. It's all in storage now. I hid a few mementos." She turned to Gillian. "I don't mean to burden you with this. It's difficult. Patrick loves both his sons, I know. But he can't accept Andy was gay and now bears the burden of regret."

"I'm so sorry for your loss and your pain. Maybe with time …" Gillian drifted off, unable to finish the statement. To do something with her hands, she topped up Sandra's tea with the last drops in the teapot.

"Thank you, dear." Sandra patted Gillian's arm. "Andy never got the chance to be himself. It's a sorrow I'll carry around forever."

"How are the family in Toronto?" Daylin turned from his mother to his girlfriend. "We have a large Quinn contingent in Toronto. My parents lived there for a while when they first left Ireland. They moved to New York right before I was born. My cousins had a cottage up in the Muskokas, and we used to visit them there. When I got the idea for the resort, I wanted it in Ontario. Fond memories."

She nodded. "I wondered why you'd pick a place in another country."

"You mean besides the excellent exchange on the Canadian dollar?"

"Okay. I'll give you that too." She smiled.

Sandra had perked up at the mention of the relatives and launched into reminiscences with Daylin. Gillian took the opportunity to make her excuses to go face the chores she'd been neglecting. Grateful the staff had helped pick up the slack, she nevertheless wanted to get back to it.

First, she went into the office to speak to Nichole. Gillian found the young woman hunched over the computer, Trevor sitting close beside her.

Engrossed in the computer screen, they didn't acknowledge her presence. Trevor's hand rested on the back of Nichole's chair, and the two looked cozy and conspiratorial.

Had they slept together? Not that it was any of Gillian's business, but whenever she saw them together, they seemed overly familiar. Perhaps Nichole built intimate relationships with everyone she worked with even if it didn't involve sex. But the way their hands strayed as they talked led Gillian to conclude they had more than a business relationship.

And why not? Trevor was attractive in a brutish sort of way. He was burly, muscular, and close in height to Gillian. His face, while not classically handsome, was rugged and masculine.

Daylin's excited voice drifted in through the open window. He was telling his mother more about his plans for the resort.

Nichole and Trevor looked up as Gillian approached the desk.

"How are things? Is Sandra crying yet?" Nichole said.

Gillian winced. "She had a moment, yes."

Nichole shook her head. "It's been years, and she still carries the guilt."

"Understandable. I doubt I'd recover if I lost my child."

"I don't know how to help her. Neither does Daylin. Seeing her suffer takes a toll on him. He has a heavy dose of survivor's guilt, and she doesn't see it." Nichole leaned back in her chair. "I don't want to point blame at a grieving mother, but it hurts him. His father doesn't help."

Gillian paused. "What about therapy?" Wasn't that the norm in New York for the upper crust? Her insides twisted. She hated generalizing. Everything she knew about Americans or the wealthy came from television and movies. She was as bad as some of the locals.

"They've both tried it. It's slow going, especially since his father won't participate."

A blanket of silence and dimming light from outside caught Gillian's attention, and she sprinted to the window.

Nichole gaped. "What is it?"

Thick grey clouds hovered over the yard and the lake. The patio was empty and the table bare. "They must have come inside. It's getting stormy out there. I'd better go tell the staff to batten down the hatches and make sure the animals are brought in and the eggs gathered. It's rolling in fast."

"Anything I can do to help?" Trevor's chair scraped across the hardwood as he stood.

Already heading out the door, Gillian absently gave him a dismissive wave.

In the living room, Daylin had settled his mother on the couch, and he sat on the armchair. He rose when Gillian breezed past on her way to the front door.

"I thought you'd left."

She paused. "I stopped to chat with Nichole. Storm coming. I have to get to the barn."

"I'll help."

She waved him away. "I'll get Rico to give me a hand."

The back door banged and Trevor ran past the window, probably on his way to the staff quarters.

Daylin frowned. "He's busy. I can help you with the animals. I'm not an invalid."

"I'll take care of it. Stay with your mom." In a hurry to get to the barn, she didn't wait for him to respond but ran outside.

The wind had picked up, swaying the trees and churning the water. She fought her way to the barn and stepped into the peace and cool.

She caught her breath and sniffed the reassuring scent of animal and hay.

The cows weren't in their stalls. They'd been milked already and sent outside. She'd have to coax them back in.

Footsteps behind her made her whip around. *Daylin.*

"I don't have time to argue with you, Day. Go back inside. It's getting worse by the second, and the cows need to be brought in."

"I'll do it."

Before she could respond, he rushed out and headed toward the pasture. She cursed and then left him to it. She checked the hens and found the eggs had been collected.

Thank goodness. She sent silent gratitude to whichever staff member had had the presence of mind to take care of all this.

The jingling of a cowbell had her running outside to help Daylin bring in the animals and settle them in their stalls. Before they'd reached the barn, fat raindrops splattered down on them.

"I can do it," he hollered over the howling wind, and she caught the irritation in his voice.

"You'll open your wound. Stop trying to be manly. I've been doing this with little help for years."

He surprised her with a kiss on the lips, slipping his tongue in while he was at it.

She laughed, unable to hold onto her irritation. "You're impossible."

"Don't you forget it. Come on. We'll do this together and then lock it up."

By the time they'd finished in the barn, the rain teemed down and the sky had turned a leaden grey with a green cast. Lightning flashed, thunder seconds behind. The clouds roiled and swirled, mesmerizing her as they ran for the house.

Beside her, Daylin cursed and veered toward the lake.

"What are you doing?" Was he crazy? She squinted into the rain.

His boat, the six-figure, newly repaired Vista, drifted away from its home in the boathouse.

Her stomach lurched.

Since the vandalism incidents had started, they kept the boathouse doors closed and locked. The Vista wasn't outside by accident.

She raced after him and caught up with him as he reached the docks, which rocked with the waves.

"Fuck." It was the first in a string of curses. He started ripping the cover off the nearest motorboat.

Gillian grabbed his arm, but he shook off her hand.

"No." She had to scream over the wind. "You can't go out there. You'll capsize or get struck by lightning."

"I'm not letting it go when it's so near. I'll snag it and drag it back."

Heart in her mouth, she grabbed him again. "No, please. You can't go out there."

He ignored her, tossed her hand off again, and grabbed the life jacket from the motorboat. As he put it on, he shouted something at her.

Her pounding pulse and the driving rain in her ears masked it.

"I can't hear you." She grabbed him again. "God damn it. You can't go out there. I won't let you."

He grabbed her by the arms. "Back off. Do you know how much that boat is worth?"

She dislodged his arms, launched into him, and wrapped around him. "Do you know how much you're worth? More than a damn boat. I'm not letting you do this." He was being as stubborn and arrogant as the day she'd met him. At least when he'd defied the weather gods then, the storm hadn't yet started.

"You're pushing your luck," she screamed. "Please. I'll help you retrieve it after the storm. Come inside." She tried one last thing. "If something happens to you, your mother will never recover from it."

His eyes went stony. He snarled something incomprehensible at her, but he removed the life jacket and tossed it back into the boat.

She helped him struggle the cover back onto it, and they ran to the house.

115

The wind whipped rain onto their faces as they raced to the porch, and when Gillian opened the screen door, it almost blew out of her grip.

Inside, she kicked off her shoes and stomped to the bathroom. As she grabbed two large, thick terrycloth towels from the linen closet, Daylin argued loudly with his mother and Nichole.

"I spent thousands getting the boat repaired!" His voice was a mix of anger and despair.

"It's just a boat. Thank God, Gillian stopped you." Sandra stood in front of him in the kitchen, hands on hips. Her face was flushed and thrust close to his chest but tilted up to meet his gaze.

"No matter what you paid to fix it, it's not worth your life." Nichole too had hands bunched on hips and a scowl on her face.

Gillian tossed him a towel and kept the other one.

"He's okay." She had calmed down now he was safe inside. "Daylin." Her eyes pleaded understanding, and then she brightened as something occurred to her. "It'll be okay. It has a GPS, right?"

His expression softened, and he nodded. "Right. I wasn't thinking. Christ. I was so afraid it would capsize or drift away, and it would take us hours of hunting to locate it."

"Someone deliberately freed it from the boathouse." Sandra vocalized what no one else dared. "Will you call the police and report this?"

He sighed. "I'll have to. They need to know whatever happens around here. These incidents are happening too frequently to let one go."

"Who was the last one to use the boathouse?" Gillian said. "Maybe they accidently left the door open?" With all her heart, she wished it were true.

"It was tied up. The boat was secured in the boathouse. It didn't slip its moorings, and it's not a coincidence the only boat out there is the one you never owned. Whoever is doing this is attacking me personally."

"He's hurting me too."

He shook his head. "Not directly." He considered. "I don't want any of you going anywhere alone—not until this person is caught. A security team will patrol the island as well." He put a hand on Gillian's shoulder. "Remember, no more visits to the bluffs alone, and definitely no visiting there at night. You promised."

She nodded, but the unhappiness must have shown in her expression.

He stroked a hand through her hair. "You worry about me?"

She nodded.

"I worry about you. This person has trespassed on my home, my boat, and my body. What if he goes after my friends and family next? What if he goes after my woman?"

"Your woman?" Instantly, her back was up. That expression had always galled her.

"That's a good thing. We're together, aren't we? Do you consider me your man?" He put his arm around her.

Nichole and Sandra moved quietly to the living room.

My man? Gillian tested it on her tongue. "My man?"

"Yes." His voice was a whisper. He pressed his lips to the top of her head and waited.

"We don't own each other."

"No." He shifted her so she faced him, and then placed a finger under her upturned chin. "We belong with each other."

She let the words wash over her. If she agreed, whatever he asked of her, she could demand the same of him. And he was in the most danger. He'd already been physically harmed. What if next time the saboteur used a real gun? The possibility always lingered in the back of her mind.

"Then you have to take your own advice and always have someone with you."

He hesitated.

"What's wrong?" She smiled. "Figure you're a big boy and can take care of yourself?"

He chuckled. "I can."

"I can too." She stroked his good arm. "But the reality is, a potentially dangerous person might decide to attack one of us."

"The security team I hired arrives tomorrow. The bastard will have a tough time getting around them."

Her brows arched. "When did you do that?"

"Before my mother arrived. I called New York." He stroked her hair. "I won't go local on this. I can't trust the townsfolk. Anyone might be behind it."

She averted her eyes. He had a point. She couldn't fault him for being suspicious of everyone. She and Daylin would just have to deal with any animosity from the town. Besides, she didn't know of any security company around here capable of handling the safety of the entire resort, and they had to consider the guests first.

She met his gaze. "Good. It'll reassure the guests."

He frowned and sadness crept into his eyes. "The next move would be to evacuate the guests and cancel all reservations for the summer."

"That's probably what he's after."

"Don't shut down."

They turned toward Sandra. She stood in the living area, facing them.

"Don't let him win." She grimaced.

Nichole shook her head. "Safety comes first. If you don't shut down, one of the guests might get hurt. It would be a good idea to close it down right now."

"He's not getting his way yet, Nicky. The security team will make sure of it."

Thunder rattled the windows as the storm raged on.

Daylin strode to the fridge and grabbed a beer. "Anyone want a drink? Looks like we'll be stuck here for a bit."

Gillian went to the window and squinted through the murk at the water. The boat bobbed and tossed on the waves. Its cover was still on, which was a blessing. If they were lucky, it wouldn't capsize. He was right: nothing to do now but wait.

"Okay," she said. "I'll take that drink."

CHAPTER 25

An uneasy peace settled over the resort after the storm ended and Daylin reclaimed his boat. It had run aground on the rocky shore and needed repairs but had survived the adventure. He reported the mischief to the police, who still had no leads. The security team arrived and moved into the main house, claiming two of the four rooms on the second level and part of the office on the main floor.

May eased into June, and Gillian, desiring to assert her independence, moved into an apartment on the mainland. Daylin asked her to stay on the island one more month, but she followed an inner compulsion to set up a place of her own. If she didn't do it now, it would become increasingly difficult to leave.

She needed to take care of herself. Slowing down their relationship wouldn't hurt either. Her heart needed the space, and her head needed time away from him to contemplate where they were headed.

Nichole backed her up on it and even helped her move.

Daylin had, however, convinced Gillian to stay on as manager of the resort, and she agreed to extend her work contract with him to the end of the season. She refused to look beyond that and didn't ask him whether he planned to stay on the island through the winter.

The day before Nichole was scheduled to accompany Sandra back to New York, Gillian and Nichole went to the mainland for the day. Ostensibly, it was to run errands, but in reality, it was to give Daylin some alone time with his mother.

All morning, Gillian had endured the sometimes polite, sometimes curious, and sometimes icy stares of the people she passed as they made their rounds.

They'd met with the contractors, who were ready to start work in a few days. At least they had welcomed the women with enthusiasm and tea.

The pair stepped into The Loon's Nest near noon.

"Interesting little place. This is my first chance to check it out." Nichole smiled at Erika as she waved and shouted a cheery "hello."

"I like coming here." Gillian sent the server a half-wave.

At the bar, Keith served drinks and chatted with customers. He caught Gillian staring and waved. "You here for lunch? I'll come and say hello."

Warmth spread through her face, and she smiled and nodded as every eye in the bar focused on her.

Keith's gaze moved to Nichole, where it lingered.

Erika appeared and guided them to a table. "This okay? Or would you prefer a place on the patio. I have one or two open."

"Oh, the patio." Nichole raised her brows questioningly at Gillian.

"Sure." There were fewer tables on the patio, so not as many people to deal with. Gillian rushed out ahead of Nichole.

It wasn't until they settled in their seats beside the cast iron railing and the potted plants that Gillian spotted Bruce Pankowski. He was with his son, Terry, a young man recently graduated from high school and now working full time for his father.

As Gillian opened her mouth to suggest they go back inside, Pankowski's gaze met hers. When his face darkened and he frowned, she swallowed and averted her eyes.

They had to remain on the patio now, or he'd know she was running from him.

Oh, God, I hope he doesn't come over here.

Nichole's cheery chatter broke into Gillian's musings.

"Pardon? I got distracted."

"I was saying, the menu looks so good, I can't decide what to have. What are you getting?"

Gillian opened her menu and stared at it. She usually got the veggie quesadilla, fish and chips, or soup and salad. Her selection had never varied from those three items in the years she'd been coming here regardless of how much she studied the menu. Maybe she'd try something different today. Live a little.

She grinned. Nichole had an energizing effect on Gillian. She wished she were more like Nichole: free, open, and self-confident.

As Gillian examined the menu, a shadow fell across the table.

"Enjoying the day, ladies?" Pankowski loomed over them, his mouth struggling to smile and busting into a sneer instead.

"Yes, thank you." Nichole gave him a genuine smile.

Gillian only nodded, her hands growing cold and the back of her neck breaking into a sweat.

Pankowski curled a finger under her chin as she stared at him wide-eyed. "What's wrong, princess? You miss me? You haven't been out this way for a bit."

She shrugged and pulled her head back. "I guess our paths didn't cross."

"Thought you'd help me get the contract with your Yankee. He never called. Must be some mistake. I heard he gave the job to Foran's boys at Tidal."

Anger bubbled up, drowning the fear. "They have what he needs for the job." *A company without an asshole at the helm.*

She smiled, but it didn't reach her eyes.

"He didn't even give me a chance. I would hate to think you had something to do with it."

"Daylin makes up his own mind. But I supported his decision to go with Tidal." Fear slammed her immediately, almost choking her, but she was tired of letting this thug bully her. "Your son is waiting for you. Perhaps you should return to your table."

Pankowski's eyes narrowed, and his face flushed deep red. He gripped her face with one hand, forcing her chin up. "You'll regret that."

Gillian froze.

Nichole leapt out of her seat. "Let her go."

"Dad." Terry rushed over and put a hand on his father's arm. "Come on."

"I should—" Pankowski didn't get a chance to finish speaking.

Keith stepped into Gillian's view, an anxious Erika behind him.

"Let her go, Bruce." Keith's voice was low and calm. "Then I'll have to ask you to leave."

Pankowski snapped his hand away, and Gillian rubbed at the throb in her jaw.

"We haven't got our food yet," Pankowski protested.

"Sorry. You're making my customers uncomfortable. Take a walk. Come back another time." Keith turned to Terry. "Tell Chef to pack up your food. Lunch'll be on me today—just take it somewhere else."

"Yes, sir." Terry faced Gillian. "Sorry for the trouble, Ms. Foster."

Pankowski snarled and grabbed Terry by the arm. "Let's go. Keep your fucking food. We don't want it." The two left, Terry's face red with shame and Pankowski's red with fury.

"You okay?" Keith brushed her hair off her face and bent over to examine her jaw.

She averted her eyes. "A little shaken."

"Sorry, ladies." Keith looked at Nichole. "It's not the first time we've had to deal with Bruce's temper, though it's usually not this early in the day he lets it loose. He hasn't had anything to drink yet."

Nichole smiled at him. "Thank you for stepping in. I thought I'd have to start a bar fight."

"Honey, I would have paid to see it." He winked at her and held out his hand. "I'm Keith Harrison, the owner of this fair establishment."

"Nichole Berringer." She clasped it.

He shook her hand and then held onto it. "Tell you what: you and Gill order yourselves a drink on the house." He released Nichole's hand and nodded his head at Erika. "Get them whatever they want."

"Thanks, Keith." The knots in Gillian's stomach eased. With Pankowski gone, she might be able to have a pleasant enough lunch with her girlfriend.

"You're welcome." He waited while they placed a drink order. When Erika left to fill it, his expression turned grim. "Let me know when you're leaving. I'll walk you to your car—make sure he doesn't cause you any more trouble."

"That's not necessary," Gillian replied.

"I hear you've been having problems out at the resort. You think Pankowski had a hand in it?"

She shook her head. "He's not the type to make covert attacks."

"Maybe you should mention this incident to the police. They might want to talk to him. He threatened you."

Gillian sucked in a breath. She was sure Pankowski had nothing to do with the attacks on Daylin. The attacks had happened before Bruce knew he didn't have the job. He wouldn't have attacked a potential client. If the police showed up to question him about it, though, it might inspire him to cause more trouble.

She shook her head. "I'll think about it. It's not him. I don't want to make him any madder than he is already by setting the cops on him."

Nichole reached across the table and patted Gillian's hand. "It'll be okay." She raised her eyes to meet Keith's gaze. "Thanks for everything. You've been great."

"Will you be around for a while?"

"I'm returning to New York for a week tomorrow. But I'll be around after that."

"Maybe I'll see you when you get back, then." Keith clasped Nichole's hand. "It was nice to meet you."

She gave him a sultry smile. "Likewise. I'll be sure to look you up when I return."

After Keith left, Erika appeared and set a white wine for Gillian and a gin and tonic for Nichole on the table. When Erika prepared to take their order, Nichole waved her away. "Give us a moment? I haven't decided yet."

"Okay, I'll come back in a few minutes."

"Make it fifteen."

"Sure." Erika smiled and walked to another table.

Gillian eyed Nichole, puzzled.

"We're not in a hurry, are we?" Nichole picked up her menu and opened it.

"No. The staff has everything under control. I only have administrative work these days, which can wait."

"Then we can have a nice, leisurely lunch." Nichole met Gillian's gaze. "I wanted to talk to you about something. Besides, this'll give that Bruce guy time to clear out of here."

"I'm not worried about him."

"Maybe you should be."

Not wanting to talk about Bruce Pankowski, Gillian opened her menu and tried to find something other than her usual. If she wanted to be more of a free spirit, she could start here. "What did you want to discuss?" She picked up her wine and sipped.

"Come with me to New York."

The wine caught in Gillian's throat. She forced it down and then covered her mouth as she coughed and sputtered.

"Easy there, girl. It's just a trip. It'll be fun." Nichole waved Erika over and asked her to bring them glasses of water. "Honestly. You'd think I'd invited you to join me in a three-way."

"Don't." Gillian gasped it out. "Are you trying to kill me?" She clutched at the glass Erika was setting on the table.

"You okay, honey?" Erika frowned, concerned.

"I'm fine, thanks. Give us another ten minutes."

Erika acknowledged the request and rushed back inside.

"Do you have a passport?" Nichole leaned forward, face alight with amusement.

Tempted to lie, Gillian gritted her teeth and admitted the truth. "Yes. I have an aunt, uncle, and cousins in New Jersey." The memory of visiting them after her parents' funeral clutched at her heart.

"Cool. Then you're coming to New York with me for a week. We'll have a great time."

"I can't leave Daylin alone." That wasn't true—he could manage much of the resort without her now, and the staff did most of the grunt work. Still, it was a straw, and she grasped it and held on tight.

Nichole didn't miss a beat. "I checked with him already. He's okay with it."

"Traitors." When Nichole opened her mouth, Gillian stopped her. "You're ganging up on me."

"No excuses. You'll be thrilled you did it."

Gillian picked up her wine, gulped it, and smiled bravely as she set the glass back on the table. She'd have to go. How else would she become more adventurous except by doing things she wasn't used to doing? "All right. I'll go. But don't expect me to act like a normal woman."

Nichole snorted. "What's that supposed to mean?"

"I'm not into shopping or spas or whatever normal girly girls do."

Nichole opened her menu. "Don't worry. You'll learn. I'm a black belt in it." She closed her eyes, jabbed her finger on the menu, and opened her eyes again. "Looks like I'm having steak and kidney pie."

Gillian stared at her, open-mouthed. "Do you like that?"

"Meh. I'll find out. Sometimes when I can't make up my mind, I let fate decide."

Erika appeared. "Well, ladies? Ready to order?"

Gillian closed her eyes and dropped her hand to her menu. "I'll have," she said and opened her eyes again. Liver and onions. What if it was bad?

The other two women waited silently.

Voice soft, she said, "I'll have the quesadillas."

Her pulse thudded in her ears, and her stomach sank. If she wasn't ready for liver and onions, what would New York do to her?

CHAPTER 26

"You and Nichole made plans for me behind my back?" Gillian tried to keep the shrillness out of her voice, but anger made it difficult. And the anger was rooted in fear.

How dare Daylin push her into this stupid trip? She had no business going to New York. If she wanted to go on a trip, she'd take one—and she was happy staying home. On her island.

His island. Damn it.

Rage bubbled up inside and poured out the end of her finger, which jabbed him in the chest.

"Ow." He smiled and took her hand in his, gently turning it palm up and skimming his lips over it.

She tried to snatch it back and failed.

They were in his bedroom.

Sandra and Nichole had long since gone to bed, Sandra to her room upstairs and Nichole to the staff quarters. Their flight was scheduled to depart tomorrow afternoon. They would catch a plane at the airport in North Bay and grab a connecting flight in Toronto.

As the reality of what she'd let them talk her into seeped into Gillian's brain, panic set in. At least she wouldn't be spending her last night alone in her apartment. Daylin had insisted she spend the night on the island.

"It'll be fun. Why are you so worried? You've travelled before, haven't you?" he said.

She nodded and tried to snatch her hand free again.

His grip remained firm, and he drew her into the circle of his arms.

"Yes, but this is different." Far from home, from the island—this time she remembered not to call it hers—among strangers. She shuddered and threw her arms around him. "I'm such a fool. The thought of going out there terrifies me. Criminals roam around in New York."

The slight edge of hysteria in her voice made her laugh. "Oh, God. Now you know I'm neurotic." This would kill whatever he saw in her. He'd realize she didn't measure up to the jetsetters he was used to dating—confident, empowered women like Nichole.

Josh had been frustrated with her reluctance to travel and her preference for solitude. Now she'd drive Daylin away with it.

He chuckled and lifted her chin with a finger. "I love you anyway. Let's make a deal. Stay for three days. If you hate it, come home." He smiled, melting the knot in her stomach.

"I could handle three days. Nichole is staying for a week, and she wanted me to go with her for the duration."

"Nichole is a party girl. She loves socializing, and the more people around her, the better she likes it. If things get quiet, she goes stir-crazy."

Gillian cupped his head in her hands and drew his mouth down for a kiss. There was an edge of desperation in it. The prospect of even three days without him daunted her.

His tongue parted her lips, and she sank into the kiss. Whenever he touched her, he awakened something in her no one, not even Josh, had been able to arouse. She wrapped around him and gave and took. If this was their last night together for a week—*no, three days, just three days*—then she'd make the most of it.

***

Afterward, they lay in Daylin's bed, limbs entangled. Daylin listened to Gillian's even breathing, relieved she was able to fall asleep. He liked to believe he'd had a hand in relaxing her. She'd been so agitated before, he'd feared she'd be up all night.

She had trouble sleeping most nights since he'd arrived. Yeah, it was silly to blame himself, but he shouldered some of the responsibility for it anyway.

Propped up on his good arm, he stroked her hair, watching her sleep by the clock radio's dim LED light. Her soft, warm body next to his felt wonderful. He'd miss her while she was in New York, but he wanted her to get out and have some fun. She spent too much time alone, though she insisted she wasn't lonely.

He rolled onto his back and stared at the ceiling. While she was away, he'd tighten security on the island and get the private investigator he'd hired to find the jerk who was harassing them. If all went as planned, the problem would be history by the time she returned. Daylin wanted the women out of here for more than to encourage Gillian to have fun. Having them around, possible targets to an unidentified menace, was a constant source of worry.

Without the women around to protect, he could focus on hunting the saboteur down—and God help him if Daylin caught him before the police did. The injured shoulder ached as if in response to his thoughts, and he slipped out of bed to take one of his pain pills.

God, he'd be glad when the wound was healed. Every throb reminded him someone was trying to ruin his plans. If he could figure out why, he might be able to find the culprit.

He went into the office to check the monitors. He flicked from one camera to another, searching the grounds.

All was still.

He spotted one of the two security guards out by the cabins. The other was near the boathouse. Both men were armed. They'd be relieved in the morning by another duo. Anyone trying to cause trouble now would have a much more difficult time getting away with it.

Satisfied his loved ones and property were safe, he took his pain meds and returned to bed. Snuggled next to Gillian, he put an arm around her and closed his eyes. A fleeting hope she would return after only three days crossed his mind, but he dismissed it. Three days wasn't long enough. Best if she took the full week, though she'd protest. Whatever it took, he'd make sure this nightmare was over before she came back.

As the medication, coupled with Gillian's touch, eased his pain, cricket song and the occasional loon call lulled him to sleep.

***

Nichole's apartment was as cute and stylish as its owner. Gillian stepped across the threshold and dropped her bags, relieved to finally be able to let them go. Behind her, Nichole's cases thudded to the foyer's tiled floor.
They'd parted company from Sandra at the airport with promises to visit her at her home in the Hamptons while Gillian was in New York.

The air was close, stuffy.

Nichole kicked off her shoes and padded to the thermostat. Instantly, cool air flowed from the vents, chilling the sweat on Gillian's back and making her shiver with relief.

They'd taken a cab from the airport, and traffic had been snarled. The sun had reflected off the steel and glass skyscrapers and roasted everything on the streets below. Vendors hawking their wares called out for attention, and large, colourful billboards distracted Gillian wherever her gaze landed. The scent of spicy foods and exhaust still clung to her nostrils, and she inhaled deeply to try to flush it out.

The noise and crowds of Manhattan had scraped her nerves, and now the muted whoosh of the air conditioner soothed her. She sank into the plush, white armchair in the living room, leaned her head back, and closed her eyes.

"No time for that. We've got places to go, people to see."

How did Nichole have energy left after the long trip through two airports and a cab ride? Gillian groaned.

"I know what'll help you. Cocktails."

Glass clinked.

Gillian peered through half-closed eyelids.

Nichole stood before an open bar cabinet, a vodka bottle in one hand and a tequila bottle in the other. "Martini or margarita?"

"Your Margaritas are deadly." Gillian paused. "I'll have water."

"And? Come on, girl, you're here to party." Nichole took a jar of olives out of the mini fridge.

"Is that why I'm here?" Regret at leaving home surged through Gillian. Three days was a long time to be in this crazy, concrete jungle. She sighed and sat up straight.

"Don't you ever slow down?"

"What for?" Nichole poured vodka into a martini glass and added a dash of vermouth. She popped two olives onto a cocktail skewer and swirled it around in the drink. After giving it a sniff, she offered it to her guest.

"I need water, Nick."

"Go on. Take it. I'll get your water. Take a swig. It's heaven after a long trip."

Gillian accepted the drink and took a cautious sip. The cool liquid slid down her throat. She wrinkled her nose but was surprised it didn't burn. "Smooth."

"Okay." Nichole clapped her hands. "After I fix my drink, we're going out. You, my friend, are having a night on the town."

"It's Wednesday."

"Doesn't matter." Nichole poured, skewered, mixed, and sipped. "Ahhh. Yummy."

She glided to Gillian and held out a hand. "Come on. We're going clubbing."

Heart thudding, she allowed Nichole to pull her up and lead her into the guest bedroom. A pin-neat room in neutral tones welcomed Gillian. The furniture's simple lines and pine construction reminded her of home. Daylin's home now, true, but it still put her at ease.

A floral bedspread covered the bed, and a Tiffany lamp stood on the bedside table. Puffy mounds of pillows on the bed invited her to climb aboard and snuggle in. She pictured herself curled up amongst them with the latest novel she was reading. If only Nichole's idea of a good time was the same as Gillian's.

Nichole set her martini glass on the dresser. "Let's grab your suitcase and figure out what you should wear."

Since Nichole had helped Gillian pack, she already had a good idea of what was available. She sighed. This would be a long night, but she'd go along with whatever Nichole suggested—even if the thought of it revolted her.

What would Josh think about his ex-wife clubbing in New York? Gillian smiled at the idea. He'd probably faint with shock.

She'd wear a dress tonight, proudly. Her heart fluttered, and her hands went clammy. It would cost her, but it was time she took charge of her life and her emotions.

"Okay, I'm ready."

CHAPTER 27

Daylin squeezed his eyes shut to help his vision adjust to the dimness when he entered The Loon's Nest. He opened his eyes in time to catch Erika waving a greeting. Keith, both hands occupied with pouring a draft beer, smiled and nodded in welcome.

"Hi, Daylin. Patio?" Erika's strong voice reached him while she was still halfway across the pub.

He grinned. "Inside's fine, thanks."

She led him to a table for two in the centre of the dining room. He took a seat facing the bar and accepted the menu she held out to him. "Whatever you have on draft, please."

"Coming right up." She swished her way to the bar. "Another draft, Keith."

Daylin grinned again. Amazing Gillian came here at all, considering the noise level and the crowd, but she'd assured him she enjoyed the ambience. After glancing at the menu, he closed it and studied Keith, who chatted with whomever sat at the bar while he served drinks.

Maybe the pub owner was the reason Gillian liked coming here so much—not to imply the two had a thing going. Keith was a nice guy and probably made Gillian comfortable enough to brave eating here alone.

Since she'd moved to the mainland, she visited the pub more often. She left the island before dinner almost every evening and commuted to work each morning. Her daily departure from the island pressed on Daylin. He'd enjoyed having her in his bed all night, and it wasn't just for sex.

He let his gaze roam around the room and caught the other patrons tossing glances his way. Some of it was curiosity, but a lot of it looked like hostility. Was the saboteur sitting here, studying him?

During his trip to town that morning, Daylin had paid a visit to the police station. The cops hadn't told him anything new on the case. They'd mentioned Gus Anders, Daylin's private investigator, had been in to talk to them. The arson investigator, Samuels, hadn't shown any resentment toward Gus but also hadn't gone out of his way to help the PI either. The same was true of Officer Purdy.

If they held Gus's involvement against Daylin, he didn't care. All he wanted was to have the problem resolved before Gillian returned.

Which brought him back to her moving out. What would happen to her if the perp were still running loose when she returned from New York?

"Ready to order?" Erika flashed her teeth at him as she set his beer on a coaster.

"Yeah. The Reuben, please."

"Sure thing." She picked up his menu and stuck it under her arm. "I hear Gilly's in New York. How did you manage to talk her into it?"

"Nichole's doing, mostly, but I gave Gillian a push. Who told you she went?" The gossip machine here was impressive. Daylin didn't think Gillian had shared the information with anyone.

"People talk."

"Who talked to you?"

She flushed. "Someone from the island."

He considered. The trip had been so last minute, only a handful of people had known about it. Now it was likely the whole town knew. "One of my staff?"

Erika brushed a hand across her face, and for the first time since he'd met her, she was speechless. Finally, she said, "I don't recall. Maybe."

"It's okay. I'm not angry." *Yet.* "I'm curious about who spread the word."

"People talked. It wasn't a secret."

"No problem." Interesting she should react so defensively. Perhaps she was worried he'd get angry at whatever staff member had spread the story. He added, "There's no issue."

"When will she be back?"

"Could be Saturday. She might stay as long as a week, though."

"I hope she's enjoying herself." Erika's tone was subdued, and he was sorry he'd challenged her on the source.

"No doubt Nichole is ensuring Gillian is having the time of her life." The whole trip was probably an ordeal for Gillian, but he refused to say that.

"I'll get your order placed." Erika headed toward the kitchen without waiting for a response.

Keith sauntered up and leaned against the post beside Daylin's table. "Everything all right here? You seem perturbed."

He gave Keith an affable smile. "No problem. How are things with you? Business doing well?"

"Sure. Get a lot of cottagers and tourists this time of year. You full up?"

Daylin took a sip of his beer. "Yes. We had a couple of cancellations for next week but filled the spots again. Gill says the resort's typically at capacity this time of year."

Keith's expression turned serious. "How's the investigation into the vandalism going?"

"Not well. I hate to see it drag on."

"Sorry to hear it. Will Nichole be returning with Gill?"

Daylin caught a hint of eagerness in Keith's question. Interesting. "Yeah. She's got more work to do here."

Keith hesitated. "She got someone in New York?"

Daylin grinned at having his suspicions about the pub owner's intentions confirmed. "No, man. Ask her out."

Keith started to reply when Erika appeared and cut him off. "Here's your Reuben. Hot off the grill." She slid the plate in front of Daylin.

"Did you ask him about Nichole? You gonna ask her out?" She spoke to Keith, nodding in Daylin's direction.

Keith shook his head. "See what happens when you live in a small town? No secrets."

Daylin leaned back in his chair, took another sip of his draft, and smiled. "I'm finding that out quickly, my friend."

***

Gillian stepped into the enveloping dim of Exquisite, the nightclub to which Nichole had dragged her. Music throbbed around them, an energizing heartbeat of sound. Sexy men and women flowed around the pair, some swaying to the music, others heading to the bar or to the tables and booths scattered across platforms of varying heights. The décor was cold, sharp, and metallic. Everything had edges, and what wasn't silver was the colour of night or blood.

She followed her friend to a booth overflowing with chattering women; her heart pounded and her palms slicked with sweat. Instinct told her she wouldn't last five minutes before she'd want to bolt.

Nichole leaned into Gillian's face. "Well? Do you?"

Gillian's face grew warm, and she scanned the sea of faces around her. She hadn't heard anything anyone had said. "I'm sorry. I was zoned out."

"What?"

She sighed. This inability to hear each other speak over the raucous music was what she hated most about these places. She spoke into Nichole's ear and hoped she was loud enough. "I didn't hear you."

"I asked you if you wanted to split a pitcher of sangria with me."

Gillian shook her head. "I can't drink half a pitcher of anything. I'll have a cooler. In a bottle." Which she'd hug to her chest and cover with her hands. What had she let Nichole talk her into? Some psycho was probably lining them up in his sights right now getting the date rape drug ready to slip into their drinks.

The desire to go home—not just to Nichole's but back to her apartment—overwhelmed her. Two more nights. After that, her promise to Daylin was satisfied and she'd return to Fiddlehead. She comforted herself with the promise that she'd call the airline in the morning and reschedule her flight.

"Sit with my gals." Nichole waved at the group of women. "I'll be right back. It's faster to go to the bar to order the drinks."

Gillian hesitated and frowned.

Nichole chuckled. "It'll be okay. Sit. These ladies are my closest friends." She crouched down to shout at the women, and Gillian heard her name mentioned but little else.

Before she could respond, Nichole disappeared into the swarm of people around the bar. The women smiled up at Gillian and their mouths moved. The tallest one, a strawberry blonde, stood and shook Gillian's hand.

Leaning in close, the woman said, "I'm Dana." She waved at her friend, an exotic black woman. "That's Jenelle. Squeeze in with us."

Gillian's face must have registered her reluctance, because Jenelle rose and put an arm around Gillian. "Don't worry. We've known Nichole since high school. Sit. Enjoy. Have some munchies."

For the first time, she checked out the items on the table. Platters of appetizers, interspersed with candles, napkins, cutlery, and a stack of small, white plates packed the table's surface. She sank onto the bench seat, squishing up against a tall, slender goddess with chestnut hair.

"I'm so sorry. It's a tight squeeze." She smiled to reinforce the seriousness of her apology.

"Sorry, what?" The goddess replied.

Gillian searched for an exit. The door they'd entered was teasingly close, but it would be a while before she could make use of it. She sighed and put her mouth close to the Goddess's ear. "I'm sorry I'm squishing you. It's a tight squeeze." Already her throat had grown scratchy and her voice was getting hoarse.

"No worries. I'm Carol. Nice to meet you."

The rest was lost in a blast of music, so Gillian smiled politely and nodded. A drink appeared in front of her—a wine cooler still in the bottle. She smiled her thanks at Nichole and took a sip. As the others chatted, Gillian helped herself to some of the food for something to do.

The offerings looked fresh, the hot foods still steaming. She delicately picked up a chicken wing with her thumb and index finger and set it on a plate. Then she added a few carrot and celery sticks, a piece of garlic bread, and what she assumed was an onion ring. When she bit into the breaded ring, she discovered it was calamari but continued to nibble on it anyway.

Absorbed in noshing her way through her social anxiety, she thudded back to awareness when Jenelle nudged her arm.

"Since it's just us girls tonight, we'll take turns on the dance floor. A couple of us will always stay at the table to protect the drinks." Jenelle shouted the words into Gillian's ear.

So I'm not the only one afraid of having something slipped into my drink. That was reassuring. At least if she got up to use the washroom, her drink would be monitored by someone she trusted.

Her stomach knotted. She trusted Nichole. In theory, that meant she could trust Nichole's girlfriends, but she had to admit she wouldn't. She'd finish her drink before getting up or order a new one when she returned to the table.

Oh, God, this was too much. Only twenty minutes had passed since they'd arrived. She smiled politely and hoped it looked more like a happy grin than a rictus of fear.

"Okay," she screamed in return. "Why don't you go first? I'll stay back."

Please don't make me get up and dance. Everyone would see how uncoordinated she was. And the dress Nichole had talked Gillian into showed off her legs and arms, making her self-conscious. At least it was loose fitting and almost covered her knees.

When Nichole had first seen the dress as she helped Gillian pack for New York, she'd vetoed it. But after examining the rest of Gillian's wardrobe, Nichole had been forced to admit it was the best of the worst.

"We'll shop for new dresses in New York," her friend had promised. "We'll bring you into the twenty-first century yet."

Nothing wrong with the twentieth century. Her dress was comfortable and unobtrusive.

Nichole looked stunning in the steel blue, off-the-shoulder mini dress with ruching at the waist. The style suited her perfectly and turned a lot of heads. But Gillian preferred a more muted look—something that wouldn't attract attention.

Jenelle and Dana slid out from the seat, allowing Nichole to slip in next to Gillian, who braced for the shouting session she knew would follow.

"Come and dance with us. Carol and Tania will watch the table."

She assumed Tania was the woman across the table to whom she'd not yet been formally introduced. "It's okay. I'll take first shift at the table."

"I know this isn't your scene. But you wanted to get out of your shell and experience things. You told me that. I'm helping you do it."

Yeah, she'd told Nichole that all right. Now she was stuck with the insane decision's repercussions. Yet isn't this what she desired? Getting out of her head, participating, socializing? Sure, she was okay the way she was, but wasn't it time she tried new things? She was thirty for God's sake, well past the age where she should be unafraid to live life to the fullest—whatever that meant.

With as much enthusiasm as her body and spirit could manage, she hollered, "Yes," and she bounded up.

The valiant attempt at enthusiasm and verve failed. On her ascent, she tripped on the table's pedestal leg. Glasses, cutlery and plates skimmed onto the floor during her descent, and she landed with an ass-jarring thud at Nichole's feet.

Tears of pain and humiliation welled up in Gillian's eyes, but she forced them back. This was part of the risk. The worst had happened, but she'd shrug it off, like Nichole would, and get out onto the dance floor anyway.

Gillian heaved a deep sigh and accepted the hand her friend held out. Back on her feet, Gillian shrugged her shoulders and forced a laugh. "Well, how embarrassing."

An angry throb in her backside made her limp when she took a step, but she ignored it. "I'll be fine," she shouted. She waved away further offers of help and bent down to help pick up the debris.

As the night wore on, she loosened up—as loose as she could get, considering. While she remained vigilant over the two drinks she nursed her way through, she enjoyed her time on the dance floor. Nichole's friends were much like Nichole, though Tania was closer to Gillian's temperament. The two spent much of the night commiserating with each other about the noise and the crowd.

A man hit on her, and she brushed him off, politely but firmly. The encounter bolstered her spirits. She'd talked to a strange man, made her wishes known, and he'd respected her decision. No one had tried to spike her drink, and no one had molested her.

The fall onto the floor had been mortifying at the time, but she'd pushed through it.

All in all, the night had been a success, Gillian thought when she was finally back in Nichole's apartment preparing for bed. She'd handled everything she'd been faced with.

As she curled up under the down comforter—a must in the frosty, air-conditioned room—her thoughts drifted to Daylin. She'd texted him to let him know they'd arrived safely, but after that, there'd been no opportunity to call him. Other than his response to her text, a cursory "Glad all's well. Love you," she hadn't heard from him either. No emails or voicemails.

It stung—she'd expected him to check in with her. What if something had happened again at the resort?

She sat up. She'd been crazy to go away when someone was stalking Daylin. Why had she let him and Nichole talk her into this? He'd insisted she go away and have a good time, relax, and enjoy herself with Nichole.

Of course, he had. He wanted her out of harm's way.

She'd been so busy fretting over her social anxiety, gnawing on it, she hadn't suspected his deeper motives: send her away for a week and take care of the situation.

She reached for her phone to call the resort but changed her mind when she realized it was past midnight. He'd think something was wrong.

She lay down again and rolled onto her side. Eyes closed, she focused on clearing her mind and failed. All she wanted to do was talk to Daylin and make sure he was all right. Surely, if he wasn't, she'd have heard—the no news is good news policy usually worked.

Tension constricted her chest and knotted her gut. This would be a long night.

CHAPTER 28

Daylin rose before the sun came up. He'd spent a restless night without Gillian beside him. Sleeping alone had never bothered him before, and it didn't so much bother him now as that he simply missed her. The nights would be long indeed if she remained on the mainland after she returned from New York.

He focused on getting showered and dressed. Afterward, he had a quick bite of toast and poured his coffee into a travel mug.

Outside, the mist hovered over the water, and the air was brisk yet humid. July approached, which meant preparations for Canada Day celebrations would get underway soon. Daylin intended to double the security for it, and only paying guests and resort staff would be permitted to attend.

He regretted the necessity, but he had to do something to control the situation. He strode to the barn to check on the animals.

Katarina, the staff member assigned to look after the cows and chickens this morning, was already there. She sat on a milking stool and deftly sprayed fresh milk into the bucket.

"Morning." He stopped to watch.

Gaze riveted on her task, the young woman said, "Good morning." When she finished, she straightened up and faced him.

"Did you need help with something, Mr. Quinn?" She swiped a hand across her forehead, tucking an errant lock of hair behind her ear.

He shook his head. "No, thanks. Just making my rounds. How are things with you? Okay?"

Since sending Gillian off to New York, he'd heard rumbles that some of the staff was unhappy dealing directly with him. He'd have to fix that as soon as possible. He owned the place now, and they were stuck with him. Gillian couldn't be mother hen to them forever.

"I'm fine, thank you." Katarina's smile seemed genuine enough, even friendly.

"Have you done this type of work before?"

"Oh, yes. My parents have a farm outside of Temagami, which is why Gillian schedules me more often than anyone else." She leaned forward again and continued pumping milk into the bucket. "I enjoy the barn, the animals. Gillian lets me take the horse for a run in the afternoons, which isn't like work at all."

"Glad to hear it. How are the rooms in the staff quarters? Any problems?"

She hesitated but only for a second. Maybe he'd imagined it.

"No. Everything's fine, Mr. Quinn."

"Please, call me Daylin." The staff all called Gillian by her first name, and he wanted to continue the tradition. He liked the family feel the Fosters had cultivated among the guests and staff.

Her eyebrows twitched, but other than that, her expression remained neutral. "Sure."

"Thanks for all your hard work here. If it weren't for you, I'd have to do some of these chores. I never caught on to the whole milking routine." He continued to study her expression. "My PI will be talking to each staff member. Please make yourself available whenever he gets to you."

This time, there was no hesitation. She gave him a quick smile. "Sure. Anytime."

After he left Katarina, Daylin made the rounds through the resort, talking to the staff and gauging their reactions. If one of them was the saboteur, he or she hid it well.

He considered the idea the perpetrator was a woman and logic discarded it. The rock that had gone through his window had been large and heavy. The glass had been thick.

A woman might have the strength to heave it hard enough to shatter the glass, but she'd have to be a bruiser. Katarina was the heaviest of the female staff at the resort, more muscle than fat. She would be the only suspect out of all the women here, but he didn't believe she was capable of the violence against him. What reason would she have?

In the restaurant, he found two employees on break and sipping coffee after prepping the day's specials.

Rico spotted Daylin first.

"Prep work's all done. We're ready for the lunch crowd." Rico not only helped with guests when the resort was short-staffed, but he spent a good deal of time in the kitchen assisting the cook.

"Where are the servers?"

"In the back. Don't worry. They're all present and accounted for." Zoey, a chef-school student, was the head cook. An artist even with the simple fare they served in the resort restaurant, she had one more year before graduating.

Daylin would be sorry when she left but understood she'd need to find year-round employment after completing her education.

"You two have been working here for at least two summers, right?"

The duo exchanged glances and then nodded.

"I've been here the longest," Rico replied.

"Notice a change in morale at all since Gillian isn't running the show?"

They glanced at each other again and then back at Daylin, both hesitant to respond.

He waited. Sometimes awkward silences were useful.

Rico broke it. "Not really. I like working for you." He paused.

Daylin kept silent.

Rico continued. "No one's complaining, if that's what you're worried about." His gaze shifted away and back again. "Some whining. Not much ..." His words dribbled off into silence.

Daylin nodded. Waited for more.

This time, Zoey spoke up. "Everyone likes Gillian. I understand why she had to sell the resort, and I enjoy working here no matter who's in charge. Some would prefer if she'd kept the place or at least continued to run it, because they're used to dealing with her." She shrugged. "Change is tougher on some than others. They'll adjust."

Rico glared at her, but then his face cleared and he turned back to Daylin. "No one's complaining about you."

"Good to hear. I'm not asking you to rat anyone out. I want to make sure things are running smoothly. Any issues, I want to deal with them head on. No one should suffer in silence. Transitions are difficult at the best of times." He raked his fingers through his hair and sighed. "Selling this place was tough on Gillian, but she did what she had to. Cooperation from the staff, acceptance of me by the staff, will make it easier on her, not just on me."

"No problem." Zoey stood and stretched. "Break's over, Rico."

The door leading to the employee change rooms opened and two servers stepped out. Each young woman wore the white shirt and navy walking shorts that was the uniform here. They greeted Daylin and carried on to the front of the restaurant where the host was setting up their station.

Frustrated he was no closer to figuring out who was tormenting him, he bid goodbye to Zoey and Rico and went outside. He headed toward the main house. It was almost time to meet with the PI.

As he reached the door to the main house, he pulled out his cell phone. He'd touch base with Gillian before getting involved in the next time-consuming item on his massive to do list. They'd talked briefly early this morning, but he wanted to hear her voice again.

After one ring, a gruff voice said, "Everything all right, Quinn?"

"Who's this?" Daylin pulled the phone away from his ear and verified he'd called the correct number.

"Guess."

"Where's Gillian?"

"You think she's safe?"

Daylin's throat closed. "What do you mean?"

"You think she's safe in New York? I shot you, I can shoot her."

Icy fear ratcheted up Daylin's spine and spread through his extremities. *Oh, God. Gillian. Nichole. Mom.*

"Where's Gillian?" he shouted, unable to keep the panic out of his voice.

"Tighter than Fort Knox there, aren't you?"

Daylin tried to think. How long would he have to keep the guy on the phone for a trace? Could they trace it using his cell after the person hung up? He raced to the office, hoping Gus Anders, the PI was already there.

Empty.

Another chuckle from the cell phone caught his attention. "So secure. Looking after yourself. It's what you do best, isn't it, Quinn?"

"Who are you? Why are you doing this?"

The breathing on the other end of the phone rasped heavily. "I've been watching her." Slow exhale. Another deep inhale. "I can see her now."

"Where is she?" Daylin tried to hide the panic, but it poured out of him. Whoever this was had Gillian in his sights.

"I've watched her on her island. It's her island, Quinn."

"Stay away from her."

"*You* stay away from her." A shout this time. Heavy panting betrayed the man's distress, but then he chuckled again. "You don't have a choice, now, do you? You're not anywhere near her. I am."

The caller was male, though he was trying to disguise his voice. Were the frequent chuckles deliberate or nerves?

"Who are you?" He didn't expect an answer to the question, but he wanted to keep Chuckles on the line at least until Anders arrived. Peering through the screen door, Daylin searched for any sign of the PI.

"A friend."

"You're not my friend." Daylin spotted Anders heading up from the docks. Thank God.

"No," Chuckles agreed. "Not your friend."

"Then whose friend are you?"

"The woman you're taking advantage of. She deserves better."

"I suppose you think that's you?"

Chuckles hissed out a long breath. "Don't push me. You don't want to push me."

"What do you want?"

When Anders opened the door, Daylin waved him inside. As the PI moved to step around him, Daylin grabbed Anders's arm.

Give me your phone. Daylin mouthed it, pointing at the cell phone attached to Anders's belt.

Puzzled, the detective handed it over.

"What do I want?" Chuckles's tone was mildly curious, contemplative.

Frantic, Daylin typed a message into Anders's phone and sent it to Nichole's number: *It's Daylin. Where are you?*

"She never saw me." Chuckles sounded wistful now. "I wanted her to see me. Looked right through me. I'm doing her a favour." Anger tinged the voice now. "Texting Nichole, are you?"

Daylin gulped. His head swam. How would Chuckles know he'd texted Nichole? He stared at the screen, waiting for a reply from Nichole, but terrified he wouldn't get one.

"She can't answer you, Quinn."

"Why not?" Fear had leaked into his voice, but he didn't care.

The phone in his hand pinged. Incoming message—an image.

Daylin opened it.

Gillian sat with Nichole at a table on a familiar outdoor patio.

He got it. On Fifth Avenue. The image viewed the women from above, and they sat on a rooftop patio.

He checked the phone number from which the image had been sent and nausea speared through his gut. The number was Nichole's.

Whoever had Gillian's phone also had Nichole's.

CHAPTER 29

Teeth gritted, Daylin dropped his voice and it became low and menacing. "Stay away from them."

Anders finally interrupted the drama playing out before him. "What's going on?"

Daylin pulled the cell phone away from his ear. "Whoever is harassing me is stalking Gill in New York. He's there, and he's on the phone with me."

Anders snatched back his phone from Daylin's hand. "I'll contact the New York police. Where are Gillian and Nichole?"

"A rooftop restaurant on Fifth Avenue." He named it and then stuck the phone back to his ear when Chuckles spoke again.

"Feeling helpless, Quinn?" The grating laugh came again. "Poor girls. Cut off from you now."

"I'll have the police track the phones and find him," Anders whispered and stepped away to make the call.

Anders's words eased the terror in Daylin's gut. If the women were in a public place, Chuckles couldn't harm them. He'd be arrested when the police tracked him using the cell phones, and this nightmare would end.

"Perhaps I'll join them for the evening. Maybe take them to my place. Maybe I'll just take Gill. I bet she's hot in bed, even if she dresses like a farmer. Maybe I'll take her pert little ass for a test drive."

There was a second of silence, which Daylin broke with a peppering of curses.

Chuckles laughed again. "They're getting up. Time to move along. It's been fun, Quinn, you son of a bitch. You want to control everything, but you can't control me. I can do whatever I want here, and you can't stop me."

The line went dead.

"Gus!" Daylin ran to the office where Anders was completing his call to the police.

"They're working on it. They've got my number. I sent them the messages you received and gave them the women's cell numbers. They'll find the phones. When they do, they'll get the guy."

"I still don't know who it is, but now I know he's in New York, it'll be easier to figure it out." He went to the computer and opened his web browser. Navigating to the staff schedules on the intranet, he checked if anyone had requested time off.

No one was missing.

"Damn it." He used his cell to call the New York police but was unable to get an update. The officer promised to call back as soon as he had news of either the man who'd called Daylin or on Gillian and Nichole's whereabouts.

Next Daylin phoned Officer Purdy. "I have information." He ran through the situation for her. "If I give you Gillian's flight number, can you check the manifest to see who from this town might have been on the flight?"

She promised to do that and get back to him.

Next, he called Keith at the pub.

When the pub owner came on the line, his voice betrayed surprise that Daylin was calling. "What can I do for you?"

"I'm not sure." He explained the situation. "Since you're up on the town gossip, maybe you know if anyone from the area has left town for two or three days."

"Haven't heard anything, but I can ask around. Erika talks to everyone who comes in. I'll check with her and get back to you." He paused. "When you locate the women, call me. I'd like to know they're okay."

"Will do. Thanks." Daylin disconnected.

"It's not someone on staff here." He heaved a sigh of relief. At least he could stop eyeing his employees with suspicion now. The bastard got cocky. Bragged about what he'd done.

Didn't he think I'd get the police to investigate?

Daylin called Nichole's apartment and left a message for her. While he waited for the phone to ring, he paced.

I need to go there. I can't wait here for something to happen. That psycho might hurt them.

He called the airport to find out when the next flight to Toronto departed from North Bay.

***

Gillian followed Nichole onto the steamy sidewalk. They'd had a lovely lunch outside on the rooftop patio, a first experience for Gillian. She'd gawked at the view, enjoyed people-watching—people were always more enjoyable from a distance—and savoured the delicious food. Nichole was fun to hang with, and Gillian, to her surprise, was energized rather than depleted by the outing.

Next, she'd tag along to the business meeting Nichole had to attend, and then they had plans to meet Nichole's friends in Central Park. From there, Gillian insisted they go home for dinner. She hated being out so long. Besides, she still hadn't changed her flight and wanted to do it this afternoon.

One more night in the big city and she'd head home.

After they'd settled into a cab, Gillian dug around in her purse for her cell phone. She'd give Daylin a call. It would be great to hear his voice. She hoped he hadn't had any trouble. When she'd called him this morning, he'd said everything was fine, but that was hours ago.

God, she was so lovesick. Maybe calling him again this soon was extreme, but she could text him.

Unable to find the phone, she pulled items out of the bag one at a time, glancing at each one and then setting it in her lap. By the time the purse was empty, she had a small pile of junk on her thighs but no cell phone.

She peeked at Nichole, who sat staring at Gillian, brows raised.

"I've lost my cell phone." Worry laced her voice. "Maybe I left it at the table. We should go back." But she didn't remember removing the phone from her purse. She tossed the stuff in her lap back in the bag and closed her eyes. Where had she last seen her phone?

"I'll give the restaurant a call. Don't worry. We'll find it." Nichole opened the front pouch of her purse where she kept her phone. "It's gone."

A sick sensation spread through Gillian's gut. "How is that possible? I don't remember taking my cell phone out at all, and the purse has been with me the whole time we've been out." Besides, why would someone steal her phone and not her wallet? Or the whole damn purse for that matter?

Nichole leaned forward in her seat and asked the cab driver to take them back to the restaurant.

Every second in the cab grated on Gillian's nerves. How could she have lost her phone? She'd kept a paranoid grip on her purse the whole time they'd been out. It didn't make sense. Could she have left it at the apartment? No. She'd dropped it into her bag before leaving her room.

The cab pulled up in front of the building that housed the restaurant and the women jumped out. Nichole tossed some money at the driver, and they raced for the entrance.

The air conditioning hit Gillian in the face when she entered the lobby, and it helped to ease the tightness in her chest. Sweat rolled down her back in a slow trickle, the sensation making her shiver.

She reached the elevator first and punched the up button. "I've never lost anything before." When the reminder she'd lost the island to Daylin popped into her head, tears welled up. Afraid she was about to have a panic attack, she leaned against the wall next to the elevator doors.

"It'll be fine." Nichole stood in front of the elevator, left hip thrust out, right foot tapping.

The doors opened, and Gillian almost barged in before she realized people were trying to exit.

"Nichole, hey." A man barred their way, and he caught Nichole in a hug. "Are you just getting here?"

"Oh, hey, Trevor." Nichole turned to Gillian. "You remember Trevor, my assistant?"

Anxious to get upstairs, she nodded and hopped into the elevator. "Sorry, Trevor, we're in a hurry."

She pressed the button to hold the doors open and focused her gaze on Nichole, willing her friend to hurry up. The air grew thick and hard to breathe.

"What's the matter? You seem tense," Trevor said.

Nichole nodded, still standing outside the elevator. "Problem. We might've left our cell phones upstairs. Where are you headed? Want to hang?"

What the hell is she doing? Gillian wanted to scream. "Nichole." She couldn't resist the verbal nudge.

Her friend grabbed Trevor's hand and yanked him onto the elevator as she stepped aboard. "Come on. We'll get the phones, scoot over to my meeting place, and then go to Central Park. We'll hit Les Blues for dinner."

Gillian snapped her head around to glare at Nichole. What happened to returning to the apartment after the park? She chose to ignore the plan change. No sense arguing about it now. She had to find her damn phone.

How could it be missing? Blood pumped loudly in her ears. She was getting worked up again. She inhaled deeply, trying to clear the tension and the fear. Every stop the elevator made on the way up made her want to hit something. People crowded her. To make matters worse, Nichole chattered gaily to Trevor as if nothing was wrong.

Nothing is wrong. It's not the end of the world. She had to believe that, or she'd get hysterical, but oh, God, she just wanted her phone back and this trip to be over.

The elevator finally reached the top, and the doors opened. The crowd spilled out, dragging her along with it.

Nichole strode up to the hostess and asked if anyone had turned in two cell phones. The hostess shook her head, and Gillian rushed to the table where they'd had lunch.

Two couples were in the midst of receiving drinks they'd ordered when she raced up.

"I'm sorry. I might have left my phone here." She scoured the table. Nothing. "Did you find a phone?" Damn it, where was it? They hadn't been gone from the restaurant long. If they'd left the phones behind, they should be sitting on the table or back with the hostess.

All four people denied seeing any cell phones.

Gillian stood staring at them as if she didn't believe it, but she finally admitted the phone wasn't there. She jumped when someone gripped her arm but relaxed when she identified Nichole.

"Come on. We'll have to cancel the phones."

"Daylin will wonder why he hasn't heard from me."

Nichole smiled, indulgently. "You talked to him this morning, right?"

"Yes." She whispered it. What if someone was using her phone? Both phones were missing. That wasn't a coincidence.

Trevor put an arm around Nichole. "Why don't I help you ladies out? You can use my phone to cancel yours or whatever you need to do. Come over to my apartment." He smiled, flashing dark puppy eyes at Gillian. "I live nearby. It'll be faster than going to Nichole's or the office."

She hesitated. "Do you have a cell phone we can use here?"

"Sorry. The battery's dead. I need to recharge it. But there's a landline at my apartment you can use so you don't even have to wait for it to charge. You can take care of this and be on your way in no time."

Nichole didn't give Gillian a chance to respond.

"Great idea. Gillian can go to your place to do what she needs to do while I go to my meeting. I'll be back in an hour. The office I'm visiting is a quick cab ride away." She took Gillian by the arm and led her away from the restaurant.

CHAPTER 30

Daylin felt as if the planet had dropped out from under his feet and left him spiralling after it. "What do you mean no one from Fiddlehead or Temagami was on that flight?"

Purdy sighed through the cell phone into his ear. "I'm sorry, Mr. Quinn. The only one on the flight from around here who then went on to New York was Gillian."

"There has to be some mistake." He paused, thinking it through, pacing around his living room while he did. "Okay, so not a resident of Ontario."

Purdy filled the silence. "I checked subsequent flights as well. A few people caught the flight to Toronto, but didn't continue to New York. I even checked the flights between Toronto and New York, in case he drove or took a flight to Toronto from another airport. Whoever you spoke to doesn't live around here. No one from here crossed the border between the time Gillian left here and the time you received the call except Gillian."

Frustrated, Daylin thanked Purdy for her help and disconnected. He returned to his office, where Anders sat, cell phone pressed to his ear. He held up a finger when he caught Daylin's stare.

After disconnecting the call, Anders said, "The police in New York found the phones on the roof of a building overlooking a rooftop restaurant on Fifth. They speculate whoever it was watched the women from there as they had lunch." Anders shook his head. "Whoever you talked to was long gone when the cops got there."

"He's not from here." Daylin parked on the edge of the desk.

"Did the cops tell you that?"

"Not exactly. Purdy told me no one from around here caught a flight from North Bay to Toronto and then on to New York."

Anders tilted his head and his eyes unfocused. "What if it wasn't a Canadian? You're assuming whoever's out to get you lives here. What if it's someone from New York?"

Daylin called Purdy again, a lump of fear growing in his gut. He asked her to check the flight manifests again to see if any resident of New York other than Nichole had caught the same flights as the women. When he hung up, he took stock of whom he had working here from New York.

He grabbed his laptop and searched the employee/contractor database for the names of those who lived in New York but had spent time here on the island. It was a short list. Most of the contractors working on the renovations and construction were locals. Assistants came and went. The architect had come and gone twice, but the timing was wrong.

There. Trevor Gianelli. Nichole's PA.

Daylin cross-referenced with the dates he'd had incidents of vandalism. Trevor had been there for all except when the rock was thrown.

He called Purdy again. First, he asked about the flights, certain she would confirm his suspicions.

She didn't. "Sorry, Mr. Quinn. No one from New York was on any of the flights to Toronto with a connection to New York. Numerous New Yorkers were on the Toronto to New York flight."

"Can you find out if a Trevor Gianelli was in Canada on the date of each incident? If so, can you find out if he was staying at a local hotel during the first incident?"

"You think he's connected to the problems you've had there?"

"I do." He wouldn't have suspected Trevor—the guy was friendly to everyone and a close friend of Nichole's. It was a long shot and based on a hunch, but Trevor was the only potential suspect so far. He gave Purdy the dates of all the incidents and waited while she put him on hold.

When she returned, she reinforced his suspicions. "He was in the country during the time each incident occurred, and he stayed at the Fiddlehead Motel the night the rock went through the window."

Daylin scanned the roster for the night in question and verified Gianelli had not been on the island and wasn't expected to be in Ontario. "He wasn't supposed to be here, Officer. He should have been in New York then."

"Thank you for the information, Mr. Quinn. Leave it to me. I'll contact the police in New York and ask them to take him in for questioning."

"I'm already booked on a flight to New York."

"When are you leaving?"

"Later on this afternoon."

After he disconnected the call, Daylin went into his bedroom to pack.

Gillian hadn't wanted to go, but he'd pressed her. Nichole had essentially browbeaten Gillian. Sure, she'd claimed she wanted to experience more, but she'd been nervous. And all he'd cared about was getting her away from danger.

He should have listened and kept her close until the trouble was resolved. But no, he'd pushed her into walking right into a trap. He grabbed his phone and speed-dialled Nichole's number at her apartment. When the voicemail kicked in, he hung up. He'd already left two messages.

Once again, he called the office and called friends. No one had seen them.

He contemplated calling Trevor's cell but decided against it. As long as Trevor didn't know they'd caught on to him, he'd be less likely to harm the women.

Daylin dropped the phone and finished packing.

***

Gillian followed Trevor out of the elevator to his apartment unit. The building was in the heart of Manhattan. Security was tight, the lobby sumptuous and welcoming, and the building clean and quiet. Despite that, she had to focus on keeping her nerves steady.

He ushered her into the apartment, and they stepped into a large living room, tastefully furnished and decorated. The furniture was leather and dark wood, the carpeting white and pristine. Paintings of cityscapes framed in a light wood accented the warm tones of the walls.

"You have a nice place." She sat, back rigid, on the edge of a plush sofa.

"Thank you. Let me get you a drink."

"No, thank you." She dropped her purse on the floor and stood. "Your phone. I'd like to report my cell phone missing and then call Daylin."

"Plenty of time for that. Don't worry." Trevor pressed a hand on her shoulder and eased her back onto the sofa. "I make a mean GT."

"GT?" She frowned.

Trevor chuckled at her confusion. "Gin and Tonic."

"I don't need alcohol." Frustration gave an edge to her voice. Didn't these people do anything besides drink?

"Oh, but you have to try this. I use the best gin, a quality tonic, in the perfect ratio."

Too tired and irritated to argue about it, she waved a hand at him. "Go ahead. I'll give it a shot." She'd take a sip to make him happy and then get on with what needed to be done.

He disappeared into another room, returning a minute later with two drinks. He set them on the coffee table.

Each clear and bubbly drink was in a unique rocks glass. He grabbed the tall glass and handed it to Gillian.

She accepted it and took a small sip.

"Refreshing." She paused, had another sip, and then set the glass on a coaster. "Thank you. Please, may I use your phone now?"

149

"Sure. There's a phone in the office."

Relieved to get to it, she hurried after Trevor, following him into a scrupulously clean and organized office.

She spotted the phone on the desk and went to it. "I'll need to find the number for my carrier. Can I use your Internet?"

"No problem." He powered up his computer, and they waited for it to load.

While Trevor logged in, Gillian picked up the phone.

No dial tone.

Puzzled, she switched it off and then on again, but the phone remained dead.

"Trevor? It's not working."

He held out his hand, and she gave him the phone. He hit talk, listened, shook his head, and shrugged. "If the phone service is down, the Internet is as well. I've been having some problems with the service lately. I'll get my cell phone charging, and in fifteen minutes, you can make your calls."

Gillian returned to the living room while Trevor plugged in the cell phone. She took her seat again on the couch. Without thinking, she picked up her glass and sipped. A fat slice of lime floated among the ice cubes, giving it a tart bite. Tension made the liquid pool in her gut. Unsure she could choke down any more, she set the glass back on the table.

Trevor walked into the room and picked up his drink.

"Cheers. It's nice to have you here, even if it isn't the greatest of circumstances." He smiled at her. "Drink up."

"I'm sorry. My stomach is bothering me." She stood. "I'll get a glass of water from the kitchen if you don't mind."

He frowned. "Sure. Allow me."

He brushed past her and went into the kitchen, but she followed him.

"I'll bring it in to you. Go sit."

His brusque tone startled her.

He grabbed a drinking glass from a cupboard and then went to the fridge.

"It's okay. I'll wait."

He poured water from a jug into the glass and handed it to her, a scowl on his face.

She left the kitchen and headed toward the living room, but when she spotted a bookcase packed with books in the den, she detoured. "Mind if I check out your book collection?"

"Treat yourself." Annoyance tinged his voice.

She ignored it. She didn't know how to make small talk anyway. She'd be better off spending the time it took to recharge the phone with her nose in the books.

As she scoured the titles and author names on the spine of the books,

Gillian forgot about Trevor. She recognized most of the authors, some of whom were her favourites. The water refreshed her, washing away the bitterness of the gin and tonic.

The sips she'd taken of the alcoholic drink were small and few, but even that little bit of alcohol had made her nauseated. Stress and alcohol did not mix—not in her stomach. She gulped more water.

Trevor's low voice broke into her reveries.

"I don't give a fuck." The rest of the conversation was unintelligible.

The tone of his voice shocked her. Uneasy, she set down the book she was perusing and listened, breath held.

His voice lowered further.

She hadn't heard the door, and the only voice was Trevor's. He was on the phone.

At least she could make her calls now.

She started to walk from the room but froze when her gaze landed on a pellet gun propped against the wall in the back corner.

Her mouth went dry as she crept over to it and picked it up. Since it would make noise to check if it was loaded, she didn't. Instead, she set it back down where she'd found it, afraid of what would happen if Trevor walked in and caught her handling it.

Was it possible Trevor had shot Daylin? Why? He was Nichole's friend. If he'd done that, then maybe he'd also been the one to set the fire.

She tried to recall if Trevor had been on the island when all the incidents had happened but failed. She simply couldn't remember.

Nichole and her entourage had come and gone regularly during the last two months. If Trevor was behind everything, he may have manipulated getting her here.

Tears threatened, and Gillian forced them down. No one knew where she was except Nichole. Daylin might have tried to call her by now, might have tried Nichole by now, but their cell phones were gone. Perhaps Trevor had taken them. But how?

She shrugged that away. She'd better focus on right now. No one could help her. She'd have to get out of this on her own.

She slipped out of the den and tiptoed toward the living room. When she got close, she pressed against the wall and listened to the conversation. Part of her felt ridiculous for doing it, but another part of her, the suspicious, paranoid, cautious part of her, made her stay quiet and alert.

Trevor raised his voice to a normal level, as though he didn't care if she heard him. "No problem. Take your time, Nichole. Gillian will be fine." At Trevor's words, a lump of icy fear balled in Gillian's gut.

Nauseated, she thought about the out-of-service phone. If he was trying to keep her here for some reason, maybe the phone wasn't broken.

Silently, she scurried back to the office and knelt on the floor to search for the phone cable. When she found the end that plugged into the wall lying on the floor, she shoved it back in where it belonged. She lifted the receiver and pressed "Talk." There was a dial tone, but at the sound of approaching footsteps, she pressed "End" a second before Trevor appeared in the doorway.

"What are you doing?" Trevor strode into the room, pried the phone from her hand, and set it down. "The phone's broken."

"I wanted to check if service had been restored." She gave him a weak smile and sighed. "It's still broken. Maybe I can try your cell now?"

"Sure. It's in the living room. I just talked to Nichole. She's been delayed. Why don't you come and finish your drink while you make your call?" His voice was normal, friendly.

"Okay. First, where's your washroom? I guess I drank too much water."

He huffed out an exasperated breath, but when he spoke again, his voice was even. "Down the hall. Follow me."

She hurried after him.

He ushered her into a small powder room off the den, and she closed and locked the door.

She pressed her ear against the door but heard only silence. If he waited for her outside the bathroom door, she'd be in trouble.

In case he was listening, she used the toilet and then washed her hands. Without flushing, she opened the door and peered out. She jumped when Trevor straightened up from where he leaned against the wall across from the bathroom door.

"Oh, I'm sorry. I almost forgot to flush." She ducked back in and flushed.

Now what? She'd have to go back into the living room.

As long as she pretended everything was fine, he'd play along. Hopefully. The charade couldn't last forever. She had to either get out of here or phone for help.

She followed him into the living room and again took her seat on the couch. Automatically, she reached out for the glass of gin and tonic. When she realized what she was doing, she snapped her hand back. "Oops. I left my water in the den. I'll go get it." She jumped up before he could move.

Back in the den, she spotted her cup resting on an end table next to a chair. She snatched it up and pivoted, almost bumping into Trevor.

"Something wrong, Gillian?"

"Yes, something is wrong. Someone stole my phone, and I want it back." She brushed past Trevor, anger displacing fear. She strode back into the living room, set her glass of water on the coffee table, and picked up her purse.

She faced him. *Let it go*, she thought at him. *You haven't crossed any serious lines yet. Let it go, please.*

"I want to go home. Tell Nichole I'll meet her at her apartment." Surely, he'd take the out she offered. Surely, he didn't want to hurt anyone, to hurt a friend. This was insane.

He remained silent.

Her request hovered in the air between them. The next one to speak would determine the direction this would take. Sweat broke out on her palms, and she rubbed them on her pants.

She braved speaking first, attempting to control what would happen next. "I'm tired, Trevor." She used his name deliberately, making it personal. "I'm leaving."

"Too late." He pulled a gun from the end table and pointed it at her. "Sit down. Drink your GT."

"Why are you doing this? We're friends. Daylin's your friend." She dropped her purse and eased onto the couch.

He shook his head. "We're not friends. I cozied up to him for business, not pleasure. You, on the other hand, will be for pleasure."

He dropped into the leather armchair across from her and took a sip of his drink. "It's good. Drink up."

"You're trying to poison me."

"Not poison, honey. Drug. There's a difference."

She twisted her hands in her lap. "I don't think so. Answer my question. Why are you doing this? Why would you hurt Daylin?" She glared at him. "You're the one who shot him with the pellet."

He smirked at her. "I'm earning my prize. The goal is to force Quinn to unload that fucking island."

"I don't understand." Nauseated, she reached for her water and sipped. "Why are we here?" He planned to hurt her. She was sure of it. But how badly, and how was he planning to get away with it?

"The drink contains a date rape drug. You should have done as you were told and finished the fucking drink. If you had, you could have survived this. Sadly, that's all changed now."

A chill traced a path up her spine. "What do you mean?"

"You'd have passed out, waking up in the hospital with no recollection of the beating and rape. I'd tell the police you got tired of waiting to use the phone and left. Not knowing the city, you ended up walking into an alley where you were attacked. The big city chews country mice like you up and spits them out. It would destroy Quinn. He thought he was so fucking clever sending you away from the resort. Joke's on him. He sent you right into my arms."

The blood drained from her face and her head spun. "Rape?" Her voice was weak, frightened. She licked her dry lips.

He leered at her. "Shame to waste the opportunity. It's not like you'd have known who did it." He drew closer to her. "I still get the bounce. I'm not giving that up. Now you'll be awake for it."

She leapt to her feet and her gaze darted from the gun to the apartment door.

"Forget it," he said. "You're not getting out of here."

"You're insane. What makes you think you'll get away with this?"

"The cops will find your body in an alley as planned. I'll tell people you left. They'll assume you went to Nichole's apartment, or, well, who the fuck cares? It'll take a while for anyone to realize you're missing."

"You're a psychopath."

"No need for name calling."

"What has Daylin ever done to you?"

His eyes flashed, and he sneered. "Fucking nothing, that's what he's done. He's rolling in success, but would he throw some my way? I can't even score with his cast-off women." He trembled with rage. "You're as bad as all those cunts he's fucked." He advanced on her. "Fucking whore."

Gillian scoured the room, taking in the knickknacks, searching for anything heavy to use as a weapon. She might go down, but she'd go down fighting. If only she had a testicle-puncturing manicure like Nichole usually wore, but she kept her nails short for farm work.

Trevor grabbed her and, at gunpoint, led her from the living room.

CHAPTER 31

Trevor shoved Gillian into his bedroom and slammed shut the door behind him. He tossed the gun onto the dresser.

Relieved he thought her such easy prey, she braced for a fight. The overpowering anger inside her surprised Gillian, but she let it fuel her.

Ironic that I'd be more afraid to have a conversation with him than I am at the prospect of him raping me. Thank God for preventative paranoia and the self-defence classes she'd taken.

She didn't wait for him to approach her, but rushed to a chair at the other end of the room and snatched it up. "You won't touch me."

He chuckled. "Well, would you look at that? The mouse that roared. Going to give me a little sport first, huh, little mouse?" He licked his lips. "I'll enjoy fucking you. It's more fun if they struggle and beg."

Rage skittered through her at his words. They implied he'd attacked women before. "You rapist bastard."

The venom in her voice only brought a sneer to his face. "You might call it a hobby."

"Does Nichole know what you are?"

"She knows I'm a wonderful assistant." He closed in on her.

When he was near enough, she jabbed out fast with the chair. She focused on hitting him hard and fast—no holding back. Fury and adrenaline gave her strength, and she was already a strong woman. Used to lifting and carrying heavy objects when she did farm chores, she was fit and muscular.

Nichole was a waif. Her friends looked like they needed a good meal and would be knocked down by a light breeze, but Gillian was well nourished and strong.

The chair's legs connected with Trevor's chest. He cried out in surprise and pain but managed to grab the crossbar on the bottom. He hauled on it, yanking her toward him.

She shrieked as she stumbled and almost lost her footing. Instead of pulling back, she shoved into him and knocked him onto the floor, but he kept a grip on the bar and pulled her down with him. The chair between them gave her the edge, and she rolled away and leapt to her feet.

He regained his feet a second after and lunged at her. He grabbed her by the arm and spun her around, pulling her tight against his chest.

"That's better." He thrust a hand down her pants and probed into her panties with his fingers.

She remained silent, breathing in hoarse gasps as she struggled against him. With nothing between them now, she had to rely on her willingness to hurt him barehanded. Wishing she had spike heels on instead of conservative two-inch rounded ones, she stomped. Her heel found the soft meat of his socked foot, and she rammed him in the solar plexus with her elbow.

He howled, and when his grip loosened, she lunged away from him. She faced him, feet planted on the carpeted floor, fists raised, and waited for him to make a move.

He laughed at her defensive posture. "I'd love to keep you around for a while. You'd make a great little plaything. Come on, baby. I'm going to fuck you. I promised Quinn."

Gillian's eyes narrowed, and she gritted her teeth. *Use the anger. Override the fear.* It might give her the ability to survive. She scanned the room, taking in the lamps on the tables and the sports equipment propped along the wall. Nothing useful. The most threatening item was a tennis racket. The gun was out of her reach on the dresser right behind Trevor.

"What do you mean?" Fear had crept into her voice, and she gulped air.

"Who do you think took your cell phones?" He didn't give her time to reply. "When Quinn called, I answered. Told him my plans for your cute ass."

He lunged as she did, and he caught her with a right hook to the face.

She staggered backward, smashed the armoire with her left hip, and fell to her knees. Ignoring the searing pain, she fought to stand as, fists raised, he closed in on her again. The next punch to connect made her head spin, and she staggered backward. She bounced off the armoire again, harder this time, and the knickknacks on it clattered as they fell over.

If she didn't act fast, this would end in her rape and murder. She had to take the offensive. Her right arm slammed out and sluiced through his defences. The heel of her hand smashed him in the nose, and he dropped to his hands and knees.

She spun around, ready to run, but he grabbed her leg and yanked it out from under her. When she was down on the floor, he grabbed her by the hair and dragged her to the dresser. He snatched up the gun and pointed it at her.

"You'll fucking pay for this." He smashed her head into the dresser as he released her hair.

She collapsed on the ground, dazed, and he stood over her, the gun pointed at her head.

The doorbell chimed. Nichole?

Trevor heard it too and glanced toward the bedroom door.

Gillian dived for the gun and screamed when it went off, the shot grazing her arm.

He shoved her back to the floor and jammed a hand over her mouth.

She bit into his flesh, and when he yanked the hand away, she screamed, high and piercing.

The sound of a door smashing and footsteps running into the apartment distracted him, and she screamed again. When one of her hands slipped free of his grasp, she hauled off and punched him in the face.

"Help, back here, please."

A male voice yelled, "Police."

Her relief was short-lived when Trevor swung the gun up at her chest. Reflexively, she shoved against his arm as the gun went off, and the bullet went wide.

"I'll fucking kill you." He screeched out the words.

Nothing more creative than "Fuck you" came to mind, so she went with that. Message delivered, she grabbed for the gun. She tried to twist it out of his hand the way they'd practiced in class but her grip slipped.

In her periphery, two cops raced into the room, guns drawn. The female officer hollered, "Freeze. Police."

A gunshot rent the air.

Trevor's weapon had fired again, the bullet smacking into the wall.

The policewoman stepped toward him. Taking advantage of the distraction, Gillian rolled away and crawled behind the male officer.

"Please. He wants to kill me. He tried to rape me."

Trevor waved the gun at the female officer. "Fuck you. This isn't the way it ends."

Her gun went off.

Gillian got to her feet and stumbled to him.

Blood oozed from a wound in his chest. His eyes were open and glazed.

The male cop put a hand on her shoulder. "Are you okay?"

"No." She dropped to her knees and buried her head in her hands.

CHAPTER 32

The cops called an ambulance, had Gillian's wounds treated, and then took her to the police station. They kept her there for hours. She answered questions, told her story, and waited around doing nothing when they left her alone.

Though she thought of it as an interrogation room, the place wasn't stark or intimidating. She sat on a couch, a cup of coffee on the coffee table in front of her. Two detectives had sat opposite her on armchairs for most of the ordeal, but now the chairs were empty. The men had been called out of the room, again, and she'd been left alone, again, with no explanation for the abrupt departure.

Exhausted, she'd broken down in tears more than once while she'd stuttered out her version of what had happened in Trevor's apartment. Three wet tissues sat crumpled on the table next to her coffee mug, and she squeezed and twisted a fourth one in shaking hands.

The silence and the locked door—she'd tested it when they'd first walked out—made her want to scream and pound on the door. Whenever the urge became unbearable, the tissue in her hand suffered the consequences.

The detectives, whose names she'd forgotten as soon as they'd given them, had claimed they knew she was a victim here. They'd insisted she wasn't a suspect, and they'd notified Daylin, who was on his way.

They'd hammered at her nevertheless. Yes, they had to verify what had happened, especially since Trevor wasn't able to provide his part of the story. But she craved to get away from here. Yet, had they released her when she first requested it, it wouldn't have mattered. She had nowhere to go until she located Nichole or Daylin arrived.

The reminder she was alone in a strange city brought the tears again. She dropped another crumpled tissue onto the pile and yanked a new one from the box next to her.

A beep sounded; the door lock clicked.

Daylin pushed his way past the officer who'd unlocked the door.

Gillian jumped up and leapt into his arms, unrestrained tears saturating his shirt when she buried her face in his shoulder.

"Oh, God. Oh, Daylin." She couldn't choke out anything else. She hugged him, released him, gripped him again, and then ran her shaking hands over him as if she doubted he was there.

"Okay. It's okay. I'm here." He kissed the top of her head and then eased out of the constricting hold she had on him.

Their gazes locked, and he winced and cupped her head in the palm of his hands. "Trevor did that?"

He meant the bruises on her face.

"Yes," she whispered.

He wrapped his arm around her and guided her to the couch. When he sat, he drew her into his lap.

With her head on his shoulder, she moulded to his body.

"I'm so grateful you're here." She put her arms around him, lightly this time. "I didn't know what to do next." Her breath hitched, and she nuzzled her face into his neck.

He stroked her hair with one hand and caressed her back with the other. "They knew I was searching for you. I'd reported you missing and in danger. They found Nichole."

Gillian gasped.

"She's fine. I'd reported you both missing. She's waiting in the car for us."

Daylin explained what had happened at the resort and how he'd figured out Trevor was the one sabotaging it. "I'm so sorry I brought this into your life."

"How were you to know? He was your friend, Nichole's friend. He led me to believe he was my friend, too, so I trusted him. He envied you. All this was about envy. I can't understand it."

"He must have had a lot of hate and anger in him."

"Thank God he never hurt Nichole. She spent a lot of time around him."

He started to reply, but the door opening interrupted him.

A police officer entered the room. "Excuse me, Ms. Foster, you're free to go anytime you wish. But if you could stay reachable for another day or two, we'd appreciate it."

Daylin helped her stand and rose with her. "She'll be staying with me. The detectives have my contact information. Is that sufficient?"

The cop nodded. "Yes, sir."

Gillian gripped Daylin's arm. "Everything I brought with me to New

York is at Nichole's place. I don't want to desert her. She must be hurting."

"Don't worry," he replied. "We'll make sure Nichole's all right. But I want you with me until we go home."

The cop held the door open for them and Daylin led Gillian from the room.

***

Daylin clasped Gillian's hand as they made their way up the stone walkway toward the red brick, two-storey farmhouse his parents owned in East Hampton. His other hand clutched the handle of her suitcase. Sandra had insisted the couple come out to the house to spend the night when Daylin relayed what had happened.

He hadn't argued, though he'd been reluctant to bring more stress to Gillian by dragging her into his family issues. In the end, he'd decided that if his having a murderous rapist as a friend hadn't scared her off, then his father probably wouldn't.

The invitation had also extended toNichole, but she elected to stay with her own family.

The door opened as they reached the large, wooden front porch. Sandra rushed out and ran to Gillian, throwing her arms around the young woman.

"I'm so relieved you're all right. I never would have believed Trevor could do what he did." She stepped back and examined Gillian, brushing gentle fingers over her bruised face and the bandage on her arm.

"I'm okay. Thank you for your concern." She squeezed Daylin's hand.

"Let's go inside. We've had a long drive," he said.

"Yes, of course. I've got hot tea and coffee made and some lunch. We'll eat on the back patio." Sandra hooked an arm through Gillian's and escorted them inside.

The farmhouse was large, but warm and welcoming, with hardwood floors, teal-blue walls, and country décor. In the heat of the day, windows were open but shaded and ceiling fans circulated the air.

Daylin always enjoyed the time he spent here. The large property had once been used as a farm, though there were no longer animals or crops raised on it. Now, everything was manicured, and the only plants growing here were flowers cultivated in a small greenhouse in the back.

"Where's Dad?" Surely, he wasn't working on a Sunday.

Daylin thought he caught a flash of annoyance on his mother's face.

"He's next door. Mr. Arnett is tinkering with a new car. Your father went to look at it."

"That's okay." Part of him was relieved to be able to put off confronting his father again after their last explosive encounter. He walked Gillian through the house and onto the back deck, an extension of the wraparound porch from the front of the house.

A hunter green, wrought-iron patio table was set for lunch. Four matching chairs with padded cushions huddled around it. Since the patio was covered, there was no need for an umbrella.

Gillian leaned out over the railing. "The flowers are gorgeous." She fluttered her fingers over a saucer-sized hollyhock dangling from the post near her hand. After drawing in a deep breath, she exhaled loudly. "The air is so refreshing."

"Sit, please." Sandra waved to a chair and Gillian obliged.

Sandra settled into a seat. "Anna will bring out the serving cart. I forgot to ask if you have any allergies. Is there anything you need to avoid?"

Gillian smiled. "No."

Daylin took a seat next to her as the patio door slid open and Anna, the housekeeper, stepped outside. She eased a wooden serving cart through the opening and pushed it over to the table.

"I'll take it from here, Anna, thanks. Daylin can give me a hand."

He leapt up and helped his mother transfer the serving dishes onto the table so they'd be in easy reach. As they settled down to eat, the patio doors slid open again and his father appeared.

Daylin stood, but when Gillian moved to do the same, he waved her back down.

"Dad." He met his father's gaze and noted the iciness in it. "Please, sit down and have some lunch with us. Come and meet Gillian."

His father ignored the invitation. "Sandra, a word?"

"Sit. Have some lunch with us." Sandra's eyes pleaded, but Patrick either deliberately ignored it or completely missed it.

Daylin's irritation rose.

"Dad," Daylin's voice held a warning. "We'd love to have you join us. Gillian and I return to Ontario the day after tomorrow, and I don't know when I'll be back here again."

To Daylin's surprise, Gillian rose and went to Patrick. She offered him her hand. "It's nice to meet you. Please, stay and have lunch with us."

Patrick looked her up and down, a frown clouding his face. "You sold my boy that island?"

"He bought it from me, yes." She dropped her hand to her side.

Daylin caught the slight tremor in her voice. The palpable tension between the members of the Quinn family must be intimidating. Her mastery of her shyness impressed him. Warmth and affection for her spread through his chest and landed in his heart.

"You know why he wants it?" Patrick said.

"Yes." Her voice was barely above a whisper, but Daylin heard her loud and clear. "In honour of his brother. You must be proud that he loves his brother so much and has the resources to create such a tribute."

"His brother—"

"—sounds like a wonderful person. I wish I'd met him. I'm sorry for your loss."

Patrick's face twisted with pain. "Andy was selfish for doing what he did, and his behaviour brought shame on the family."

"Dad." Daylin went to his father and put a hand on Patrick's arm, but Patrick brushed it aside.

"There's no need to build a monument to a corrupt lifestyle." His jaw clenched. "I have to attend to business." He turned to Gillian. "I'm sorry my son dragged you into our personal affairs. He shouldn't have. If you'll excuse me." He spun on his heel and went back inside.

The silence on the patio dragged on until they heard the garage door open and the car start. Tires squealed when Patrick tore off down the long, winding driveway.

"He's in a lot of pain," Sandra said. "He won't admit he blames himself for Andy's suicide, and he takes it out on Daylin. I'm sorry you witnessed that."

Gillian stepped over to Daylin. He released the breath he'd been holding when she put her arms around him. Her body, pressed against his, relaxed him, and he threw a tentative smile at his mother.

"I'll talk to him later. Let's eat."

Gillian's deep brown eyes showed compassion.

He kissed her on the forehead and escorted her back to her chair. This was why he loved her. When they returned home, he'd find a way to convince her to move back onto the island.

CHAPTER 33

Later that night, Gillian slipped a nightgown on as Daylin used the en suite bathroom. She was surprised Sandra had allowed them to share a room, but Daylin laughed when Gillian mentioned it.

"My mother doesn't judge, and my dad is just relieved you're not a man."

Maddeningly, she'd blushed at his words, but as she recalled them now, she giggled.

She climbed into his bed—the one he'd used when he'd lived here. Thankfully, it was queen size. The furniture in the room had grown up with him.

It was nice of his mother to maintain the room for him here, but it hinted at Sandra's fear of letting go after the loss of her youngest son.

Daylin emerged from the bathroom, naked, and joined Gillian in the bed.

"I've been looking forward to getting you alone in here all day." He pinched the thin strap of her nightgown between two fingers. "What's with the dress?"

She pursed her lips. "It's not a dress. Besides," she said, bunching it up around her waist, "no panties."

"It's clothes," he muttered and stroked his hands along her hips to her belly and then lower.

She put her arms around him and nuzzled his neck. "Behave. We're in your parents' home."

He chuckled. "Then quit turning me on."

"I want to touch you." She pressed her lips to his and kissed him. Need and want made her frantic, and she parted her lips to him.

He pulled back. "Your lips say yes. You're driving me crazy."

"I know. I'm sorry. I want to behave, but I need you." An image of her

163

confronting Trevor flashed through her head, and the fear of never seeing Daylin again came rushing back. She feathered her hands along his firm biceps and solid chest.

He was her man, the man she wanted to be with, and she needed him right now.

His palms brushed across her body, leaving tingles of desire in their wake. The strokes and touches were urgent, firm, demanding. His gaze focused on hers, and his eyes glazed over with lust. "I won't be gentle."

"I don't want you to be." She was alive and wanted to experience his body, to have every solid piece of him on her or in her. "Take."

What she'd refused Trevor she wanted Daylin to demand so she could surrender it to him.

His knee parted her thighs, and he pressed hard between her legs.

"Don't hold back. Don't wait." She arched into him.

His mouth captured hers, frantic. His lips were the only softness he offered—everything else was steel flesh. He nipped her lips, and the pleasure-pain had her growling low in her throat. When he penetrated her with a quick thrust, she clamped her legs around his back, pressing him into her.

It wasn't enough. She needed more.

Her arms locked around him, and they rolled and she was on top. She rose over him, conquering, rocking on him. "Mine, and I'll take it."

This time Daylin growled feral lust. He spun her over and now he was on top. "Mine, and you'll give it."

"Yes." She gripped his head in her hands and drew his mouth back to hers. The wild ferocity of their mating drove her to the cliff edge and over it. "You too. Now. Now."

He was planked over her, his chest hovering above hers.

She couldn't take her gaze off his eyes. It was as if she glimpsed into his soul. When the moment came, she felt his release and closed her arms around him tight, pulling him down to her, pressing him onto her.

The sudden body weight huffed a gasp of air out of her, but when he tried to ease off and roll to the side, she stopped him.

"I need to feel you on me a little longer."

"Okay." He kissed her, and it was tender this time. "I love you, Gill. The fear of losing you hasn't diminished even though you're here with me and I know you're safe."

She kissed his lips, equally tender. "Me too. I'm trying not to think of what might've happened, but I can't get it out of my head. If he'd have raped me, killed me—"

He pressed a finger to her lips. "It would have destroyed me. We can't dwell on that. But we can make the most of our second chance." He did move off her then but draped his arm over her chest. His hand stroked her cheek.

"Ever since you picked me up at the police station, I need you touching me. When you're not, I panic. What's wrong with me?"

"It'll be okay. You're traumatized. I'll help you get through it."

"I fought him."

He smiled. "Yes, you did. When we first met, you told me you could take care of yourself. You survived. You kicked ass before the cops arrived."

The image in her head of Trevor's dead-eyed stare haunted her, nauseated her. She'd stopped him from raping her, but it had cost her. "Paranoia and fear paid off."

"Were you paranoid and fearful? I'd say you were proactive. You were living alone on an island. Taking self-defence classes was a smart decision."

"I never expected to be tested like that." She slid her hand across his chest and tugged his earlobe. "I love the feel of your skin. You're a miracle." She kissed his shoulder. "Thank you for coming to get me."

He ran his hand through her hair. "I had to come. The police beat me to Trevor's, but no matter what, I had to come after you. Will you be okay? Can you sleep?"

"Yes." She closed her eyes, fatigue and passionate sex catching up to her. She turned her back to him and snuggled into his warm body, his arms cradling her. "I know I can kick ass, but I feel a lot safer when you're holding me."

He kissed her shoulder. "When we return to Ontario, move back to the island with me."

Her eyes popped open and she spun around to face him. "I can't."

He frowned. "Why not?"

She opened her mouth to reply, but he held up a hand, forestalling her.

"Before you argue about it, just listen." He rose up on one elbow, facing her, his curly hair and broad shoulders silhouetted in the dim light of the clock radio. "Yes, we've only known each other for two months, but we've worked together every day since I landed on the island. I've gotten to know your quirks, your habits, how you think."

She didn't know what to say, and the silence expanded until he broke it.

"I love spending my days with you. I love you."

She stroked his arm. "I love you, too. But I need to be sure. I don't want to move in with you just because I almost lost my life. We can't do this out of fear."

"I'm not doing it out of fear." Annoyance laced his voice. "I want to wake up to you every morning. I want to go to sleep with you every night. We'll run the resort together."

"And what? You'd pay me a salary and I'd sleep with you? No. It's complicated enough. I've got to live on my own. I want to be in a relationship with you, but I'm not ready to move in with you." As soon as the words were out, she wanted to take them back. What was she saying? She loved him. She wanted to go to sleep with him, to wake up to him.

What he proposed sounded like heaven. Why was she turning him down? She didn't want to live without him, but moving in with him wouldn't work. She needed more than that, and more, right now, would be moving way too fast.

"Not now. It's not the answer. I'm sorry."

He switched off the lamp and lay back down, drawing her to his body. "Okay. We'll see how things go when we get home."

Gillian didn't reply. What was there to see?

CHAPTER 34

An hour later, Gillian rolled out of bed. Sleep eluded her, and she finally admitted defeat. She'd go into the kitchen for a glass of water and then maybe nose around in the library she'd glimpsed when she'd toured the house. The Quinns had walls of books, and they called to her.

She slipped on her robe and tiptoed down the stairs and out toward the kitchen in the dark.

Shadows in the darkened living room drew her gaze as she passed by. She jumped and cried out when a figure shifted in the big leather armchair across from the couch.

"It's only me." The voice, gruff and dripping with fatigue, belonged to Patrick Quinn. "Sorry to startle you."

He switched on a lamp.

While the light wasn't overly bright, it speared into Gillian's dark-accustomed eyes, and she squeezed them shut.

"Can't sleep? Come join me for a drink." Ice rattled in a glass.

She opened her eyes.

He held up a rocks glass with a sliver of golden liquid and some ice cubes. "Whiskey. You got a taste for it?"

"I came out for a drink of water." She squinted, trying to gauge his mood.

He didn't appear drunk, and he didn't seem angry. He looked sad.

She entered the room and sat on the couch. Perhaps if she talked to him, she could help him. "I can have one small drink."

He went to the liquor cabinet and grabbed the whiskey bottle and a rocks glass. "Ice?"

"Yes, please."

Her gaze followed him as he fixed her drink and delivered it to her, his movements slow and deliberate. "Cheers."

"Thank you."

He returned to his drink, tossed back the remnants, and poured another one. When he was seated again, he leaned back, legs stretched out, ankles crossed. "Bed okay? Trouble sleeping?"

Her face flushed at the reminder that she shared his son's bed. The familiar sensation of self-consciousness hit her, and her mind went blank. As a distraction, she took a tiny sip of her drink, letting it sit on her tongue before she swallowed. She tasted a hint of vanilla and a smoky flavour. It went down smoothly.

"Just restless, I guess."

She could see where Daylin got his looks.

Patrick's dark hair was peppered with grey, but he still had a lot of it. It curled around his ears as his son's did. Their eyes were similar as well—the colour of dark rum and framed with enviably long, black lashes. Patrick had maintained his lean physique, and his hard body reflected his hard personality.

"Are you having difficulty sleeping as well?"

He shook his head. "Not difficulty. Avoiding it. Sandra says I was rough on Daylin earlier and won't stop nattering about it. What do you think?"

How was she supposed to respond? *Yes, you were quite the asshole to your one remaining son, sir.*

"Is this something you want to discuss with me?"

His eyes narrowed as he studied her. "He bought your place, and you included yourself in the bargain. Tell me why I should be okay with what he's done. You okay with being chattel?"

She gasped at the insult. But he'd asked a question, and her default under these circumstances was to answer honestly.

"I wasn't part of the bargain as you put it. He doesn't own me. I had a contract to help him run the resort for two months." She set her drink on the coffee table and hugged herself. How long would she have to sit here before she could return to bed?

You don't have to wait. He has no right to intimidate you and make you feel small.

The thought reassured her, but it didn't get her off the couch and back to her room. Unsure of what to do or say, she waited for Patrick to speak again.

"And then you found out how rich he was?" He slugged back half his drink.

Her blood boiled and gave her the courage she needed. "And then I found out what an amazing man he is." She glared at Patrick. "I have my own money, thanks. Selling the resort ensured that, even when half the money from the sale went to my ex-husband."

"Ah. An ex. Why'd you split up?"

"Not your business, Dad."

Gillian jumped up, but before she could move, Daylin strode to her side and put his arms around her.

"Don't let him needle you. He's an angry old pisser. Come back to bed." He scowled at his father. "If it wasn't for Mom, I'd never see you again."

"I didn't mean anything by it. I want to know about the girl who's banging my son right under my roof." A slight slur had crept into Patrick's voice. He licked his lips, chugged the rest of his drink, and went to the cabinet to get another one.

"Don't you think you've had enough for one night?" Daylin eyed Gillian's drink on the coffee table and raised his brows. "Yours?"

"Yes." It came out a whisper. "When I couldn't sleep, I got up to get a drink of water. Your dad was in here alone and asked me to join him for a drink. After that one, I planned to return to bed. I thought if I talked with him, things might get better between you." She shook her head. "I was wrong. I'm sorry."

The sound of glass smacking wood brought their attention back to Patrick. He'd slammed his empty glass down on the liquor cabinet's shelf. "Why did you leave? He wasn't like that until you left."

Daylin staggered backward as though he'd been slapped, and Gillian rested a hand on his shoulder.

"You pushed me out. You wanted Andy to take the company's reins and he did, even though he hated it, until you drove him out. My position as director of international operations demanded I travel. Surely, you understand. I didn't abandon anyone." His jaw clenched and irritation seeped through in his voice.

"You don't have much of anything to do with the company anymore. We'll lose it because of this fucking project for a dead faggot." Patrick's voice grew louder with every word, and his face went scarlet. "No one's running it now except me. Who can I hand it to now? I built it from the ground up and gave you and your brother everything. You both threw it away. He preferred to live in poverty than have anything to do with the business."

"No one threw anything away except you. Nothing Andy and I did was ever good enough for you. Andy preferred to live in poverty rather than let you hold his lifestyle choices hostage. I haven't walked away from the company. I've got good people in place handling things for me while I get the resort up and running. Gillian's helping." He put an arm around her and pulled her to him. "I don't want to talk about the future of the resort without considering Gillian's place in it and in my life."

He released her and moved to stand before his father. "Your unreasonable demands and homophobia drove Andy and me away. We've lost Andy forever, and you were part of the reason why." Daylin turned to

Gillian. "He wouldn't even come to the funeral."

He glared at Patrick. "As if the rest of us would turn our backs on a loved one. It was emotional blackmail."

Patrick's face contorted with grief and tears spilled down his face. Hand shaking, he grabbed the bottle of whiskey and fumbled to open it.

Daylin rushed over and laid a hand over his father's, stopping him. "Enough. You're already drunk. Don't make it worse." Gently, he pried his father's fingers off the neck of the bottle. "You miss Andy, don't you?"

Patrick nodded but didn't speak.

"We all do. We all wish we could have stopped him. But we didn't, couldn't. Now we have to live with the consequences. We were never close to you, but we wanted to be. Andy went out of his way to impress you, get your approval. He failed because you didn't approve of who he was." Daylin led Patrick to the armchair and eased him into it.

With a glance at Gillian, Daylin sat on the edge of the coffee table and faced his father. "Andy was an artist, not a businessman. He was gay. You didn't accept the man he was. Try to accept him now, even though he's gone. Help me honour him. Accept me."

Patrick slumped forward, head hanging, elbows on thighs, hands dangling between his knees.

Afraid to move, Gillian stood rooted by the couch.

Sandra, still blinking sleep from her eyes, stepped into the room. She paused, her glance taking in each of them, and then went to her husband's side. Crouching next to him, she draped an arm around his shoulders.

"We'll work this out. Please." She lifted her head to meet Daylin's gaze. "Take Gillian to bed. I'll handle this."

"You've been handling this for years. It's got to stop." He rested a hand on his father's shoulder. "We never tell each other how we feel, Dad. I love you. No matter what, I love you. I hope you feel the same about me, about Andy."

Patrick raised his head slowly, as if it were heavy. "You're my sons. I loved you from the moment I watched you enter the world." His voice was thick with emotion and Irish accent. "I wanted the best for you. I wanted everything for you. Everything I worked for was all for you. I don't know how things got so twisted around."

"We'll figure it out," Daylin replied. "What do you say we call a truce for now?"

Patrick patted his son's hand. "Sure enough." He gazed at Gillian. "I'm sorry. I was rude and insulting. I hurled anger at you because you were handy. Because you're with my son and I was angry with him."

She clasped her hands in front of her, unclasped them, and then gripped her elbows with her hands. The fidgeting didn't help her think of anything helpful to say, so she nodded. "It's okay."

"Go to bed. It's late." Patrick stood and offered his hand to Daylin. "We'll talk in the morning." His accent had faded again as his voice levelled out and the emotion eased out of it. His face relaxed, and he turned exhausted eyes on Sandra. "Let's go to bed."

Sandra took his hand and guided him from the room.

Daylin strode to Gillian and took her in his arms. "Did we scare you away?"

The concern in his voice was so strong she drew away to look him in the eyes. "If anything, it makes me love you more. The love you expressed is so powerful. Why wouldn't I want to be with a man capable of that?"

"Thank God for you, Gilly." He wrapped an arm around her waist and walked her back to their room.

CHAPTER 35

Back on Gillian's island, Daylin dropped his suitcase on the floor inside the front foyer of the main house. In his head, he still referred to the place as hers. She belonged here now more than ever. With him—especially after the scene at his parents' place. She'd helped him maintain his sanity and mend the ravaged relationship he'd had with his father.

Their talk the next day had been anti-climactic compared to the eruption during the night, but it had been cathartic and healing. His father still had a long emotional journey to make before he would allow himself to love his sons unconditionally, but Daylin believed he'd arrive there eventually.

Grateful to be home at last, he wished Gillian were here instead of at her apartment on the mainland. Sure, she was coming to work the next day. But he wanted her with him every day, every night. Everything in this house, on this island, spoke of her absence.

He kicked off his shoes and, though the temptation to procrastinate burned in him, he took his suitcase to the bedroom. After dropping it on the bed, he opened it up and started putting away his clothes, pitching the dirty laundry into the hamper.

A movement at the patio door startled him, but he grinned and opened up the door when he recognized Nichole.

"I hope I'm not disturbing you." She carried a bottle of red wine. After kicking off her shoes, she strode toward the bedroom door. "Keep doing what you're doing. I'll pour us some wine."

She disappeared, returning with two filled glasses. After handing one to Daylin, she set the other on the nightstand.

"Unpacking? I'll take care of mine tomorrow. I'm too wiped to do it today." Nichole plunked down on the bed. She wriggled, trying to get comfortable. "Blasted phone." She reached into the front pocket of her skirt and yanked it out.

He marvelled she'd been able to slide it into such a tight skirt. No wonder it made her uncomfortable when she sat.

He set his glass of wine on a table and returned to his suitcase. "Thanks for the drink and for coming back here with us. Are you sure you're okay to work tomorrow?"

Trevor's betrayal had been hard on Nichole. She blamed herself for leaving Gillian alone with him.

Nichole sipped her wine and leaned back against the headboard. "I can't stop thinking about what might have happened. She was a sitting duck."

"She was more like a sleeping tiger. Or an Amazon warrior."

Nichole smiled. "Exaggerate much?" She scrunched up her face. "I couldn't have done what she did."

"Self-defence. You should take a class in it. He could have come after you instead of Gillian."

She shrugged. "He wouldn't have." Her tone was firm, confident. "What will you do now? She doesn't want to move in with you."

"She told you that?" Women talked, he got that. Still, he wished Gillian hadn't discussed it with Nichole—not that he had anything to hide from her. He just hadn't been ready to air that bit of laundry yet.

"I pried it out of her. You know our Gill—a woman of few words." Nichole set the glass of wine on the night table, stretched and yawned. "Oh, I'm so tired."

She curled up on her side, propping herself on one elbow. Her skirt rode up, exposing her thighs almost to her panties. She tapped the bed next to her. "Come. Sit with me."

"Maybe you should go to your room and get some sleep." How much had she drunk? Her glass was half-full, so not much, unless she'd started before she showed up here. He wasn't in the mood for this.

"You're right. If I stay here much longer, I'm liable to do something naughty." Her eyelashes flickered and her lips puckered.

"Come on. It's getting late and we're both tired. I'll walk you back to the staff quarters."

Daylin moved to the bed and offered her his hand. She grabbed it and, giggling, yanked him down on top of her.

"Hey, cut it out." He tried to roll off her, but she pulled him close.

"Nichole, what the hell?" He pushed away from her.

"Oh, come on, spoilsport. Lighten up."

He scowled. "Not funny. Come on." He hauled her off the bed and handed her back her wine glass. With one hand cupping her bent elbow, he guided her to the patio door.

"You're no fun anymore." She winked. "You're not drinking your wine. Sit down. Relax. Have a drink with me."

He sighed. "One drink. We've got a lot of work to do tomorrow, and it'll start early." He picked up his glass of wine and sipped.

She sashayed back to the bed and sat, curling one leg under her.

He finished unloading his suitcase and stuck it in the closet. "Let's go into the living room." Nichole had always been a flirt with him. He wasn't worried she'd seduce him, but he'd be more comfortable having her around if they weren't in the bedroom.

She followed him out. When they reached the living room, she brushed past him and dropped into the armchair, so he took a seat on the couch.

"Cheers." She held out her wineglass, and he clinked his against it.

"Cheers." He smiled and sipped.

She chattered to him about her plans for the resort, and Daylin relaxed. He sipped his wine, threw in the odd comment, and let her ramble on. When his head bobbed and the room spun, he figured fatigue must be catching up to him.

"I'm not feeling well."

She stood, took the wine glass from his hand, and set it on the coffee table.

"Let me help you back to bed."

He tried to stand, staggered, and fell against her. His stomach was bothering him. Maybe something he'd eaten on the plane disagreed with him. The wine sloshed in his stomach and nausea threatened. Sleep. He had to lie down and sleep.

Nichole propped him up and guided him toward the bedroom.

"Nick. Whaz dern iz." His lips and tongue refused to form words. He stumbled again and they both almost went down, but by now they'd reached the bedroom and she tumbled him onto the bed.

"Relax, sweetie." Nichole leaned her face close to his. "I'll take good care of you tonight."

Everything went dark.

CHAPTER 36

Gillian woke before dawn and rolled out of bed. Without Daylin beside her, she couldn't get a decent night's sleep. She would reach out to touch him and then snap awake when she realized he wasn't there. How many restless nights would she have here before she got used to sleeping alone?

She went into the tiny kitchen to start the coffee. On the island, one of the staff would be setting out to the barn to do the chores. Everyone else would be snatching some more precious moments of sleep. She'd get there early, which was okay. Maybe she'd surprise Daylin with breakfast in bed.

An hour later, she moored her boat at the dock on the island.

The eastern sky grew pale against the cloud cover as the sun started its ascent on the horizon. Gillian grabbed her backpack from the boat and headed toward the main house without taking her flashlight out of the bag. She easily made out the shapes of trees, boulders, and anything else in her way.

As she reached the front porch, the jangle of cowbells and the cluck of chickens reached her ears. The cows were already in the pasture, the eggs already retrieved. In the distance, Katarina strode from the pasture and waved as she reached the barn door.

Gillian decided she'd go to the restaurant kitchen and make breakfast after she got the coffee on. He'd appreciate waking up to hot coffee and fresh scrambled eggs with bacon and toast. It was so blissfully domestic she smiled.

She slipped quietly into the house, not wanting to disturb him. Immediately, her gaze locked onto the two glasses of wine on the coffee table. Next to the glasses stood two empty bottles of wine.

Her stomach knotted and a lump formed in her throat. She shook her head. Nichole had probably come over last night to keep Daylin company.

175

That's all it was. Daylin wasn't Josh.

But two bottles of wine?

Daylin didn't typically drink a lot. He'd been tired from the trip. They'd agreed it would be best for Gillian to go to her apartment and come to the island in the morning.

She set her backpack on the couch and went to the kitchen. And froze.

An outfit she recognized as Nichole's and a fragment of cloth lay on the hall floor in front of the open bedroom door.

Gillian tiptoed along the hallway, her gaze locked on the clothing and what turned out to be a pair of panties. When she reached the doorway, she stiffened.

Dim morning light filtered through the sides and top of the blinds shielding the bedroom windows enough to illuminate two bodies lying in the bed. Unable to stop, Gillian crept closer despite the horror clutching at her throat.

Exactly like Josh.

Tears spilled from her eyes, but she didn't close them, not even to shut out the sight of Daylin's arm curled around Nichole's body.

He slept, at peace, carefree. The blanket covered him from the hips down, leaving his bare chest exposed. The covers had slid off Nichole in her sleep, displaying her naked body. One of his hands cupped her breast.

Gillian stumbled from the room without waking them. She grabbed her backpack on her way out and raced outside, leaving the front door wide open.

***

Nichole waited until Gillian slammed from the house before she slipped from Daylin's bed and slunk to the kitchen window.

Gillian lurched down to the dock, climbed back into her motor boat, and roared off.

Instantly, Nichole hurried back to the bedroom and yanked her clothes back on. She tiptoed out to the living room and grabbed one of the empty wine bottles off the table. Working quickly, she rinsed it out and put it in the bag of empty bottles to be returned to the beer store.

She crept back into the bedroom and curled up on the edge of the bed, as far from Daylin as she could go.

In sleep, he had the face of an angel. An urge to stroke his hair had her lifting her hand, but she pulled back. She didn't want to wake him. For him, today would be a bad day. Why force him to begin it before he was ready?

Nichole closed her eyes. Had that idiot Trevor done his job, Gillian would already be out of the picture and Nichole would be picking up the pieces of Daylin's shattered heart. She resented not having him to herself yet.

But she could wait.

By tonight, he'd be free of Gillian forever, and this time, Nichole wouldn't depend on someone else to do the job for her.

***

Daylin opened his eyes.

Immediately, Nichole sat up. "You okay?"

She reached behind her and grabbed a damp washcloth, which she draped on his forehead. "You must have come down with a bug or something. I stayed here last night to make sure you were okay."

"I don't remember anything about last night." He frowned, striving to recall the night before, and noticed his bare chest. Was he naked? He lifted the blanket. He wore underwear.

"I thought you'd feel more comfortable if I took your shirt and pants off." She sounded apologetic.

"No problem." He pressed the cool cloth against his aching head. "Thanks for taking care of me. I don't know what the hell happened."

"Maybe it was the combination of air travel and the wine we had when we got home. Sorry. You don't drink a lot. I shouldn't have refilled your glass the last time."

"It's not your fault. I'm my own liquor control board." He laughed. The nausea was diminishing. Some coffee and food would perk him up. He licked his dry lips and got out of bed.

"I'll get the coffee going." She left the room.

He went into the bathroom. His mouth tasted like he'd been licking the inside of a sweaty gym bag. His stomach lurched.

After he'd washed and dressed, he made his way to the kitchen. Coffee was ready, and he gratefully accepted the mug Nichole held out to him.

Outside, the day brightened. Birdsong filtered in through the open window.

He peered out through the screen and searched the docks for Gillian's boat. Disappointed at the sight of the empty spot where she'd have tied it up, he finished his coffee and considered what to do.

Nichole cleared the wine glasses from the living room and set them in the sink. "I'll do these dishes and then work in the office."

He stopped her before she turned on the water. "I'll do it. You've done more than enough."

She reached for the wine glasses. "Let me take care of these glasses for you. The red wine is drying in the bottom of the glass."

"I'll clean them. I need you to get out there."

Hammering echoed across the island, as the renovations got underway for the day.

"Make sure the guests are okay and staying away from the construction areas, please, Nicky. Someone besides the foreman should look in on it. I need to do the rounds, so it's you."

"Okay. I'll run back to the staff quarters and change first, but then I'll scope things out for you." She headed toward the door, but turned back before she left. "Make sure you rinse out those wine glasses."

Absently, Daylin nodded his head. "Yeah, don't worry about it."

When the door slammed shut, he faced the sink. Through the window, the empty spot where Gillian docked her boat mocked him. He twisted away from it, hunted up his cell phone, and called her.

No answer. Voicemail kicked in.

"Hey, it's me. I hope everything's all right and you're on your way over. Call me back when you get this. Love you."

Frustrated, anxious, he went to make the rounds of the resort. She'd just have to hunt him down when she arrived

Two hours later, she still hadn't appeared.

He went to the admin offices inside the restaurant and found Rico sitting at the desk.

"Have you heard from Gillian, Rico?"

"She called about an hour ago. Said she's not feeling well. Maybe still recovering from the flight?" Rico's expression told Daylin the other man didn't believe what he was saying.

"Is she okay?" Why hadn't she called him directly? He grabbed his cell phone from the clip on his belt. Nothing. No voicemail messages. Not even a text.

What if she was seriously ill? He'd been sick last night. What if she had the same thing but worse?

"She didn't sound good. Sad, if you ask me. When I asked her if she was okay, she said yes, but she was off. I meant to tell you, but I got distracted. I told Nichole when she came by. She said she'd go to Gillian. You don't have to worry. Nichole will take care of her."

CHAPTER 37

Daylin returned to the main house. He should call Gillian before he headed over—check if Nichole was there and everything was all right. They might already be heading back here, and he'd be wasting his time going to the mainland.

He picked up his cell and placed the call, but hung up when he got her voicemail. Nichole might answer. He punched in her number.

"Hi."

Relief flooded through him at the sound of her voice.

"Where are you? Gillian's not answering her phone."

"I'm at her apartment. I'm leaving to pick up groceries for her. Listen, I'll have to call you back. She's not feeling well. She'll be okay—just needs rest and lots of liquids." Nichole sounded chipper, upbeat.

Shock speared through Daylin. "What's happening?"

"Don't worry. I'll call you back."

"Wait." When she disconnected, he had an urge to throw his phone across the room.

There was a knock on the door and Katarina peered in at him through the screen. "Can I talk to you for a moment?"

"I'm busy. Can it wait?" He didn't know what to do, but he refused to sit here and wait for Nichole to call him back.

"I guess. It's about Gillian." She turned to leave, but he rushed to the door and threw it open.

He gripped her by the arm and pulled her into the house. "What about her?"

"I wasn't sure I should say anything, but she looked upset when I saw her this morning. Since then, I've been wrestling over whether to tell you about it, and, well, obviously I decided to rat her out."

"It's not ratting her out if it helps her. What's wrong?"

179

"I don't know. Did something happen here this morning to make her run away? I don't want to gossip, and I don't want to interfere with anything. But Rico told me you were asking about her as if you hadn't seen her today. That's why I decided to say something." She hesitated.

"Go on."

She sighed. "I was outside, taking care of the animals, and waved to her when she got here this morning. She looked happy walking up from the dock. Next thing I know, she's running out of the house like demons are chasing her, and she's crying. She took off in her boat and I haven't heard from her since. I tried calling her, but she's not answering her phone. I'm worried."

His heart thudded against his chest. "Thanks for letting me know. I'll take care of it."

After Katarina left, he returned to the kitchen. His gaze landed on the dirty wine glasses. They'd sat on the table this morning, along with the bottle of wine. Gillian, who'd dealt with a cheating husband, had probably walked into the bedroom and seen Nichole in bed next to him.

But she hadn't been near him, and Gillian would know they hadn't had sex, wouldn't she? And if she'd jumped to the conclusion that they had, why wouldn't she have confronted him? The least she could have done was ask him. She knew he and Nichole were just friends.

Well, he would go and straighten this out right now. Why hadn't Nichole told him what the problem was when he'd called? He could have set Gillian straight long ago—as could Nichole. What was going on?

He called Rico and told him to step into the role of manager for the rest of the morning. The young man expressed surprise, but didn't question the order and assured his boss everything would be fine.

Relieved, Daylin hurried to his boat.

***

Gillian stirred but something tugged at her wrists and ankles. Her head pounded and nausea quivered her stomach. After she opened her eyes, she waited for her vision to adjust to the dim room.

The blinds in her bedroom were closed, and she lay on her bed, padded wrist and ankle cuffs securing her to the bedposts. A petite figure she slowly recognized as Nichole sat in an armchair across from the bed.

Confused, Gillian struggled to sit up and moaned when the restraints tugged her backward and snapped back her aching head.

"Good morning." Nichole sounded pleasant, chatty.

"What happened?" How had she ended up in her bedroom? The last thing Gillian remembered ... "You came over to discuss this morning." She'd only been home an hour before Nichole had arrived at her door, demanding to be let in. She'd claimed to have an explanation for what Gillian had witnessed.

"Yes."

After some arguing through the closed door, she'd let the other woman in to keep the neighbours from overhearing them.

"How did you drug me? Why did you drug me?" Gillian squinted, trying to see her friend's expression.

The sun pressed in through the cracks at the side of the window blinds, but Nichole's face remained in shadow. She shifted in her chair, crossed her legs.

"Your memory will be a bit sketchy. I'm surprised you remember that much. I guess I didn't give you enough."

At the amusement in Nichole's voice, Gillian gritted her teeth. "What did you use?"

"Date rape drug. Handy stuff. I slipped it into the glass of water you were drinking when you went to get one for me. You're such a sweet girl—good hostess. So sure I was fucking your boyfriend, but you offered me a glass of water when I burst into tears of sorrow and regret."

"What are you doing?" Gillian's hands shook, and she wasn't sure if it was from fear or from being restrained. "How long have I been here?"

"One thing at a time." Nichole approached the bed and loomed over Gillian. "I had to incapacitate you. After what you did to my boy Trevor, I had to make sure you wouldn't take me out the same way. Fuck. If only I'd known you had the moves, we would have been more prepared. Who'd have thought a bumpkin like you could fight?"

"Why would we need to fight? Over Daylin? I've already left one cheating bastard. I can leave another."

"You didn't leave Josh. He left you. Remember? You were too stupid to know he was gettin' some strange on the side until you walked in on them fucking."

Gillian's head felt like it was stuffed with hamster bedding. Her shoulders and arms burned. She shifted, but nothing eased the strain. "Untie me."

"No, sweetie. We have work to do, and you won't like it. I'm sorry, but you'll have to stay where you are."

What Nichole had said about Trevor finally seeped into Gillian's soggy brain. "Trevor was working with you."

"Not with. For. He worked for me—on every project—the one to get Daylin off your fucking island and away from you included."

"But he shot Daylin. Why did you have Trevor shoot him?"

"I told that idiot to shoot whoever was next to Daylin—to get at a staff member. He's lucky Daylin wasn't seriously hurt. Still, I could use it …"

"Why? Daylin's your friend, your business associate." Her fingers strained to reach the locks on the cuffs and failed.

Nichole must have lost her mind. Gillian struggled to recall the last two months, to find anything that should have indicated the woman was about to snap.

"Why are you doing this? We're friends."

"Friends? No. From the first time I met you I hated you. He wasn't supposed to want you. He'd be with me if it wasn't for you, you dumb bitch." She shrieked out the words. "You made him consider living in this hick dump. The middle of fucking nowhere. Well, when we're married, we'll live in New York."

Gillian hoped the neighbours heard the shouting and became suspicious. "Obviously, you've got what you wanted. I saw you in bed together this morning."

Nichole smiled. "Yes, you did. And it sent you racing home, didn't it? Must have been traumatic to catch him in bed with me." She paced across the room.

Dropping into the chair again, she leaned back and crossed her ankles. "Anyway, this plan is better." She grabbed a sheet of paper off the table beside her. "This is your suicide note. I'll read it to you: *I can't live with another betrayal. There's no love here for me. I can't go on.*"

Below the printed words was an exact copy of Gillian's signature.

She set the paper back on the table. "Short and sweet, right? Says it all."

"How'd you get my signature?"

"Easy. I forged it. Daylin's office has plenty of documents with your signature on it. I used the pen from your purse, too."

Gillian yanked on the restraints. "You're out of your mind."

"Plan one lousy murder and everyone thinks you're nuts." Nichole sneered. "I've got it going on, bitch. When you're out of the way, I'll be right there to comfort Daylin. Poor sweetie. Losing his brother and his woman to suicide will fuck him up, but I'll be there to help him get through that difficult time."

"Oh my God." A hard ball of horror formed in Gillian's gut at the realization. *And I walked right into it.* "But why pretend to be my friend? Why buy me clothes? You bought me clothes." Who did that?

Nichole snorted. "It worked, didn't it? No suspicion on me at all. You both trusted me enough for me to take you to New York—just us gals." She puffed out her chest. "I should have been an actress."

Gillian opened her mouth to scream when her phone buzzed. She craned her neck trying to see it.

The phone sat on the night table next to her bed, the call display out of her range of vision, and the phone out of her reach.

Nichole picked it up and let out an exasperated tsk. "I told him you were resting. Bloody hell. I must get this show on the road. He can't come here and find you alive now, can he?"

She switched off the phone and set it down. "I'll be right back. Gotta head him off." She went to her bag and pulled out a ball gag. "Yeah, I know. I have all this bondage stuff. I bought it just for this occasion. I don't want tape residue on your mouth. Clever, huh?"

Gillian struggled, whipping her head from side to side.

"Bad girl." Nichole gripped Gillian's head. "You know I can't punch you, much as I'd like to. It'd leave a mark. But I can do this." She pinched Gillian's nose closed, and when her mouth popped open, the ball slipped between her lips.

"Be patient, sweetie. I'll be right back and we'll finish up." Nichole hopped off the bed. She grabbed her cell phone from her purse, and left the room dialling.

"It's me." Her voice receded as she walked down the hall and into the living room, her words becoming unintelligible.

How could she talk so casually about murder? How was this happening?

Only two days ago, Gillian had been in New York at Daylin's parents' place. Five days ago, she'd gone to the bar with Nichole and her friends. She'd stayed at her apartment, and trusted Trevor because she trusted Nichole. He'd been acting on her orders? Why?

Nichole returned, and after setting her phone down, removed the gag from Gillian's mouth. Gillian flexed her jaw, loosening it up. She attempted to bring a hand up, but the cuffs held her fast.

"You told Trevor to rape me? Kill me?" She tried to keep her voice steady and failed. Maybe if she kept the other woman talking, Daylin would show up and put a stop to this.

"The rape was his idea. I had to let him have some fun. He was supposed to beat you up. Though, in hindsight, I should have told him to kill you. He screwed up when he didn't drug you first. How fucking hard is it to get a gin and tonic down a person's throat? Idiot." She walked to the table by the window, picked up a large goblet of red wine, and brought it to the bed.

Nichole wore gloves.

Gillian's gaze riveted on them.

"You'll have to drink this now."

Her head snapped up. "You're crazy if you think I'll do what you want."

She struggled against the restraints. The padded cuffs kept her wrists and ankles from getting chafed. Oh, God, that was the point. No evidence of the bondage would show.

Nichole set the drink on the night table and grabbed Gillian by the hair. Shoving her face into Gillian's, Nichole said, "Understand this. You'll drink the wine. If you don't, we'll have to go with a much messier alternative. I've got razor blades in my bag. A vertical slice up each arm will do the trick just fine. I'll make sure your prints get on the razor. But surely you don't want to go out that way. So drink the fucking wine."

"What makes you think he'll go for you if I'm dead? He wasn't with you before he met me. You'd slept together, but he wasn't in love with you. You told me that."

Talk. Keep her talking. Daylin, please, you have to know something's wrong. He'd come. He had to.

"He'd have realized I'm the one he wants to be with eventually. But then you showed up. You lured him into your bed."

"No, I didn't. We fell in love. Stop this. You need help. It's not too late to stop this."

"Drink. When you're asleep, I'll remove the restraints and leave you here with the note. You'll die in your sleep—a much better way to go than bleeding out. Less messy. It won't take long, I promise, and it won't hurt. I'll go to the supermarket and pick up some groceries. When I get back, I'll find you dead in your bed. I'll get hysterical and call an ambulance, give you mouth-to-mouth, but it'll be no use." She patted Gillian's cheek. "So, what's it going to be?"

Gillian stared at her, wide-eyed, unable to speak. She struggled to find her voice, and when she did, she screamed, high and loud.

Nichole leapt up and jumped on top of her prisoner, covering her mouth with a gloved hand. "Shut up. You bring company to the door and I'll fucking slit your throat and leave through the window. Not the way I want to do it—suicide works better for me than obvious murder—but I'm flexible."

Nichole picked up the glass of wine, lifted Gillian's head, and held the glass to her lips.

"Drink."

The liquid flowed into her mouth, dribbled down her throat, out the corners of her lips. She coughed, and Nichole pulled back the glass and checked the quantity. "Lost some, but you swallowed it. Good girl."

"Please. Don't do this. You'll break his heart. If you love him as you say you do, you'd put his happiness first."

Her captor shook her head. "You certainly have a high opinion of yourself. He'll get over you. Drink." She lifted Gillian's head again, and tipped more of the wine into her mouth. This time, she spat it out.

Nichole squealed. She yanked Gillian's hair, shaking her head until her eyes blurred with tears.

She cried out as pain speared through her scalp from the roots of her hair. "Let me go. You won't get away with this. It's insane."

Nichole flung Gillian's head onto the bed with teeth-rattling fury. Gillian squeezed her eyes shut and tears dripped down her temples onto the pillow. Again, the fist gripped her hair and yanked her head up.

"See this?" Nichole waved a razor in Gillian's face. "I'm not fucking kidding. One way or the other, you'll die today. Which way do you prefer?"

Gillian sobbed, but when the edge of the razor pressed against the inside of her arm, she begged. "Please, no. Not that way."

"All right, then. Work with me. I'm trying to be considerate here."

The razor disappeared and Gillian's head thudded back onto the pillow as Nichole exchanged one weapon for another.

"Drink. Careful you don't spill any."

CHAPTER 38

Daylin leapt from the boat as soon as it was tied off and walked to where his car sat in the public parking. His phone alerted him to a waiting voicemail message. Hoping it was Gillian, he paused to retrieve it.

Nichole's voice, chipper, greeted him. "Hey, don't worry. I've got our Gilly girl tucked into bed. She's nursing a vicious headache—probably a migraine. Must be some jet lag. But she's not up to company, and I'm about to go run some errands. Meet me at the pub for lunch at noon, and then we'll go back to her place together and check on her."

Why would Gillian talk to Nichole but not Daylin? If Gillian was upset from what she'd thought she'd seen this morning, wouldn't she be angry with Nichole, too? Was it a migraine after all?

Enough of this nonsense. They'd have it out whether she liked it or not.

He got into his car and headed toward the apartment.

Fifteen minutes later, he swung into the guest parking for the squat, six-unit building and parked. As he stepped from his car, the lobby door swung open and Officer Purdy emerged.

She waved. "Mr. Quinn. Got a minute?"

He strode to her side. "Sure. What can I do for you?" Probably something to do with Trevor.

"I wanted to talk to Gillian again, ask her a few more questions about what happened up here. One of the incidents at the resort doesn't point to Trevor. I went to her apartment, but she doesn't appear to be home. Since you're here, maybe I can talk to you instead. I'll need to talk to Nichole as well."

"Gillian's home." His gut twisted, but he shrugged it off. She was probably sleeping, and Nichole had likely already left for the supermarket.

"I rang the bell and knocked, but there was no answer."

186

"Come on. I've got a key." He led the way, and they took the stairs up to the second floor to save time.

When they arrived at the door, he didn't bother to knock or ring the bell. He whipped out his keys and unlocked the door.

Gillian's cell phone sat next to an empty water glass on the coffee table. As they walked by it, it vibrated, signalling waiting messages.

"I'll see if she's in her bedroom."

The door opened and Nichole emerged, panic on her face. She shut the door and blocked his path. "What are you doing here?"

"Officer Purdy wants to talk to Gill." He tried to brush past her, but she put a hand on his chest and held him back.

"She's sleeping. She shouldn't be disturbed."

His gaze landed on her gloved hands, and he grabbed her by the wrist. "What is this?" Panic rose, gut to heart. "Purdy! Nichole's here."

He shoved her aside, keeping a grip on her wrist, and threw open the bedroom door.

Gillian lay on the bed, eyes closed. A pair of padded cuffs dangled from her left wrist. Her right arm was thrown carelessly across her stomach. Another pair of padded cuffs rested next to her right thigh. A cry escaped Daylin, and he flung Nichole's arm away in his hurry to reach Gillian's side.

Behind him, Purdy rushed noisily into the room. "I'm calling nine-one-one, and you, Miss Berringer, don't move."

In Daylin's auditory periphery, Nichole protested, and Purdy shut her down.

He crouched at Gillian's bedside and lifted her shoulders. Her head flopped back, and he cupped it with his hands.

"Gillian, wake up." Fear laced his voice. He sat on the edge of the bed and pulled her into his arms, cradling her like a child.

Her eyes fluttered opened; her lips parted, but no sound came out. Her eyes rolled back in her head and her eyelids closed.

"What happened here, Nichole?" Purdy held up her hand when the emergency line dispatcher picked up on the other end of the line. "This is a medical emergency. I need an ambulance." Purdy gave the address and explained she was a police officer. "I'll need guidance."

She dragged Nichole farther into the room, snapped cuffs on her, and shoved her into the armchair. "Don't make a move. What did you give her?"

"I found her like this. I left the room and came back, and she was like this."

"Cut the bullshit. It's obvious what happened here. What did you give her?" Daylin snarled the words, his face a mask of anger and fear. He ignored the urge to attack Nichole and pound the answer out of her.

"What did you give her?" He screamed it as he tapped Gillian's cheek, trying to get a response from her. "She's barely breathing. Oh, God." He checked her pulse. It was faint but there, and her skin was icy.

Nichole didn't reply.

The seconds ticked by like hours as Daylin listened for the ambulance. It would be coming from Temagami, which was close even though it seemed as if they were driving from across the country.

Purdy upended Nichole's bag on the floor and rooted around in the clutter. She snatched up a prescription bottle and read the label.

"Sleeping pills." She provided the name for the dispatcher. After a pause, she said to Daylin, "Induce vomiting."

He held Gillian's head, opened her mouth, and prayed they weren't too late.

***

Gillian's return to awareness started with hearing. Someone shuffled next to her and breathed audibly. A hand held hers in a loose grip. She lay on a mattress that could only be in a hospital. The disinfectant smells verified this guess. Her mouth tasted foul, and rinsing it with some cool, clean water became her mission in life. She opened her eyes.

Daylin blinked when they locked gazes, and bewilderment crossed his face.

"Gillian." He pressed his other hand to her forehead and stroked her hair. "You're okay." He spoke as though he were telling himself as much as he was her.

She smiled, her heart flooding with love. "You got there in time. Nichole?"

His face darkened, and he shook his head. "Arrested. Purdy was with me when I found you. We caught her in the act. She'd been working with Trevor, and we had no idea until she went after you. She set you up. I'm so sorry."

"It isn't your fault. We both trusted her." A weight pressed on her chest. "It never occurred to me she'd want to hurt me. She'd told me she didn't love you. She pretended …" She trailed off, unable to continue. Tears welled up in her eyes at the thought of how close Nichole had come to succeeding.

"I spoke to a cop shrink who works with Purdy, and she believes Nichole is a narcissistic sociopath. Can't say for sure without a formal assessment, but that's her opinion. They can be charming, act like they're your friend, but they're manipulative." He skimmed a hand through his already tousled hair. "She had us fooled all right."

He shook his head, sadly. "Poor Keith had been fooled enough to want to ask her out."

Gillian gasped. "Oh, no. He must be devastated."

"Yeah, but he'll get over it. We talked when he came in to visit you. He brought you those flowers." He pointed to a large vase loaded with daisies, carnations, and two different kinds of lilies.

"I'll give him a call soon. Tell him thanks. Ask if he's okay. I still can't believe it. And Trevor? How did she force him to do what he did?"

"He went along with it voluntarily. He's as culpable as she is—or would be if he'd lived." Daylin's grip on her hand tightened. "At least you're safe now."

She closed her eyes. Her mouth was Sahara dry, but she didn't have the energy to sit up. "Help me? I'm thirsty."

"Of course." He jumped up and pressed the button to raise the head of the bed. He picked up a cup with a lid and straw from the table and held it out to her.

"I had this ready." He sat next to her in the bed and held the cup for her while she sipped.

When she'd taken two mouthfuls, she leaned back, and he set the drink back on the table.

He drew her into the circle of his arms. "No one will hurt you again." He leaned in and kissed her lips. "I'll take you home as soon as possible."

When she nodded, he smoothed the tears from her cheeks with gentle fingers. "My home. You're not returning to the apartment."

She opened her mouth, but he stopped her. "The island. You'll be more comfortable there, and I want you with me. I'll take care of you. When you're better, we'll talk."

The thought of returning to the island, even if only for a short stay, comforted her. After all she'd been through, it would be a relief to hide there for a while.

Not wanting to think about the coming winter and what it might mean to her relationship with Daylin, she snuggled into the warmth of his body. "Okay. I'll go back to the island with you," she said, "for a little while."

CHAPTER 39

Time passed in a haze for Gillian. The last remaining guests went home after the Canadian Thanksgiving long weekend in October, and renovations on existing cabins got underway. Landscapers continued work on the lawns and gardens, and the new buildings were completed.

So far, she'd spent all of her nights with Daylin. She returned to her apartment every couple of days to make sure everything was okay, but both she and Daylin wanted her on the island at night. While they'd talked about the resort management and the ongoing construction on it, they hadn't discussed their relationship.

And nothing had been said about the morning she'd caught Nichole in bed with him. Yet, because it continued to intrude on Gillian's thoughts, she knew she had to broach the subject sooner or later.

As she stared out the kitchen window at the beauty of a bright October morning, she decided the time had come to break her silence. Today was sunny and mild, but soon the cold would set in and the lake would freeze over. Travel between the island and the mainland would stop until the ice got thick enough to drive on.

She needed to know what side of the divide she should settle into.

Daylin had come to mean more to her than she'd ever expected. She loved him—enough to consider making a life with him if he wanted it. But that one incident hung between them. Whatever the fallout, she had to tell him what she'd seen.

She'd fully recovered from the drug overdose. If the worst should happen and their relationship cooled, she could still return to her apartment and make a life on the mainland.

She sensed him before she heard him approach.

He came up behind her and put an arm around her waist.

She leaned into him, soothed by his touch.

His breath tickled her neck. "You're lost in your thoughts. What's up?"

"I guess it's the time of year. It's making me contemplate the future."

"Me too." He kissed her shoulder and her neck and trailed his way up to her cheek.

"That day Nichole came to my apartment ..."

"It's over. She's in jail. She'll be staying there for a long time. Are you having difficulty coping? Is it PTSD?" He turned her so she faced him. "Whatever help you need, we'll get it for you." He frowned. "It should've occurred to me before. But you're eating well, sleeping okay."

Her heart swelled. He'd been keeping close tabs on her, had cared enough to pay attention.

"It's not that." How could she broach this? She sucked in a breath and plunged ahead. "I saw you in bed with Nichole that morning. I came to the resort, walked into your bedroom, and there you both were."

"Yes, but I thought you knew she'd staged it. Do you think I had sex with her?" Shock crossed his face. "Nothing happened between us."

She swallowed. Quietly, she said, "That's not what I saw. Yes, you were set up, too, I know. But I need to know the truth of what you did or didn't do." She paused to collect her thoughts.

He waited, one hand resting on her shoulder.

She relished the contact, was grateful for it. "Her dress and panties were on the floor in the hallway in front of your open bedroom door. I walked in, and she was ..." Her voice broke, but she soldiered on. "... snuggled against you. Your arm was around her, and your hand was holding her breast. A sheet covered you from the waist down, but you were naked from the waist up. She was completely naked—not even a sheet covered her."

A tear slipped out of each eye at the memory. She didn't try to stop them. "I thought you'd had sex with her. I ran away." It's how her marriage had ended. The image of Josh and Candi in bed together still haunted her. To have the same thing happen with Daylin had been too much.

"Oh, baby. You were wondering all this time? Why didn't you ask me?"

"I didn't want to accuse you, because whatever happened wasn't your fault. I have no right to pick at you about it. But I can't let it go. I'm so sorry."

He took her hand and led her into his office. From the file cabinet, he pulled out a sheet of paper. "Purdy faxed me this after you left the hospital. I'd asked her to analyze the wine glasses Nichole and I had used."

He handed her the paper, and she read it. "Rohypnol? The date rape drug?"

"Yes. But I didn't understand why she'd trouble to drug me. When I woke up, she was in bed with me, but she was fully dressed and had about a foot of distance between us. She'd removed my shirt and pants, but I had briefs on. Now I understand. She knocked me out and staged the scene for you." He pulled her into his arms. "I'd never betray your trust. I love you. When I almost lost you, I didn't know how I'd carry on without you."

He pressed his lips to hers, a tender touch, overflowing with affection and love. When he lifted his head again, he held her tight against his body. "We'll build a fabulous place here, offer scholarships so those unable to afford it don't get left behind. I want you to be a part of it, and you can continue to write during the winters. Stay here with me. Marry me."

He reached into his pocket and took out a ring box. "I bought a ring while you were recuperating, but I wanted to wait until we were alone again to give it to you. Marry me, Gillian. I know you don't need a man to take care of you. I don't need a woman to take care of me, either. But maybe we can take care of each other without the need."

She pressed her hand to her heart, her gaze riveted on the white gold engagement ring. Five round, brilliant diamonds sparkled back at her. "Oh, it's beautiful."

She hesitated. Where would they live? "New York?"

"I want to live here with you. Always. I've been happier here than anywhere else. I love it here. I love you. We can have a wonderful home here."

"But your father—the family business."

"I can continue to help him. It'll mean some travel, sure, but you can come with me. Or I can go alone for short trips. We'll make it work."

The prospect of what the resort would become tantalized her. She envisioned creative people enjoying their island, honing their talents, freeing themselves to do what they were born to do. It was something she knew she could be passionate about.

As for the man embracing her, he'd brought her to life—made her want to live it. She loved him more than anyone, and she trusted him with her soul.

"Yes, I want to marry you. I enjoyed visiting your parents, and I'm not afraid to leave my island anymore." She rubbed her cheek against his. "But Daylin?"

"Yes?" He squeezed her.

Today, my life changes forever. Gillian squeezed him back. "Mind if we have a small wedding?"

###

SAMPLE CHAPTER: *INJURY*

Eyes closed, sheet covering her face, Daniella Grayson groped for the phone and dragged the receiver to her ear. "Hello?"

"This is Tobey Ames from TNN, Miss Grayson. Do you have any comment on last night's arrest of your mother?"

Were she not so hung over, Dani would've bolted up. Instead, she drew her legs to her chest, assuming the fetal position. "No comment." The hand that held the phone dropped to the bed. Thumb probing for the "End" button, she found it and disconnected the call.

The phone rang again as she contemplated whom to call first. This time, she let it go to voice-mail. The machine in the living room clicked on after the third ring. The message and beep played, and John Madden, her manager, came on, sounding intense. "Dani. Are you screening? Pick up. I've been getting calls about your mother …"

Dani sat this time, resting her aching head on bent knees, and answered. "What's going on, John? Tobey Ames just called, asking about my mother's arrest."

"I don't know the details yet. They're accusing your mother of killing your father twenty years ago. You would have been what, then? Five?"

Silence. Dani tried to understand what John was telling her. "My father left us when I was five." Dani's mouth went dry, and her hands and feet grew cold. "Lilli was a bitch from hell." Nausea threatened and her spine prickled as she processed the awful news. *Could it be possible? Oh, God.* "She's capable of it. If they've arrested her for killing Daddy, she probably did it." An edge of hysteria had crept into her voice.

"Listen," John said. "Don't answer the phone or open the door until I get there. I'll call the lawyer on my way over, and we'll figure this thing out. There must be a mistake."

Dani said goodbye to John and hung up the phone. She shivered as she

193

slipped out from under the covers and got out of bed. A glance at the clock on her nightstand showed seven-twenty in the morning. No wonder she felt like shit—she'd just gotten *into* bed at four-thirty, helped up to her apartment once again by her trusty chauffeur, what's his name? She always had trouble remembering. Oh, yeah, Cope.

Good looking as hell, but too young for Dani's tastes, and her employee, so she barely gave him a second glance. But he was kind and helpful and made sure she got home safely no matter how drunk she was.

Dani grabbed her bathrobe and snuggled her naked body into the warm terry cloth. As she slid her feet into a pair of slippers, the phone rang again. She returned to her nightstand and disconnected the phone. It continued to ring in the living room until the machine kicked in.

She listened for the caller's voice.

"Hello, Miss Grayson. It's Mark Rutherford of ASN. John Madden suggested you give me an exclusive interview. I'd love to hear your side of the story. Please call me back at ..."

Dani shook her head in disgust while Rutherford recited his phone number. She pulled the plug on the living room phone as well. Anyone she'd want to talk to could call her cell.

She sank onto the couch, switched on the TV, and clicked over to the news channel. An eternity seemed to pass before the stories cycled to the one about her mother. Finally, the newscaster returned to the headline news.

A somber Toby Ames faced the camera, eyes filled with compassion. "Ms. Lillian Capshaw, mother of Oscar-nominated actress Daniella Grayson, was arrested last night in her apartment in Toronto on charges of first degree murder in the death of her husband Paul Grayson. Grayson's skeletal remains were discovered yesterday morning in a capped well at a Sharon, Ontario residence once rented by the family. Ms. Capshaw was taken into custody late last night."

Dani's childhood home flashed on the screen behind the reporter. Plywood covered the windows, and two police cars sat in the driveway. Video footage of Dani appeared on the screen next, showing her exiting a limousine.

The newscaster continued in voiceover. "Miss Grayson, seen here arriving at the premiere of her movie, the Academy Award-winning best picture *Injury*, lives in Los Angeles and has not commented on last night's events. We will update you as the story progresses."

Dani flicked to a channel that focused more on entertainment news. After a few minutes, her photo appeared behind the news anchor, and he gave the same spiel as Ames had though without the premiere clip.

The footage then switched to a taped interview with Gregory Henderson, caught leaving a restaurant with a date. Dani swallowed past a lump in her throat and hugged herself, terrified of what Henderson might say.

Always an attention hog, Henderson leaned toward the female reporter and into the microphone. "No, I haven't talked to Dani. She's not speaking to me these days."

Dani noted the slight slur in his speech. Henderson's arm rested around the shoulders of a gorgeous blonde, who looked delighted to be with him, getting her fifteen minutes of fame.

"Did you meet Lilli Capshaw when you were dating Miss Grayson?"

"No ma'am." Henderson swayed and steadied himself by leaning on his date. "Dani kept me all to herself." He looked into the camera. "Call me, sweetheart. I'm here for you, baby."

The date lost her look of delight.

After a few more inane questions from the reporter and more slurred responses from Henderson, the interview wrapped up.

What an ass. Dani switched off the television, recalling the premiere. She'd stepped out of the limousine and had smiled for the cameras while voices of people she didn't know had cried out for her to look their way.

She hooked her arm through Greg Henderson's and hoped her four-inch heels wouldn't catch on the red carpet. "Greg," she whispered, "don't let go of my arm."

He smiled at her. "Relax, baby. I've got you covered."

Dani loved tall men. At five-foot-ten, she usually looked most men in the eyes—looked down on them, let's be honest—especially in four-inch heels. Henderson was the perfect height for her, and their chemistry on screen and high-profile romance off screen had helped make *Injury* the hit of the season.

She tried to get in front of the cameras as much as possible and had worked hard at looking particularly stunning for that premiere. Her body-hugging gown had shown off her slender figure. She'd let her long, dark hair hang loose in a wild and carefree way that took hours with a curling iron to achieve.

Maybe my father is watching this, she'd thought, as she always did when she put herself on display in public. It's why she put herself on display in public.

Daddy's never seen me. All those times, I thought he'd see me and feel sorry he left us, and he wasn't even alive.

The doorbell rang. *John.*

She unfurled from the couch and waited for him to enter. When the door didn't open, she walked over, reached for the deadbolt, and then remembered John's warning to not open the door. She checked the peephole. Nothing there. If that was John, he wouldn't be hiding. She waited. The doorbell rang again, but whoever was there took pains not to be seen.

Dani left the door, went to her room, and opened her closet. *There'll be a media feeding frenzy. What am I going to wear?*

Did it matter? Yes, she supposed it did, but it felt strange to know that her father wasn't out there somewhere perhaps noticing her and thinking about contacting her.

At eighteen, she'd tried to find him, to ask him why he'd turned his back on her. She could understand that he'd want to escape controlling, abusive, obsessive Lilli. Dani herself had moved out of her mother's home at sixteen. But Dani was a child when her dad had disappeared, and she'd taken the rejection and ensuing lack of contact personally.

The knocking on the door penetrated her thoughts. *How'd that asshole get into the building?* Multiple fists pounded the door, she realized. More than one asshole was out there in the hall stalking her. Then she heard voices arguing, demanding. She hopped back into bed, pulled the covers under her chin, and waited.

A key rattling in the door told her John had arrived. Dani sighed and slid out of bed. Peering out of her bedroom, she waited for him to step inside. John, handsome, rugged, older. But assertive, protective, kind. She itched to touch him.

Would he sleep with her now she was over twenty-one? It'd been five years since she'd tested those waters. When she'd first hired him to be her manager, she'd thrown herself at him.

She'd almost fired him when he'd rejected her, then had decided she didn't give a shit after all. One by one, she'd seduced his associates, until she'd gotten it out of her system. The older men had been eager to accept the offer of her young body.

When John had complained, like he had any right to say anything about whom she fucked, she'd told him to butt out. He'd almost quit on her then, and she'd had to beg and plead and promise the moon to keep him as her manager. Fear of him abandoning her reined in her reckless, wanton behavior, and she'd battled to keep him in her life.

They'd had a holy alliance since then, focusing on her career, which had skyrocketed. She'd kept her attraction to him locked away, taking it out only in the darkest of nights when she took comfort from and pleasured herself on thoughts of him.

But now that ache for him was back, fierce, hot. Dani slid a hand down her robe and loosened the knot on the belt at her waist. The robe parted slightly, exposing her body in a thin, vertical line of curves and shadows. Her nipples hardened, and she parted her lips.

She tilted her head to the side and watched John struggle to shut the door as hands holding microphones jammed themselves into the opening, and voices shouted her name. John pushed against the door, and a man cried out in pain. The arms disappeared, and the door slammed shut.

"Don't worry, Dani. I've alerted security. They'll be gone soon," John said, his back to her.

The normality of seeing him there shook her back to reality, and she closed the robe. When he turned to her, she faced him head on. "John." Her voice caught in her throat, and his name came out low and throaty, but it was grief, not lust that did it. "What happened to my father?"

###

ABOUT THE AUTHOR

Val Tobin lives in Newmarket, Ontario with her husband, Bob, and Scully, their cat. She spends her days writing, reading, and searching for the perfect butter tart. Her educational background includes a diploma in Computer Information Systems, a B.Sc. in Parapsychic Science, a M.Sc. in Parapsychology, Reiki Master/Teacher certifications, and Angel Therapy Practitioner® certifications.

CONNECT WITH VAL TOBIN

Facebook: www.facebook.com/valtobinauthor
BookBub: bookbub.com/authors/val-tobin
Web Site: valtobin.com
ALLi: allianceindependentauthors.org/members/val-tobin/profile/

OTHER BOOKS BY VAL TOBIN

Paranormal Sci-Fi Thrillers
The Valiant Chronicles Series
Earthbound (prequel): A spirit becomes earthbound after refusing to cross over in order to solve her murder and prevent more deaths, some of which might be predestined.

The Experiencers (book one): A black-ops assassin atones for his brutal past by helping an alien abductee escape capture.

A Ring of Truth (book two): A rogue assassin triggers an apocalypse when he attempts to rescue a group of alien abductees.

The Valiant Chronicles books are also available as a complete set in e-book and paperback.

Romantic Suspense
Injury: A young actress at the height of her career has her personal life turned upside down when a horrifying family secret makes front-page news.

Gillian's Island: A socially anxious divorcée confronts her greatest fears when she's forced to sell her island home and falls for the dashing new owner.

About Three Authors: Poison Pen: Three wannabe authors suffering from various mental disorders find love in unexpected places when they interfere in the investigation of a colleague's murder.

Forever Young: You Again: Complications arise when an accounting tech is assigned her former lover as a client and his company's previous financial controller is found dead.

Paranormal Romance
Walk-In: A young psychic woman fights an attraction to a handsome but sceptical novelist while she battles a power-hungry sorcerer determined to make her his next conquest.

Horror Suspense

The Hunted: A Storm Lake Story: A monster hunter revisits her terrifying past while helping a reporter uncover the origins of Storm Lake's creatures. A stand-alone sequel to the short story "Storm Lake," The Hunted takes place twelve years later.

Urban Fantasy
Tales from the Unmasqued World Series

The Fool: New Beginnings (book one): A newly divorced woman suffering a midlife crisis gets involved in the search for a missing half-vampire teen.

The Magician: Infinity's End (book two): After getting expelled for setting a demon loose on campus, a student mage searches for the real culprit and finds his troubles have only just begun.

The High Priestess: Persephone's Return (book three): Stuck in the spirit world, Jaycie struggles to find a way out. But others want to keep her there forever. Will she make it out of Hades alive?

www.ingramcontent.com/pod-product-compliance
Lightning Source LLC
Chambersburg PA
CBHW031424250626
47155CB00004B/1618